By Evelyn Waugh

A LITTLE LEARNING

A LITTLE LEARNING

The First Volume Of
An Autobiography

by
EVELYN WAUGH

LITTLE, BROWN AND COMPANY · BOSTON · TORONTO

LIBRARY OF CONGRESS CATALOG CARD NO. 84-080134

MV

PRINTED IN THE UNITED STATES OF AMERICA

TO MY GRANDCHILDREN,
ALEXANDER AND SOPHIA WAUGH,
EMILY-ALBERT FITZHERBERT
AND EDWARD JUSTIN D'ARMS.

CONTENTS

PUBLISHER'S NOTE

A LITTLE LEARNING is the first and only volume of an autobiography which Evelyn Waugh was never to continue. Drawn largely from the diaries which he kept from the age of twelve, it covers his early childhood, his schooldays and time at Oxford in the early 1920s, and ends with an account of his experiences as a schoolmaster at a private school in North Wales.

A LITTLE LEARNING

Chapter One

HEREDITY

ONLY WHEN ONE has lost all curiosity about the future has
one reached the age to write an autobiography.

I lately took up and re-read after many years H. G. Wells'
The Time Machine (conjecturing, incidentally, who of modern
critics, if presented with the sentence out of context, would
identify the author of: 'The soft radiance of the incandescent
lights in the lilies of silver caught the bubbles that flashed and
passed in our glasses'). At the end of the volume, the first
edition, were sixteen pages of advertisement of the popular
novelists of 1895, all eulogized by reputable papers with an
extravagance seldom accorded to me in my professional life;
all, today, quite forgotten. It seemed I had taken a little hop in
the Time Machine and had seen displayed before me the futility
of contemporary esteem.

I longed for the loan of the Time Machine – a contraption
with its saddle and quartz bars that was plainly a glorification
of the bicycle. What a waste of this magical vehicle to take it
prying into the future, as had the hero of the book! The future,
dreariest of prospects! Were I in the saddle I should set the
engine Slow Astern. To hover gently back through centuries
(not more than thirty of them) would be the most exquisite
pleasure of which I can conceive. Even in my own brief life
I feel the need of some such device as a failing memory alien-
ates me daily further from my origins and experience.

I

In middle life my father gradually lost the hearing of his left
ear. He used to attribute this affliction to having, years before,

slept on damp ground in camp with the Somerset Volunteers. At the same age I suffered in the same way. I blame it on heredity.

Sir Osbert Sitwell named his grand autobiography from the left hand, which by repute reveals the characteristics we inherit at birth, and the right hand on which are scored the experiences and achievements of our subsequent lives. In childhood the left hand leads us; in manhood we seem completely right-handed, in control of our fate; then with age, not only infirmities, but foibles and mannerisms in ourselves remind us of our parents. Knowing whence we derive, it is easy to draw analogies between ourselves and our forebears. But we are the conjunction of so many and so various influences that any idiosyncrasy is explicable in these terms. In physiognomy there are not half a dozen distinct shapes of nose or lip, nor colours of hair or eye, nor formations of cranium, cheekbone or jaw; any face, beautiful or hideous, can be composed of a few elements that can be recognised piece-meal in family portraits; so with talents and temperament. The succession of our progenitors recedes into obscurity; any one of them may emerge in us as the dominant component.

Mankind none the less is stubbornly curious of genealogy; or, at least, that part of mankind which is interested in the past; and the past is the sole concern of biographers.

Most elderly people find it hard to take an interest in the young – or, indeed, to remember their names – unless they have known their parents. Ignorant of fashions in biological theory we still look to heredity – as our forebears looked to the stars – as the source of character. When one of the young misbehaves, we muse: 'How like her poor uncle'; when one shows talent, we ask: 'Now where does he get that from?' and daily give intuitive assent to a proposition which confounds our reason.

None of my ancestors was illustrious. I can therefore be acquitted of vainglory if I follow the old fashion and preface my own history with some account of theirs.

My eight great-great-grandfathers comprise three Englishmen, two Scotchmen, an Irishman, a Welshman and, sole exotic strain, a man of Huguenot family, naturalised for a century in Hampshire; three were lawyers, two soldiers, one a clergyman, one a mathematician, one a painter. Of these, four only preserve recognisable personalities; the others are mere names: S. P. Bishop, who died with the rank of lieutenant-colonel in the Bengal Army, leaving many children (he had seen service in most of the local campaigns in the first thirty years of the nineteenth century); Thomas Raban followed the law in Calcutta; John Symes followed the law in Bridport. The fourth, whom I suppose to have been a soldier, cannot be identified with certainty. He died young, probably in India. He was reputedly of the family of Mahon of Strokestown, Co. Roscommon, who were briefly ennobled at the Union (the second and last peer died insane and childless) and are best known for the murder in 1847 of their head, Denis Mahon. My great-great-grandfather belonged to an earlier generation; perhaps he was an uncle of Denis, but the destruction of the Dublin archives in 1922 has left much Irish genealogy conjectural. My great-grandmother was christened Theodosia, as was the sister of the first baron. She was presumably left an orphan early, as she was brought up by a General Price in Bath, doubtless a brother-officer of her father. He had seen service in India and to India she was sent to find a husband. She married my great-grandfather, a major in the East India Company's army, who died of cholera shortly after the birth of my grandfather.

There is some slight mystery about Theodosia. She was not much spoken of in the family. I have her portrait in miniature, painted during her brief widowhood; she is *décolletée* in black velvet with a jet necklace and black net gloves. Her ringlets are dark, her skin very fair. She is not mourning deeply. Her smile is smug, her fine eyes inviting and she did not wait long for a second husband.

Her interest for me is that she, alone of my immediate

forebears, was a Roman Catholic. How this came about, I do not know. It was an unusual event in an Anglo-Irish Protestant family. Her expression is not that of a recent, zealous convert. Perhaps her second husband, named Devenish, was a Catholic. It was her change of religion which caused her sisters-in-law, when she remarried, to remove my grandfather from her keeping and take him into their care. My mother remembered these great-aunts of hers as demonstrating the insidious character of popery by the tale that many years after the little boy's reclamation he was found to have retained a rosary (perhaps less as an aid to devotion than as a memento of his lost mother), which he kept in secret and slept with, until detected. Theodosia had other children by her second marriage, but my grandfather was never allowed to meet his popish half-brothers and -sisters.

Of the John Symes mentioned above one curious experience is recorded; a preternatural summons one night enjoining him: 'Arise, get thee to Launceston.' As seems usual in such cases, he was sceptical and obeyed only on the third command. Bridport is some eighty miles from Launceston. Providence furthered the journey by providing a ferry-man, awake and ready to cross the dividing stream, and a coach at the inn with the leaders just being put in. He arrived at Launceston to find the Assize Court sitting, recognised the prisoner, who was on trial for murder, as a sailor he had spoken to at Plymouth on the night of the crime, and so secured his acquittal. That is the tale my great-grandmother, his daughter, used to tell. One of my aunts put it in writing. True or fictitious it provides little light on his shadowy character; still less does it adumbrate a transmissible gift or defect.

The Symes family became extinct with the death of Sir Stewart Symes, sometime Governor-General of the Sudan. He outlived his only son, who was killed in action in 1944.

The other four progenitors had the attention of biographers and portrait painters.

The Reverend Alexander Waugh, D.D. (1754–1827), was a

4

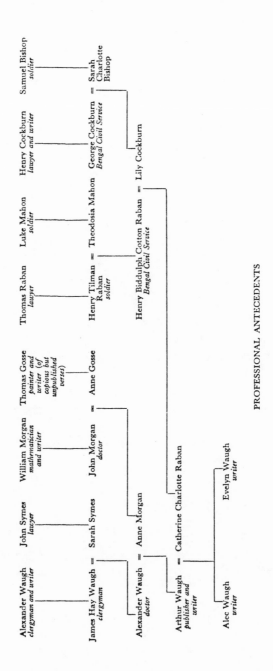

PROFESSIONAL ANTECEDENTS

minister of the Secession Church of Scotland, a body which came into being in 1733. It consisted for the most part of scattered yeomen and labourers who believed that the hard-won establishment of Presbyterianism in 1690 had betrayed the revolution of John Knox by laxity in doctrine and the acceptance of patronage in Church appointments.

Alexander Waugh's father, Thomas, joined the Secession. He held the rather bleak upland farm of East Gordon, near Greenlaw in Berwickshire, as had his forebears for four generations certainly, probably for longer. But he was the last of the family to do so; his elder son, Thomas, on his succession, sold up and bought a larger farm in the more clement district on the banks of the Tweed, near Melrose, and his son emigrated to Australia.

My great-great-grandfather was educated for the Ministry at Edinburgh and Aberdeen. In 1782, at the age of twenty-eight, he was sent to London to the chapel, now demolished, in Wells Street, off Oxford Street, which he served until his death. He became one of the most prominent Nonconformist preachers of his day and, among other public activities, helped found the London Missionary Society and the Dissenters' Grammar School at Mill Hill.

His biography, compiled by two colleagues, enjoyed considerable popularity; it is a work designed purely for edification, consisting of extracts from his sermons, letters and diaries, and the testimony of many admirers. I cannot conceive of anyone, not actuated by family piety, reading it today, but it is possible to discern, through all the unqualified eulogy and the effusive evangelical diction, an admirable and entirely likeable character.

There was nothing dour about this staunch Calvinist. He was tall and handsome, athletic in youth, patriarchal in age. Everyone speaks of him as genial, hospitable, open-handed, affectionate, humorous and scrupulously charitable in judgement. He played the fiddle, enjoyed wine and sea-bathing; on his travels he was a keenly observant sightseer. He was widely read in the classics and in his own branch of theology. When, during the Peace of Amiens, he spent some weeks in Paris, he seems to have had no difficulty in conversing in French. He was rigidly faithful to the tenets of his sect, but quite without rancour. He was wholeheartedly dedicated to his ministry. It was computed that in total he preached 7,706 sermons. His private prayers were long and fervent.

His congregation was drawn from all over London, mostly from recent immigrants in humble circumstances. These, whose employment made them inaccessible during the day, he visited regularly in their homes, tramping the streets at night from lodging to lodging. His sermons and lectures are all in pure English, but in private he delighted to resume the dialect of his youth, remaining fervently Scottish throughout his long exile. Almost every year he revisited his homeland, travelling by sea. In London his house in Salisbury Place was the centre of the expatriates to whom he acted not only as religious director, but as banker, employment-agent, almoner and host. One of his daughters records, with the sole hint of irony which the biography admits: 'Of my father it may most truly be said that he was "given to hospitality" and that at times when the exercise of the virtue was neither strictly necessary nor convenient. His house, though small and scarcely affording accommodation to his own family was ever open to his brethren, especially those of his own communion, from Scotland; and no sooner was he apprised of their intended visit to London, than, if at all consistent with previous domestic arrangements (and he was not very particular on this point) he hastened to offer them, with a sincerity of invitation that could not be mistaken, a place at his family board and a bed under his roof; though his pressing avocations necessarily called him so constantly from home during the day that he himself seldom enjoyed the pleasure of their society or was able to press his kindly offices upon them till late at night on his return.'

How many tedious days spent in trying to entertain the

rough and dazed immigrants of the Secession find their memorial in this sharp little record!

His stipend was small, but he had a childless brother-in-law, John Neill, a Scotchman also, who came to London at about the same time as himself, set up as a corn-merchant in Surrey Street, Strand, and did well. To him, my great-great-grand-father was indebted for what his biographers describe as 'constant and delicate attentions to his domestic comfort'. When Neill died he left £150,000 entirely to his nephews and nieces in trust to their children. In the following hundred years this legacy was subdivided to vanishing-point, but in the first generation it provided a substantial contribution to 'domestic comfort'.

The beauties of Scottish scenery were something of an ob-session with Dr Waugh. He seems seldom to have spoken in public without introducing some rhapsodic passage on the subject. He sent all but one of his sons to Scottish schools and universities, but none returned to farm in his homeland; only one entered the ministry and he died prematurely. The three remaining sons became anglicised and married English women. My great-grandfather, as will appear later, became a clergy-man of the Church of England. His brothers went into com-merce and prospered. One, trained for medicine, rightly decided that there was more money to be made in pharmacy, set up on a large scale in Regent Street, kept a house in Ken-sington and a country villa at Leatherhead adorned by three beautiful daughters, one of whom married Thomas Woolner, the sculptor; the other two successively (and, in the case of the younger, in defiance of English Law) married Holman Hunt. A study of her in widowhood appears in Diana Holman Hunt's (Mrs Cuthbert) delightful book of memoirs, *My Grandmothers and I*. I do not know the other's business. He must have been a solid citizen, for he was Master of the Merchant Tailors Company in 1849.

I know only one action of this great-great-grandfather's that is at all discreditable and it is most uncharacteristic. Quite early in life he adopted armorial bearings to which it is scarcely conceivable that he had any right. They were almost identical with those of Wauchope (estoiles being substituted for mullets) and were displayed illicitly and rather profusely by his descendants until my father's time, when their use, slightly modified, was regularised.

Thomas Carlyle came first to London in 1824, when my great-great-grandfather was aged and ailing. Forty years later he wrote to congratulate Thomas Woolner on his engagement: 'In early times I used to hear a great deal of Dr Waugh, oracle of all Scotchmen in that strange London and much talked of at home among Dissenting Religious Circles:—an excellent, reasonable, solid kind of man, I do still understand.'

My great-great-grandfather never sought to move outside his own community; he was a prominent man in an obscure world. Those who bore witness to his scholarship and culture were not hypercritical. He would not, I think, have shone in the company of my two other notable forebears, William Morgan and Henry Cockburn.

William Morgan, F.R.S. (1750–1833), settled in London ten years earlier than Dr Waugh and lived there throughout the whole of the other's ministry. One may be confident that they never met. They had nothing in common. Morgan was a Unitarian by profession, perhaps an atheist at heart. Alexander Waugh belonged to no political party, but he abhorred the Revolution and described Robespierre in his diary as 'a most execrable, bloody monster'; Morgan's Jacobin sympathies were so notorious that he went in danger of prosecution for treason in 1794. He was the close associate of Francis Burdett and Tom Paine and bequeathed as a venerable relic to his heirs Horne Took's buttons embossed with the name 'Reform Club'. (I own them today.)

He was club-footed and clever. Lawrence, painting him full-face, has made the best of his looks, lending him a meditative, almost poetic air, but a profile of him in carved ivory betrays a long nose, a protruding under lip and a face drawn down into an expression of contempt.

He came of an ancient but impoverished family of Welsh gentry, unambiguously armigerous, who in his day held small properties near Bridgend, on one of which, Tylyrcoh, coal was later found, which for two generations provided sustaining royalties to their descendants. His pedigree extended into legend. Half-way down the roster of barbarous vocables there appears the hero, Cadwgan Fawr, who in 1294 led a war-band against Earl Gilbert de Clare. After they had hewn many of the occupying force of English and had driven the rest from the field, his companions in arms settled down to celebrate the victory. Not so Cadwgan Fawr, who, ready for more, turned to a henchman with the command: '*hoeg fy mywall*' (Anglice, 'sharpen my axe'), which the family adopted as its motto. As the genealogist of Glamorganshire, George Clark, wrote: 'A Welsh pedigree does not pretend to accuracy of detail.' The pedigree of the Morgans of Tylyrcoh is as good as most and it certainly fortified their self-respect as they declined into obscurity in their remote valley during the five centuries after Cadwgan Fawr until William and his brother, George Cadogan, came to London and made themselves known in advanced intellectual circles.

George Cadogan Morgan also held revolutionary sentiments and was in Paris at the fall of the Bastille; he attracted attention by his lectures on electricity and died young as the result of inhaling poisonous fumes during a chemical experiment.

William Morgan studied, and briefly practised, medicine, then turned to mathematics and physics. His first paper to the Royal Society was a description of electrical experiments 'made to ascertain the non-conducting power of a perfect vacuum', but it was as a mathematician that he was elected Fellow five years later, and it was as a mathematician that he earned his living by becoming actuary to the Equitable Assurance Company.

Before Morgan's day insurance policies had an affinity with

9

the gaming book. Many companies were bankrupted. Morgan was one of the first to apply science to the computation of contingencies. The Equitable prospered greatly during the fifty-six years in which Morgan directed. He was paid the salary, high for the times, of £2,000 a year, which was continued in full strength after his retirement. He was a close friend of Samuel Rogers (thirteen years his junior) in the days before the poet established himself in fashionable society, and married his son, William, to Rogers's niece, Maria Towgood. Their association was commemorated in the Tory weekly, *John Bull*, with the lines:

> *Cries Sam, 'All human life is frail,*
> *E'en mine may not endure.*
> *Then, lest it suddenly shall fail,*
> *I'll hasten to insure.'*
> *At Morgan's office Sam arrives;*
> *Reckoning without his host;*
> *'Avant!' the frightened Morgan cried,*
> *'I can't insure a ghost.'* [An allusion to Rogers's notoriously cadaverous appearance.]
> *'Zounds! 'tis my poem, not my face;*
> *Here list while I recite it.'*
> *Said Morgan, 'Seek some other place,*
> *I cannot underwrite it.'*

William Morgan served on the Council of the Royal Society and published numerous papers on public finance. He was popular in progressive, intellectual circles but alienated many by his asperity. To the end of his life he remembered his native tongue and on one occasion after dinner made an extemporary translation of a Welsh ballad into what was described as 'elegant English verse'.

Lord Cockburn (1779–1854) was of border family, a junior branch of the Cockburns of Langton; no Celt, but of Saxon-Norman origin. His portrait by Raeburn, taken in middle age, was regarded as so typical of his race that it was lately used on the bank-notes of the Commercial Bank of Scotland. His

Memorials of my Time gives a classic description of Edinburgh society when it bore the sobriquet of 'the Athens of the North', but eschews personal revelation.

His father, sheriff of Midlothian and baron of the Scottish court of exchequer, was a rigid Tory. My great-great-grandfather turned Whig, a defection which in early life occasioned some loss of preferment from his uncle Henry Dundas, Lord Melville, the Tory dictator. He was a keen politician and rose to the bench by his eloquence and success at the criminal bar. In 1837 he was appointed a Lord of Justiciary. He wrote and spoke on almost all topics of public policy. He was Presbyterian by profession, but not notably devout, and was one of the dissenting minority of judges in the decision which, by confirming State control over the Church, brought about a further secession in the formation of the Free Kirk; but he did not ahere to that body. In the Second World War I was sent on a company commanders' course held in a pretty, sham castle in the outskirts of Edinburgh where I noticed the Cockburn arms in a stained-glass window. This, I learned, was Bonaly Tower, which Lord Cockburn built in emulation of Abbotsford.

The *Edinburgh Review* of January 1857 described him as: 'Rather below the middle height, firm, wiry and muscular, inured to active exercise of all kinds, a good swimmer, an accomplished skater, and an intense lover of the fresh breezes of heaven. His face was handsome and intellectual; a capacious brow which his baldness made still more remarkable, large lustrous, and in repose rather melancholy eyes, which, however, when roused by energy or wit, sparkled like a hawk's.

'A dash of eccentricity mingled with the originality of his character. Attired with the scrupulous precision of a well-bred man, he set the graces of fashionable dress at defiance. His hat was always the worst and his shoes, constructed after a cherished pattern of his own, the clumsiest in Edinburgh.'

Confirmation of this peculiarity in footwear comes from his granddaughter, my maternal grandmother. At the age of eight she was staying at Bonaly when the portrait which now hangs in the National Portrait Gallery of Scotland was being painted by Watson-Gordon. When asked her opinion by the painter, she replied after long and grave scrutiny: 'Well, it's *very* like his boots.'

Carlyle described him as 'small, solid and genuine, by much the wholesomer product' (than Wilson, 'Christopher North' of *Blackwood's Magazine*, who died at about the same time); 'a bright, cheery-voiced, hazel-eyed man; a Scotch dialect with plenty of logic in it, and of practical sagacity; veracious, too. A gentleman, I should say, and perfectly in the Scotch type, perhaps the very last of that peculiar species.'

His library, which was dispersed at a five days' auction in 1854, contained besides the normal classical sets, a fine collection of rare works on Scottish history and antiquities and ten sixteenth-century carved oak portraits taken from the roof of the banqueting hall at Stirling Castle. No indication is offered in the catalogue of the manner of his acquiring these pieces of royal property.

Thomas Gosse (1765–1844), the only other great-great-grandfather of whom it is possible to form a clear impression, was an itinerant portrait-painter. His family came from France at the revocation of the Edict of Nantes and for a century prospered as clothiers at Ringwood in Hampshire. Then trade shifted north and the southern weavers were put out of business. Thomas, the eleventh son, felt the impact of this turn of fortune while he was studying painting at the Royal Academy Schools in London. Brought up in easy circumstances, he was abruptly left to earn his living, which he sought to do by engraving. But on July 22nd, 1790, he was turning into Fleet Street from Chancery Lane, thinking of the difficulties of his trade, when he was confronted by a vision of the risen Christ, who assured him that his 'accepted righteousness' had been 'received into heaven'.

He returned to his lodging much moved by this experience, brooded on it, and for the rest of his life evinced a confidence in his eternal salvation which rendered him indifferent to his own worldly prosperity and, later, to that of his family. He did not join any particular sect, preferring to rely on his own direct inspiration, and in his travels worshipped in public on Sundays wherever he found it congenial. His son, Philip Henry, the naturalist, became a Plymouth brother and records that in old age his father often 'broke bread' in his chapel. It is this son who was the protagonist of Edmund Gosse's *Father and Son*.

Thomas Gosse was constantly on the move, usually on foot, travelling from house to house and town to town making portraits, once or twice in oil but normally in water-colour on ivory for a few guineas each. One miniature of a dentist was paid for with a set of false teeth.

At the age of forty-two he married a young and handsome girl named Hannah Best, who was something a little higher than a housemaid and a little lower than a 'companion' in a family at Worcester, where he was employed in painting. It was his habit to leave his wife and children in lodgings for long periods while he tramped the country in search of custom. When well over sixty he walked from Bristol to Liverpool. He was sometimes bizarre in dress, returning home from his travels on one occasion in yellow-topped boots, nankeen small cloths, leather breeches, snuff-coloured cut-away coat and brown wig. When rebuked by his wife he replied: 'Pooh! The tailor told me it was proper for me to have.' But a portrait in oils scrupulously painted by himself in old age shows him soberly dressed, rather clerical than bohemian. He has a long, thin face and thick, rather short white hair, and his large eyes seem to glance beyond the spectator with an air of detachment quite unlike the heroic, mesmeric gaze common in self-portraits. He has contrived to make himself look both demure and dotty.

In periods of repose he wrote a number of allegorical epics with such titles as *The Attempts of the Cainite Giants to re-conquer Paradise*. They did not find a publisher. His daughter,

Anne, married the son of William Morgan mentioned above, and was the mother of my paternal grandmother. There must be many of Gosse's miniatures preserved in cabinets all over the country, but his name is little known and collectors and dealers have never shown interest in them.

There is an element of fantasy in the thought of these four totally dissimilar men, quite unknown to one another, entering, as it were, into a partnership to manufacture my brother and myself, who, apart from a common aptitude for story-telling, are antithetical – though not antipathetical.

2

When I leave these eight progenitors, four of them mere masks, I come into the full light of my father's memories, which he set down some thirty years ago in his autobiography, *One Man's Road*, a book of much charm, which lacks general interest only in its latter half, when his life became uniformly uneventful. His accounts of childhood are vivid; in particular his recollections of his paternal grandfather, which it would be otiose to repeat in detail.

The Rev. James Hay Waugh impressed his grandchildren as the embodiment of patriarchal authority; nor did he lose stature as they grew. My father was nineteen when his grandfather died and he had long been conscious of some absurdities in his manner, but he and his siblings rejoiced in them, without ridicule, accepting them as the picturesque survivals of an earlier age.

James Hay Waugh suffered from a trembling hand, which he attributed to excessive snuff-taking in youth, and he employed an amanuensis to whom he dictated numerous memorials for the information and edification of posterity, but he left no record of how or where he spent his early manhood. It seems probable that, until he was in his late thirties, he worked with one or other of his brothers in their London businesses. Nor did he leave any description of the circumstances in which he decided to become a clergyman in the Church of England. Did he resist the claims of the rival theology? The bland majesty with which he surveys the lens of the camera betrays no scars of spiritual anguish. Did he receive a call, a revelation? He has not, as did Thomas Gosse, recorded it. Whatever he experienced would now be dubbed 'a late vocation'. He made no decision until after the deaths of his father and his uncle, John Neill. Throughout his subsequent life he professed deep reverence for his father's memory, but he had done something clearly contrary to his father's precepts; there is no line of guilt on that placid brow.

Not that Dr Alexander Waugh would have made any acrimonious opposition to his change of communion. Anglicans and Presbyterians were nearer in his generation than in the next. When one of his sons, Alexander, who became a minister of his father's church and died young, showed an interest in Anglicanism, the father showed affectionate moderation, writing: 'In regard to the Church of England you will be expected to express your assent and consent to the whole system of the doctrine and policy of the establishment. It is said there are many in that church who believe neither her Articles nor the Scriptural authority of her orders and that it is not expected a young man should trouble himself with nice scruples on these points. But subscription is too serious and awful a matter to be trifled with . . . Search the Scriptures, consult the candid and upright tutor whose instructions you are to enjoy; let your eye be single; and should the conclusions to which your inquiry leads you be different from my views, I shall not respect you the less, but very cheefully aid and assist you to the utmost of my power.'

But there is some ambiguity here; does he mean he will reinforce the arguments of the candid tutor and help him to a better disposition, or that he will cheerfully assist him into the Church of England? He seems to assume that no son of his could accept episcopacy and the Thirty-nine Articles without equivocation. And of John Neill's temper we know nothing. It is not uncommon for laymen to be more bigoted than their clergy. James Hay had large expectations from that direction which, in the event, were fully realised. The face in the photograph is not only that of a man of untroubled faith but also of a man who suffers no anxiety about money. Could he have been sure of his legacy if he apostatised?

Is it an unworthy conjecture that, when he asked for the hand of Sarah Symes, the Bridport attorney pointed out that an Anglican clergyman, with private means, enjoyed a position more congenial to his daughter than a dissenting minister or a London businessman?

James Hay Waugh married as an Anglican and as a married man went up to Oxford, to Magdalen Hall; he led a domestic life in the Broad Street and can have had little to do with undergraduates twenty years his junior. He was up in the heyday of the Tractarians, and though reading for the Church, he does not appear to have come under their direct influence. He was older than either Newman or Pusey. Presumably he heard them preach, but his own style in the pulpit derived from an earlier, more prosaic, more declamatory model. His religion partook, rather, of the robust, Tory, High Churchmanship of Dr Johnson.

In the early nineteenth century most of my forebears, who were not already there, converged on South West England. James Hay Waugh unconsciously followed them. His first, brief curacy was at Warminster; there my grandfather was born. He was then offered two rich livings by the Bishop of Salisbury, but refused them 'on the ground that [as he himself said] he had taken Holy Orders late in life and was possessed of some private means, and he would never put it in the power of anyone to say that he had taken of the loaves and fishes of the Church, which were due to men who had been longer than himself in the sacred profession'. This from his obituary is quoted as 'proof of noble disinterestedness'. The bouquet would have smelt even sweeter had he not, himself, been the source of the anecdote, and had his motive been pure generosity to his fellow clergymen, rather than solicitude for his own reputation; but it seems to have been in a mood of self-abnegation that he accepted the living of Cerne Abbas, in Dorset.

This was anything but a plum; it lacked a parsonage; the stipend was a mere £81 and few of his predecessors had ever resided there. Cerne Abbas now is much restored and much embellished; garden-plants spring from its cobbles and stand in tubs beside its brightly painted cottage doors. In 1841, when my great-grandfather went there, it was remote, impoverished and decrepit. The people, long neglected, were intractable. The flagrant prehistoric giant who stands in the turf of Trendle Hill, and brandishes his club over the abbey ruins, seemed then to celebrate the victory of paganism. This was the sort of opportunity which has from time to time inspired young saints to heroism. My great-grandfather started work with the energy of a missionary and at his own expense built the present vicarage, repaired the chancel and made a large contribution to the foundation of a village school. But he was no saint and he was in middle age. After three years he abandoned the effort of reclamation and accepted the living of Corsley from the Marquess of Bath. He was forty-seven when he went to Corsley; he remained there for forty-one years and never showed any inclination to move.

It was, and is, an agreeable place. He was happy in the favour, which with the years became the friendship, of Lady Bath. (Did he, I wonder, discuss with her the act of patronage for which she is best remembered, her purchase, to please the governess, of Rossetti's first painting?) He was happy in the respect, which with the years became the awe, of his rustic parishioners. He reigned and ruled in his small community, seeing that errant girls were made honest women and that no ailing cottager lacked broth or port. Unlike his father who, as we have seen, aspired to convert the infidel French and the superstitious Irish to the tenets of the Secession Church of Scotland, he never sought to extend his influence beyond his parish. In 1854 he was invited to the pulpit of St Mary's Oxford for the University sermon, but he was not greatly in demand as a preacher; or, if in demand, he did not often accede. It was in his own well-filled church that he proclaimed his message; a message whose peroration, even in his earlier years, usually foretold his own imminent death.

He drew up many detailed plans for this eventuality. On the death of the last of my Waugh aunts I inherited an iron box of family papers, most of small interest. Among them was the following signally humourless memorandum in my great-grandfather's own shaky hand, dated in May 1876:

My beloved children

I have sketched the record I would wish to be made of myself – on a brass let in on the wall of the church. I believe it to embody the Truth.

Sacred

To the Memory of James Hay Waugh

Rector of this parish who for —— years laboured therein as The Peacemaker – The Friend – and the Father of the people entrusted to his care.

He departed this life —— in the —— of his age.

'Thou wilt shew me the path of Life.'

This memorial is placed by his Children, not to eulogise his memory nor to delineate his character but simply to record the Love – the Gratitude – the Reverence in which they cherish the name of their Father.

This wording was not used when he died nine years later, but an injunction dated in July of the same year was observed:

I desire my funeral to be as plain and simply conducted as is consistent with my Station as Rector of Corsley, and that the most worthy of the communicants carry me to my pillow beside her whom I loved in life and in death.

This, it is scarcely necessary to say, referred to my great-grandmother who had died the year before he issued this direction. He mourned her sincerely, if luxuriantly. Her modest jewellery he had broken up and set in a chalice and flagon which, together with a patten, he gave to the church.

On the Sunday after her funeral he thought it appropriate to remain in seclusion, but he dictated a panegyric to be read by a clerical son-in-law, which nicely reveals his conception of his own authority and obligations; it reads in part:

'You need no pencil of mine to give you a portrait of her life; this was ever before you . . . her piety the ornament of a meek and quiet spirit, which is in the sight of God of great price; such ornament being that only "putting on of apparel" she ever wore; setting thus before you all of every condition in life an example worthy of imitation *at all times* but in *these days especially* when such unseemly monies are spent in dress. I beseech you then to shew your love for her memory by imitating her example in these particulars.'

It concludes:

'It is then due to God's grace to add that a large portion of my usefulness in this parish is to be traced to the consistent life of her who has so lately departed from among us.

'And now, finally, pray for me that her death may help me to labour more and more abundantly and for yourselves that you may more and more listen to the injunction: "Obey them that have the rule over you and submit yourselves" . . . I beg to assure you how I have valued your sympathy with me and my family, assuring you that in proportion as you shew your loving obedience to your Spiritual Mother, the Church, you will be scattering in the soil of your hearts seeds of flowers which shall continue to bloom in the Paradise of God, when those flowers which loving hands have so liberally scattered on her grave, shall have with all the things of the Earth faded away for ever.'

A more extravagant form of memorial was the case which he had constructed, covered inside and out with black velvet, which held not only her portrait in miniature, locks cut from her head in youth and in age, a gold cross she had worn, and similar tokens of sentiment, but also by a macabre whim specimens of lead from the lining of her coffin.

Husband, father, grandfather, it was in his large family

circle that he felt the greatest scope for his benign mastery. All his grandchildren were brought to Corsley to be baptised with his own hands. When their parents were on holiday they were sent to Corsley for weeks on end. No member of the family, young or old, was allowed to leave the Rectory, even for a short visit a carriage-drive away, without kneeling at his feet to receive a formal blessing.

There was more than humble duty in these family assemblies. They were greatly enjoyed. He was no puritan. Private theatricals and card-playing were encouraged except on Sundays. He lived well in mid-Victorian style, with long, abundant meals and an ample installation of servants and horses. He never tried to cut a figure in the county. His family comprised his social world. Dr Alexander Waugh's portrait on the dining-room wall was often invoked as an example during family prayers. Near it hung an illuminated scroll: the inscription

Quisquis amat dictis absentem rodere vitam
Hanc mensam indignam noverit esse sui
(Backbiters are not welcome at this table)

is a precept to which those I have known of his descendants, have not proved conspicuously amenable.

Few pleasantries are remembered of him, some rebukes, much demonstrative affection, much bounty. The reader may discern certain points of resemblance to Samuel Butler's elder Pontifex, but they are largely superficial. He seems to have been exceptional even for his age and calling in his regard for his own dignity, but whatever his exorbitance, he was a benevolent man and that cannot be said of my grandfather, in dealing with whom, my father, in his memoirs, was less than candid. Out of deference to my aunts, who in this particular were oblivious of their childhood and professed uncritical respect for their father's memory, he was in writing strictly and uncharacteristically reticent. My mother never made any bones about her dislike of her father-in-law.

He was a doctor. As a young man at Bristol and at Bart's he showed high promise, winning gold medals and prizes. Had he wished, he could undoubtedly have made a career in London, but he was devoted to sport and country-life and was possessed, as have been so many of his family, with the desire for stability and the preference for eminence in a small world over competition in a larger. At the age of twenty-four he settled in Midsomer Norton, near Bath, then a large and pretty village, now a small and unsightly town, and lived there until his death forty-two years later.

I never knew him, nor my grandmother, who was by all accounts a fond, timid woman, skilled in water-colour painting, embroidery and the making of salmon-flies, entirely subject to his will and his moods.

His practice was as wide as his horses could carry him. He maintained, as did many general practitioners of the time, a welfare system of his own, charging guineas to the county families and shillings to the cottagers; often remitting his fees entirely. He was the doctor of Downside Abbey and School and old monks have described him to me as a welcome figure, very smartly turned out, always with a button-hole and a jolly word of greeting. He was the first Protestant to be elected to the Gregorian Society (of Downside old boys); he was president of the local Conservative Association, the Cricket Club, the Choral Society; he sat on countless committees. He was a first-class shot and latterly leased some coverts from Ammerdown and reared his own birds. He fished every year in Scotland. He led in amateur theatricals. When president of the Bath and Bristol Medical Association, a post to which he was elected at the early age of forty, he entertained his colleagues to lavish dinners, whose menus survive, at the Swan Hotel in Wells. He was pugnacious in a cheerful, hearty way and on one occasion brought an action, unsuccessfully, against a political opponent for defamation of character. People liked him the more for it. There can be no doubt that he was well liked in the district. That was his sunny public performance. But in the evening shadows the sound of his carriage-wheels between the dense evergreens of the drive was heard with apprehension. He stepped down between the stucco pillars of the porch, entered a hall which in winter was angrily lit by a red-glazed hexagonal iron lantern of gothic design (which now hangs in a privy in my own house) and stamped on the tiled floor shouting imperiously for the attention of his family, who were required to stop whatever they were doing and hurry to greet him. Had he spent an agreeable or a vexatious day? Had his patients obeyed his orders? Had he been given good stands at the shoot? Had the birds been plentiful? The happiness of all depended on his temper.

Would he be jocose? Would he be loving in his demonstrative hectoring way? Would he be cross? When cross, he sometimes laid about the drawing-room ornaments with a poker. And he was easily put out. My mother remembered a disastrous wet afternoon, at the time when she was engaged to my father. The family were surprised by my grandfather's premature return, playing snap with his cards. An appalling outburst of rage resulted, such as she had never witnessed in her own family; it was provoked not by any damage to the cards, but by the curious belief that a pack used for whist was in some way disabled by any other game, so that a good hand could never thereafter be dealt from it.

He was not simply a man lacking self-control. There was in him a strain of what today would be diagnosed as 'sadism'. Indeed when my father first had this unfamiliar expression explained to him, he said: 'I believe that is what my father must have been.' It is related that once when he was sitting opposite my grandmother in the carriage, a wasp settled on her forehead. He leant forward and with the ivory top of his cane carefully crushed it there, so that she was stung. He flogged my Uncle Alick fiercely; my father, who was delicate, he deliberately frightened, sending him as a small child into dark rooms alone and swinging him on high gates, ostensibly to fortify his character. At table he nagged and bullied so that it was a common occurrence for one or other of my aunts, when nearly adult, to leave the table in tears.

The openhanded generosity for which he was extensively known did not begin at home. He provided my father and uncle with a respectable education, but he did little for my aunts. My uncle, who was in the Navy, married a Tasmanian girl and brought her back to Midsomer Norton to a house in the village which it was thought would be her home while he was at sea. He died young and she was left with an infant son in a strange land. Not only did my grandfather see that she packed up and returned to the Antipodes; he gave her as a parting present a bill for the funeral expenses and my uncle's unpaid account at his tailor's, much of which had been incurred before she met him. My grandfather himself was found, when he died, to have been disconcertingly negligent in paying his way.

3

My mother's family was named Raban, an uncommon patronymic which, until 1914, they believed to be German in origin. In that year the enormity of the invasion of Belgium disabused them. Later a cousin with genealogical interests traced them to Penn in Staffordshire, where they had lived as yeomen for five recorded generations until 1706, when they went into business in London for two generations. Towards the end of the eighteenth century they emerged into the professions and services, but chiefly in India, where four generations served in the army or in the administration, first of the East India Company, later of the Empire. They built a commodious bow-fronted house, now a nursing home, at Hatch Beauchamp in Somerset; there, and to an old house named the Priory at Shirehampton, they sent their women-folk and children as refugees from the climate and there those of them who survived, retired. In fact, none of my direct male forebears did survive. There are memorial tablets and stained-glass windows dedicated to their widows, brothers and cousins in Hatch

Beauchamp Church, but the bodies of my last three Raban progenitors lie in India. Thomas Raban, my great-great-grandfather, was killed in Calcutta in 1811 in a carriage accident. Henry Tilman Raban, who married Theodosia Mahon, died of cholera with the rank of major. His son, my grandfather, Henry Biddulph Cotton, the lonely little boy with the rosary, passed from Trinity, Cambridge, into the newly formed Bengal Civil Service, which recruited young men of promise by offering unprecedented security for their dependents. He was magistrate at what was then called Pooree in Orissa, the shrine of Juggernaut. For more than a generation the notorious bloody extravagances of the festival had been suppressed. The chief danger to the pilgrims in my grandfather's day was from cholera. An inspecting officer's report expresses surprise and admiration at his familiarity with all the insalubrious purlieus of the city. On marriage he moved to what should have been the healthier station of Chittagong, but he succumbed to one of the endemic diseases during my mother's infancy. To the confusion of the family tree his widow, Elizabeth Cockburn, married a cousin of his, a clergyman, and bore a second family, also named Raban, half-aunts and half-uncles of mine, who, following the call of the south-west which seems to have summoned so many of my family, settled in Somerset near my present home, where my step-grandfather owned the advowson of a living.

The Rabans' connection with India ceased in 1917, when my half-uncle Basset was killed in action. He served in the 1st Bengal Lancers and never married. When he came home on long leave he always stayed with us, for he was one of my mother's relations for whom my father had a particular liking. My chief memory of him is indistinct, but very glorious, when he set out to attend the coronation of King George V.

Gentle reader, have you ever – except in the cinema, where nothing is credible – seen a Bengal Lancer in full rig? If not, conceive that it took the fancy of some sportive djinn to transform a cornet of the Household Cavalry into a Mogul

Emperor, and that he was distracted half-way through the operation. My father, though volatile and even somewhat theatrical in temperament, was always strictly subfusc in appearance. Now down that short paved path from front door to front gate, where my father made his grey regular passage, there passed a being reserved in mien, but bearing on his person the panoply of the gorgeous East. Detail eludes me, though I had watched him dress; he was all scarlet and gold and canary yellow; he wore a sash, epaulettes and spurs, sword, great buckskin gloves and crowning all a towering turban. He was, I have since learned, small and slightly built, but in my childish vision he was a figure of commanding splendour.

He served as A.D.C. to the King-Emperor at the Durbar of 1911 and in 1914 had passed into the Staff College at Quetta. He could, without reproach, indeed with official approbation, have finished his course and accepted a safe and useful posting. Instead, when the casualties in France and Flanders mounted, he cut it short and volunteered for an attachment to the English army. He was killed in the trenches commanding a battalion of the Royals.

Such, then, are the physical materials of which I am made. The body, which includes the mind and nerves, is a link in a heterogeneous concatenation; the soul is a separate creation.

My brother and I are composed of precisely the same ingredients. We are of the same height (the Waughs shrank in height throughout the nineteenth century, perhaps because it suited their bossiness to choose small wives). If there is one characteristic common to all my father's family, it is the habit of setting up house and staying there. I have inherited this propensity. My brother is indefatigably nomadic; a legacy, it might be claimed, from Thomas Gosse, from whom, perhaps, I got my youthful aspiration to become a painter. Most of my father's family were pious, some extravagantly so. I have theological and ecclesiastical interests. My brother is indifferent in matters of religion – the spirit of William Morgan? Most of our forebears of whom we have any account have been hospitable and gregarious; my brother is all of that, retaining in his sixties an undiminished zest for life and a delight in human society in every form. I am easily bored and fond of solitude. My brother was athletic in youth: I never; Cockburn's skating there gaining mastery, Morgan's club-foot here? As I suggested at the start of this chapter, precedent can be found in a few generations for every idiosyncrasy. The newspapers, I see, have now taken to the expression 'genes' for what was once described as 'blood'. A happier metaphor perhaps is a game of poker. One is dealt a hand the value of which depends on the combined relationship of its components, not on the sum of its numerals. One can 'stand' on what one is given or discard and draw, not always improving the hand by doing so. Every card, high and low, is in the pack of heredity. No two hands are identical.

So, sceptical of its relevance, I close this account of my inheritance and start on my own experiences.

Chapter Two

ENVIRONMENT

I WAS BORN in the late autumn of 1903. I have no more memory of the house where this occurred than of the event itself. It was in a cul-de-sac called Hillfield Road, near the Hampstead cricket ground, off the Finchley Road; we left in my infancy. I was christened Arthur Evelyn St John: the first name after my father; the second from a whim of my mother's. I have never liked the name. In America it is used only of girls and from time to time even in England it has caused confusion as to my sex. At my private school I would silence ridicule by quoting the precedent of Field-Marshal Sir Evelyn Wood. (Once during the Italian-Abyssinian war I went to a military post many miles from any white woman, preceded by a signal apprising them of the arrival of *'Evelyn Waugh, English writer'*. The entire small corps of officers, shaven and polished, turned out to greet me each bearing a bouquet. I was disconcerted; they were overcome by consternation.) St John was more absurd. I had a High Church godfather who insisted that I must be given the name of a saint. They might have left it plain John, but instead added the prefix of sanctity, thus seeming to claim a spurious family connection.

In the backwash of the psychological speculations of the last generation there flounders a naive curiosity about early childhood. A year or two before the time of writing I submitted to an interview for the television. My questioner was plainly much more interested in my life in the nursery than in any subsequent adventures. His task, presumably, was to reveal to his public the influences and experiences which had formed the character of a writer and his work. Travel, for example, and my service in the army have stimulated my imagination. He cared for none of these things. Instead he seemed eager to disinter some hidden disaster or sorrow in my childhood. I was a disappointing subject. Save for a few uncertain flashes my mind is dark in the years of illiteracy; or rather, save for a few pale shadows, it is an even glow of pure happiness.

My father's childhood was haunted by terrors, those his father imposed and those of his own invention compounded of overheard scraps of servants' gossip about criminals and ghosts; nightly dread of the moment when his nurse shut her bible, put out the lamp and went downstairs to supper; dread even of the movement of a grandfather clock (familiar and friendly to me in my father's hall), which uttered a small premonitory rattle and rumble before striking. My grandmother had been imbued with the expectation of the imminent end of the world and with the fear of Hell. She scrupulously guarded my father from such alarms. She could not preserve him from the secret fear of a breaking coffee-cup (never heard) which was said to re-echo in Corsley Rectory on the anniversary of the sudden death of a previous incumbent.

I was entirely free of such afflictions. In compensation I have few memories of early joys – the first sight of the sea or of snow – which others, more impressionable than I, have poetically recorded.

My first visual memory is of a camera obscura on the pier at Weston-super-Mare. On that day, I have been told, I suffered an absurd and nearly fatal accident. I was biting a hard-boiled egg when the yolk suddenly shot from its white case and lodged entire in my throat, threatening me with asphyxiation. Apoplectic of face I was thumped and shaken by the heels. It was a close-run thing whether that hard ball came up, went down or stuck there to throttle me. It went down. Others, rather often, reminded me of the alarm I caused. My only recollection of that picnic is of the luminous, circular table-top in the dark hut, over which there mysteriously moved the reflections of passing holiday-makers.

I remember a small sharp disappointment on the death of a pet rabbit. It developed a growth in the jaw and was sent to the vet to be killed. This was explained to me and I was reconciled to its loss. But the vet on his own initiative decided to operate. He sent the animal back a week later pronouncing it cured. I greeted it ecstatically and it died that night.

I have also been told that at the age of four or five I fell into an unholy passion with my father, who, after a long and fully indulged morning at Hampstead Heath Fair, sought to lead me home to luncheon. I rolled in the sandy path abusing him as: 'You brute, you beast, you hideous ass', a phrase which became part of our family language. These are the only untoward incidents of my first age which remains for me paradisal – warm, bright, serene and quite featureless – lived in joyous conformity to the law of two adored deities, my nurse and my mother.

My nurse, though the fact never occurred to me, was quite young and, in my eyes, very beautiful. She came from Chilcompton, a village near Midsomer Norton, and her sister was nurse to two girl cousins of mine with whom I spent much of my holidays. She wore the nanny's uniform of the time, but we always called her by her Christian name, Lucy. Until 1914 all our servants came from the bounds of my grandfather's practice and none left us except to be married. Most were recruited from my aunts' bible classes. Lucy cannot have been one of these, for she was strictly 'chapel'. I think it grieved her that my mother played bridge and that my father drank wine, but she had no responsibility for their salvation. I was not subject to these temptations. But I was taken to the theatre during her régime and on my return she was markedly unresponsive to my excited descriptions of the event. Her father had risen from labourer to smallholder and had a milk-round on which, on rare and delightful occasions, I accompanied her brother, and took the reins while he delivered from churn to jug. I believed without question that Lucy's father was faultless. No comparison was ever directly drawn between him and my father. Lucy's father was a saint and hero with whom all comparisons would have been frivolous. He had only once betrayed anger, when her brother wantonly destroyed a sitting of eggs, and then only because the eggs were the property of a neighbour. Like most nannies Lucy was a regular bible-reader. She cannot be said to have searched the scriptures. She read undeviating, right through genealogies, law and minor prophets, accepting them all with the same confidence in their life-giving properties. This office took her six months when she turned back to Genesis and started again. Years later during the second war I found myself with two other bored Englishmen snowed up in Croatia in what was called 'a pocket of resistance'. Our few books included a bible. One of our number was garrulous and argumentative. For the sake of quiet we offered him large bets that he could not read the whole bible. It was a book with which he had little acquaintance. For three blessed days he was absorbed, interrupting his reading only to expound the new truths revealed to him. But Leviticus beat him. He gave up and paid up. Not so Lucy. For her the volume itself was the object of veneration, handled with especial care. No other book was ever laid upon it.

I think Lucy fully returned my love. She was never cross or neglectful. I remember only one quarrel. We used to frequent an enclosed garden near our house which had lately been bequeathed to make an extension of the Heath. Here my brother and some friends of his played a trick, hiding me, and telling Lucy that I had fallen into an ornamental pond. Her agitation was extreme and when I was restored to her I joined in the laughter. She led me straight home, where to my abject consternation I found that she was in tears. When she reported the matter to my mother she emphasised, not her own humiliation, but the fact that I had connived at a lie.

Throughout all her time with us she was engaged to a serious young lay preacher and carpenter. Once or twice he travelled up from Somerset to visit her. When he did so he would walk out from his London lodgings rather than make use of bus or tube on a Sunday. When I was eight she left to marry him. They settled in Chilcompton, where he rose to be a prosperous builder and timber-merchant.

My mother was small, neat, reticent and, until her last decade, very active. She had no special literary interests, but read a book a fortnight, always a good one. She would have preferred to live in the country and from her I learned that towns are places of exile where the unfortunate are driven to congregate in order to earn their livings in an unhealthy and unnatural way. She had to be content with walking her dog on Hampstead Heath and working in the garden. She spent hours there, entirely absorbed; not merely snipping off dead heads but potting, planting, watering, weeding. (A man came one or two days a week to dig or mow or roll.) When my father in middle age, after the fashion of his family, chose epitaphs for himself and my mother, he directed that on his side of the gravestone should be inscribed: 'And another book was opened which is the book of life' and on my mother's 'My beloved is gone down into the garden to gather lilies'; but her flowers did not interest her more than her fruit and vegetables. There was nothing pre-Raphaelite about my mother. I associate her less with lilies than with earthy wash-leather gloves and baskets of globe artichokes and black and red currants.

Her rustic tastes were formed by her childhood at Shire-hampton, where she and her sister were sent from India at an age which left them no memories of their place of birth, to the care of two maiden great-aunts and a bachelor great-uncle, a retired sailor. It was by these great-aunts and in this house, the Priory, that my grandfather had been detected with his rosary. Shirehampton is now a suburb of Bristol. The Priory has become a vicarage and its meadows have been overbuilt. In my mother's childhood the place was rural and my mother was entirely happy there. All her life she looked back on that elderly *ménage* as the ideal of home. The various households established by her stepfather fell far short of it. He had retired from his army chaplaincy in India and during my mother's adolescence her family were unsettled. With dwindling fortune and growing family they moved to Clifton, to Paulton, to Weston-super-Mare; my step-grandfather 'took duty' at churches which were without regular incumbents. My grandmother, after a few years, found each house unhealthy. The furniture was packed up, new curtains and carpets ordered; the family moved on. It was not until after my mother's marriage that her stepfather finally presented himself to the living of Bishop's Hill, Taunton, where my half-uncle succeeded him.

My grandmother, brought up in the idleness of British India, spent most of her day on a sofa, knew nothing of housewifery, lived in what in retrospect seemed to my mother continual, avoidable discomfort. It was an early principle of my mother's in domestic matters to 'think what mama would do' and to do the opposite. She taught herself the arts of housekeeping. I remember her as always busy with her hands, sewing, making jam, bathing and clipping her poodle (in a time when these dogs were much larger than they are today), and with hammer and screwdriver hanging shelves and building rabbit hutches from packing-cases.

It was she who gave me my first lessons. I shared them with a little red-headed girl of my own age, Stella, the daughter of our neighbour Ernest Rhys, a bearded poet and literary man, the first editor of *Everyman's Library* in the days when that series was embellished by the fine end-papers now unhappily abandoned. The Rhyses were strongly Celtic, he Welsh, his wife, also a writer, Irish. Stella's gifts proved to be musical. My mother was unable to help her there. There was no piano in my home and neither my mother nor Lucy ever sang to me. The few nursery rhymes I knew were learned as verses not as songs. Stella and I learned our rudiments from *Reading without Tears* and *Little Arthur's History*; we had our multiplication tables by rote and did simple sums; on our walks we were taught to name the then abundant wildflowers. By the age of seven, when I first went to school, I was, I think, better equipped than most modern children; certainly better than my own have been at that age.

For my first seven years my father was a figure of minor importance and interest. I remember the smell of the preparation which he used to burn to relieve his asthma, the sound of his coughing and choking on winter mornings, his voice calling my mother down from the nursery when he returned from London, the sweet smell of his mild pipe-tobacco, the quiet imposed on Saturday mornings when he was at home, writing.

I think he paid a visit to the nursery every evening and often made brief efforts to entertain, but I never particularly welcomed him; in fact, I regarded his appearance as an interruption and, in what I suppose is an entirely normal fashion, grudged his usurpation of my mother's attention.

My brother slept with me during his school holidays, but seldom came into the day-nursery. The five years that separated us made, in childhood, a complete barrier. There were other beneficent likeable grown-up persons who passed in the middle distance of my small world, but my mother and Lucy were the sole objects of love in the lustrum between pram and prep school which love permeated and directed.

2

More than once already in the preceding pages mention has been made of the obliteration of English villages. The process is notorious and inevitable. Expostulation is futile, lament tedious. This is part of the grim cyclorama of spoliation which surrounded all English experience in this century and any understanding of the immediate past (which presumably is the motive for reading a book such as this) must be incomplete unless this huge deprivation of the quiet pleasures of the eye is accepted as a dominant condition, sometimes making for impotent resentment, sometimes for mere sentimental apathy, sometimes poisoning love of country and of neighbours. To have been born into a world of beauty, to die amid ugliness, is the common fate of all us exiles.

'Composition of Place' is one of the preliminaries of medita-
tion recommended in old-fashioned books of devotion. It
should be an essential service of writer to reader, but it is
impossible for the young, difficult for the elderly, to focus the
'dissolving view' in the magic lantern and see plainly the
outward aspect of the world of even fifty years back. Place-
names once evocative of quite other associations now bear an
alien accent. It is easier to stir the emotions than the visual
imagination. I was four years old when my father built his
house in what was then the village of North End, Hampstead.
He was, in fact, the first of its spoliators. When we settled there
the tube reached no further than Hampstead. Golders Green
was a grassy cross-road with a sign pointing to London,
Finchley and Hendon; such a place as where 'the Woman in
White' was encountered. All round us lay dairy farms, market
gardens and a few handsome old houses of brick or stucco
standing in twenty acres or more; not far off there survived
woods where we picked bluebells, and streams beside which
we opened our picnic baskets. North End Road was a steep,
dusty lane with white posts and rails bordering its footways.
North End, the reader may remember, was the place where
Bill Sikes spent the first night of his flight after the murder of
Nancy.

My father celebrated the building of the house with an essay
in which he said: 'We who were bred by country pastures and
educated under the shadow of that golden Abbey in the West,
must always feel like pilgrims and sojourners in a land of
lamp-posts and kerb-stones. . . . If this book should fall into
the hands of any reader who, imprisoned in some sunless
back-room in a crowded quarter of the town, still feels the
stirring of spring in his blood, as the dingy lime-tree opposite
begins to break into leaf, let him come to Hampstead and learn
for himself the wisdom of making a home.

'Oh, but I have done an unselfish thing in telling him this!
For I know he will yearn to be about the business of Balbus,
and, as likely as not, he will plant himself upon the meadow

with the willows, that looks so spring-like from my book-room door today. Nevertheless one must not repine. My work in this line is done. Balbus has built his wall. It is a plain wall enough and Mr Voysey or Mr Baillie Scott could better it with a pennib stroke; but at least it encloses a hearth of homely comfort, a hearth that cherishes green thoughts in a green shade.'

His expectations were realised. The meadow with the willows was sold to the builders. Soon after ours other new houses sprang up alongside us. Opposite us stood a large late Victorian villa named Ivy House (where Pavlova spent her last years) with wooded grounds. Soon these were built on, leaving only the garden and a pond for the ballerina's privacy. Then the tube emerged into the open at Golders Green and round the station grew shops, a theatre, a cinema and a dense spread of new brick and rough cast dwellings not unlike our own. Eventually (I think soon after the first war) our postal address was altered from Hampstead to Golders Green. My father deplored the change, and, as far as was possible, ignored it, because Hampstead had historic associations, with Keats and Blake and Constable, while Golders Green meant, to him, merely a tube station. I, at that self-conscious age, minded more, for I knew, as he did not, that the district had somehow acquired a slightly comic connotation; but the new nomenclature was appropriate enough, for by that time it was in Golders Green we did our shopping and took the trains and buses. But in our first years there North End was a distinct village separated from the town of Hampstead to which we resorted for general extraneous purposes, by a strip of the Heath.

Its nucleus comprised an old bow-fronted inn, the Bull and Bush, famous in Cockney song, standing back from the road in a beer-garden in which the tables stood in bowers of creeper and climbing rose; a building called 'the Rooms' which served as an infant school, a village hall and on Sundays as a place of worship; a post office and village shop kept by an irascible man named Mr Borely. He was surly with all his customers

and positively savage with children until he got into some
trouble with the postal authorities. He used the same till
whether he sold stamps or bulls-eyes and he kept no accounts.
There was a question of his dismissal and my father was able
to put in a word which reprieved him. After that he became
very much more affable, to us at any rate. My father refused to
have a telephone in his house and it was to Mr Borely that we
went on the rare occasions when the doctor was summoned.
There was also a dairy named Tooley's. The Misses Tooley
ladled milk out of large china bins and sold sponge cakes and
gingerbread. Their father pastured his cows in a field nearby
and drove his rounds in a float, like the one at Chilcompton,
morning and evening. He wore white whiskers and sang
strongly in a kind of independent refrain at 'the Rooms' on
Sundays. Round these institutions clustered the cottages, their
gardens full of flowers and washing and gossip, such as were
portrayed at Cookham by Stanley Spencer. Of all this no trace
survives except in the name of the Bull and Bush, now quite
rebuilt with an asphalt car park covering its lawns and arbours.
As though to accentuate the desolation the brewers have
painted the first verse of the old song on a board outside it.

Two large houses dominated the hamlet, North End House
and North End Manor, each owned by a maiden lady. The lady
of the Manor was an aged misanthrope with whom we had no
communication except by letters of complaint about trespasses
of my own. It was in a meadow of hers, fronting North End
Road and backing on her kitchen garden (where my trespasses took place, usually with the innocent purpose of
retrieving a ball) that my father bought his plot. In fact, he
bought two plots (for the field was already divided into building lots) and later the kitchen garden also, so that my mother
had as much ground as she could manage. Between us and the
Manor gates was a waste space used all my childhood by the
builder as a depository for his materials. We called it for this
reason 'cistern land'. (After the death of the cross old woman
a co-educational school set up in the Manor. In the first war it

became a military hospital. It is still, just recognisable in parts, a hospital, much patronised by socialists.)

The lady of North End House, Miss Hoare, was very different. When I read descriptions, such as Mr E. M. Forster's, of the evangelical philanthropists of a century ago who were dubbed by Sydney Smith 'the Clapham Sect', I am reminded of her. She came of Quaker-banker stock much allied to the Gurneys and Buxtons of Norfolk. Like the Clapham Sect she had relations in politics (Samuel Hoare, Lord Templewood, was her nephew) and on the bench of bishops, but she eschewed string-pulling and devoted her whole life to practical benefactions widely ramifying but primarily centred in her own village. She must have been about sixty when we first knew her, rosy faced, white haired, blunt and cheerful in speech. When she first came to call she did so in her carriage. Apart from that occasion, except when she drove into London, I remember her as always on foot, shod in large, shapeless boots, plainly dressed and followed by two or three Scotch terriers. I rather suppose that my mother was the last neighbour on whom she called formally. She could not keep up with the new immigrants, for, besides the conurbation at Golders Green, another building enterprise was soon begun – Hampstead Garden Suburb. The houses there were better designed and their tenants were under particular restrictions about the height of their garden fences. They were inhabited not exactly by cranks, nor by bohemians, but mainly by a community of unconventional bourgeois of artistic interests. *Punch* of that period is full of drawings of the Garden Suburb by Townsend, who lived there. This utopia had its own presiding genius, a lady named Mrs (later Dame Henrietta) Barnett. My father, who had some difference with her, would sometimes wander about singing a ditty of his own composition which began:

'Blast it! Darn it!

'Henrietta Elizabeth Barnett'

so that I grew up to regard this, I now believe, exemplary lady as a ludicrous monster, but he was drawn into the community later by church-going and his perennial delight in amateur theatricals. All this was quite outside Miss Hoare's sphere of influence.

My mother said that Miss Hoare reminded her of her great-aunts at Shirehampton; she conceived a warm admiration for her (which my father professed to resent) and became her close associate in all her multifarious activities. They managed a 'clothing club' and, to inculcate thrift, a kind of private savings bank which entailed weekly visits to the neighbouring poor and much filling up of little shiny black account books. Besides the cottages round the inn there was in North End Road, a few hundred yards below us, a row of seedy old proletarian dwellings named 'the Terrace'. These were my mother's especial care, and I am sure she was a welcome visitor there. Miss Hoare and my mother also shared 'a district' in Shoreditch where they regularly visited very much poorer families than any in North End. On the days of Hampstead Heath Fair they set up a refuge, much frequented, for lost children and a first-aid station for those of all ages who fell out of swing-boats or cut themselves opening bottles. Miss Hoare played the harmonium on Sundays at 'the Rooms' and was a woman of deep, unemotional piety, but she did not confine herself to charitable work. Cricket was played in the meadow in front of North End House. Handbell-ringers were trained and at Christmas-time used to set up their trestle table and storm lanterns in, among other places, our front garden and give a performance of carol tunes. No one in North End, I think, except my father, went to work in London. That city seemed quite remote from the village. Except to reach Paddington Station on the way to Somerset, I do not suppose I went there eight times in my first eight years. One could see its smoke from Parliament Hill where in the summer a telescope was supposedly focused on St Paul's Cathedral. For a penny one could peer into the murk, but I never descried anything to attract me.

I do not know how long or how often Stella Rhys and I did

our lessons. Certainly I remember many mornings shopping with Lucy. The more impressive shops were in Finchley Road. For ordinary household purposes we frequented Heath Street and High Street. And our way up there became the most familiar in my life, for later I followed it daily to and from school. We crossed the road not troubling to look right or left, for there was very little traffic. Carters and coachmen going into London went either east through Highgate or west along the Finchley Road to St John's Wood. The only vehicles to pass us had business in Old Hampstead and of these rather a large proportion seemed to come to grief opposite our gate. It was quite common, or so it seems to me in retrospect, to see a dray-horse which had lost its footing, plunging, until a man sat on its head while others disentangled the traces, and bicyclists coasting down often spilled in the ditch. My mother was occupied on many Saturday afternoons bandaging the injured riders and sustaining them with tea.

Ivy House, as I have said, stood opposite with its grounds for a time unravaged. Once when the fence was being repaired I wrote my initials in the wet mortar of the low supporting wall and there I found them fifty years later under a mat of moss, somewhat eroded, so that they read 'FW', but still an infinitesimal private landmark where all else was changed.

I think that the reason we took the right-hand path was Lucy's reluctance to pass too near the Bull and Bush and another pub which stood by it. After North End the road became a cutting embowered in trees, its sandy banks shored up into little terraces with planks and stakes, on one side the Heath, on the other a grim empty house where the elder Pitt once confined himself. There was a turret room with double doors through which he had been fed when in extremes of melancholy and wrath and grey squirrels bred in the trees in the time before they infested the whole land. Indeed, I have heard it said that the pest began there with a pair which escaped from Regent's Park Zoo. Our path lay above the road past the seat where an old blind beggar read aloud from a

Braille bible. At his back lay the huge trunk of a fallen tree named 'the gibbet elm'. Highwaymen had been hanged on it, I was told; falsely, I have since learned. It was planted to mark the site of the gallows where a murderer named Jackson was executed in 1673 on the scene of his crime.

Next came the Italianate house which was then under construction for Lever, the manufacturer of Sunlight Soap; after that two large eighteenth-century houses behind trees and high walls and then Jack Straw's Castle where, I was told, rebel bands had twice been defeated, once in Wat Tyler's time when they were marching on London, once in the Gordon riots when they were coming out to burn Kenwood. A more recent and fully authentic incident occurred just behind the inn; Sadleir, the fraudulent railway speculator who formed the model for Dickens's 'Merdle', drank prussic acid there from a silver cream jug and was found with his legs stiffly protruding from a sand-pit. I do not think that Lucy gave me these lurid scraps of history. They must have come to me from my father a year or two later when he walked with me every morning to school.

Then came the Whitestone pond under a wide, windy sky, full of flying kites, with the Heath falling away from it leaving uninterrupted tree-tops stretching to Harrow on one side and to Highgate on the other. It is much the same today save for some nasty new flats. The banks have been tidied up and one no longer sees horses watering in the track that led through it. The pond was in my childhood already an archaism. In the summer saddle-donkeys were for hire in the Vale of Health and on the height on Sundays there were often a punch-and-judy show, a sparsely attended political meeting and a band of the Salvation Army. It was also loud with barking, for people took their dogs to exercise, throwing sticks for them to retrieve from the water.

From this point the narrow streets led down, some to the fine old houses of Frognal, some to the small shops that were our object. There was very little 'window-dressing' except at

Christmas-time, when a few paper chains and tinsel streamers would appear. The corn-chandler had a kind of panel in his window of various grains ornamentally arranged. There was also in the jewellers' window a clock in which a glass spiral revolved simulating a jet of water issuing from the mouth of a bronze lion. But in general it was not the merchandise that fascinated me but the dexterity of the shop-keepers and their assistants, who were deft with butter-hands, weights and scales, shovels and canisters, paper and string. The chemist had a gas burner on which he melted the wax to seal our purchases. Always from my earliest memories I delighted in watching things being well done.

The Hampstead of my childhood still bore plain marks of the character given it in the late eighteenth century; a pleasure garden; not a place from which people travelled to work in London, but where Londoners resorted on summer evenings and week-ends for refreshment and jollity.

Before Fair Days – Easter, Whitsun and the first Monday of August – the polychromatic procession of travelling shows passed our door – great tumbrils heaped with canvas and scaffolding, caravans of gypsies and freaks, cages of wild animals, the ponderous steam engines of the roundabouts. In a night whole streets of booths sprang up along the sandy tracks of the Heath.

Other Hampstead residents were inclined to lock their doors and lower their blinds. We always went, sometimes as a family party, sometimes I alone with Lucy. My mother, as I have said, was on post in a first-aid tent most of the day. I was taken in the morning or early afternoon, for in the evenings it was reputed to be rowdy, but the costers were there before us, streaming out of London in pony traps and donkey carts, many of the men in caps and suits covered with pearl buttons, almost all the women in the clothes which were said to be left in pawn between celebrations, velvet coats and skirts and ostrich-plumed hats such as Phil May used to draw. I jostled through the crowds joyfully. Their speech was unintelligible but they had a kind of pentecostal exuberance which communicated nothing but goodwill. They formed lines with linked arms and jigged to the music of concertinas. They sang songs. They rolled about the grass. They squirted one another with water pistols and tickled one another with feathers. I never saw a fight. Perhaps that came later in the 'rowdy' hours. The only hygienic restriction I can remember was a ban on ice-cream as sold from the bright barrows. I was told, as of something very obnoxious, that the Italians kept the mixture under their beds, and since I had a pot under mine, I surmised that it was made of urine and did not press for a relaxation of rule.

Monkeys still capered on hand-organs in those days and collected pennies in their tarbooshes. I believe I have seen a dancing bear led by its nose on a chain, but I am told this is improbable. Nothing, as I remember it, cost more than a penny; certainly two shillings afforded hours of pleasure. The smell was exhilarating – orange peel, sweat, beer, coconut, trampled grass, horses. On Hampstead Heath I saw my first cinema film; it did not attempt to tell a story, still less to move the passions. It merely portrayed figures in motion – very irregular motion – and I thought it a very poor counter-attraction to the menagerie and the fat woman.

When it ended, the fair disappeared as fast as it had grown. It travelled down the hill and away to other grounds. The rubbish was speared and basketed and the breeze blew clear through the gorse.

I have attempted no description yet of our home. It was perfectly suited to my father's needs and means; he remained there for some twenty-five years until the traffic under the windows obliged him to move to a quiet backwater in Highgate. It was a typical, unpretentious house of its period, of the kind that could then be put up for little more than £1,000. He named it Underhill after a lane near Midsomer Norton and was aggrieved when after some years the post office authorities insisted on attaching a number to it. He always spoke of it by name – 'When are you coming to Underhill?' – and, until he moved, retained it as his address in *Who's Who*.

My day-nursery was decorated with a pictorial wallpaper representing figures in mediaeval costume; it opened on a balcony overlooking the garden. The night-nursery was on the floor above facing the road. I spent few waking hours there and remember little of it. I was a healthy, if not particularly robust, child and was seldom kept in bed. My few trivial illnesses are not in retrospect associated with any kind of suffering; they were treats. When my temperature rose above 99° I was given a kind of delicious aspic jelly known as 'Brand's Essence'.

My mother and Lucy did not pamper me. Any attempt to malinger was sharply corrected. When I fell and grazed hands and knees they were scrubbed, not disinfected. I was not discouraged from hazardous climbing except so far as I endangered roof-tiles and branches. I was never harassed, as some children were and are, by warnings of physical danger from edged tools, animals, microbes, poisons or dirt. Gypsies, in those early days, often camped near us. I was never taught to fear them as possible kidnappers who would, as was their reputed practice, stain me with walnut-juice. They seemed to have a plethora of swarthy children of their own and the life of the caravan with its dogs and foals and stew-pots looked inviting.

There was one spare bedroom which in retrospect seems almost always to have been in use by some guest or relation. My mother had a small sitting-room where I sometimes sat with her. Its particular attraction was an ivory work-box made in India for one of her great-aunts, divided into many trays and compartments of sandal wood and fitted with numerous ivory spools for winding silk, needle cases, boxes of various sizes and delicate embroidery scissors and stilettos. I lunched in the dining-room, but had my other meals upstairs in the nursery so as to be out of my father's way. The main room of the house, the book-room, I seldom used except in transit to the garden through french windows, across a verandah and down some steps.

The furniture, almost all of which survives today in my house or my brother's, was mostly inherited oak and mahogany of good character. There were bookcases everywhere, leaving little wall space for the few prints and water-colours. It was a light, bright, warm house, to which 'I always returned with delight, but I never had any particular love of it as distinct from my love of home, and I always, from the moment I became critical of him, regarded my father's devotion to the actual structure as slightly absurd. He wrote of it sometimes as though it were a ship, referring to its 'stout timbers'. His attachment was sentimental but unaffected. He beat me only twice, on each occasion when I had done wilful injuries to its fabric; once by paring the corners of a chimney-piece with a new knife, once by excavating a tunnel through a boot-cupboard into the foundations where, until detected, I was able to crawl about under the floor joists.

The only part of my home to fascinate me was, when we acquired it, the narrow area of the old kitchen garden at the back of the green-houses. There weeds grew rank, head-high, and lightless steps led down to a derelict furnace-house. This cellar and this wilderness I took as my special province, thus early falling victim to the common English confusion of the antiquated with the sublime, which has remained with me; all my life I have sought dark and musty seclusions, like an animal preparing to whelp.

This taste was richly indulged at my aunts' house in Mid-somer Norton.

When my grandparents died these three maiden ladies elected to stay on in their old home and, when I first knew it, little had been changed since the 1870s. I suppose that in fact I seldom spent longer than two months there in any year, but the place captivated my imagination as my true home never did. One of the reasons, I am told, that I gave for my preference was that 'people had died there'.

From outside it seemed a regular, prosaic habitation, well hidden in its small grounds by walls and shrubberies. I suspect that the stucco-covered front rooms and porch had been imposed in early Victorian days on an older farm-house, for inside it was rambling and haphazard, with rooms all at different levels, stone-flagged passages and a tiny interior courtyard where stood a pump. There were other pumps in the garden, the stables and behind the kitchen and these for a child brought up with 'main' water were things of mystery. My grandfather's old coachman, who now cleaned boots and pottered in the garden, drew water from them with much display of energy.

There were many quaint features; one a small room off the smoking-room called 'the dark pantry', which was lit by only a single pane of red glass; it had once been used for developing photographic plates. Another was what had been the nurseries but were now lumber rooms. They were approached by a very steep staircase, gated at the top, and were themselves on two levels. In one a small window on the level of the floor opened on a large rain-water tank whose surface was vivid green and totally covered in thick scum.

The library had few books, none to interest me at my age, but a series of glass cases containing fossils which the miners used to give my grandfather.

I also delighted in the lighting – oil-lamps in the rooms downstairs, gas in the passages, candles in the bedrooms. Winifred Peck has recorded the elation of Ronald Knox and his brother on their first introduction to electricity. My own experience was antithetical.

I was alarmed but exhilarated by the bath-room. There was one only for the entire household and a bath had to be prepared half an hour in advance. It stood in a tall, narrow room which had no window save for a small sky-light. A geyser, already, in my first knowledge of it, what would now be called a 'vintage' model, was set aflame. Presently the whole room was full of steam and gas-fumes so that the fishtail burner shed little light. What it shed fell on the grinning teeth of a stuffed monkey which had been brought to England by (I think) a great-uncle and had died of sunstroke when being exhibited at Corsley at a school-treat. The steam condensed on its glass case, where it stood high overhead, so that only the teeth were visible to the child sitting in the rapidly cooling water below. I was certainly frightened of this creature, but in a pleasurable way, as I was frightened by my Aunt Connie when she sang, at my insistence, the ballad of 'Lord Randal'. There are, as is well known, many versions. My aunt's was wholly anglicised in diction, long and throbbing with cumulative horror. As she sat at the upright piano of the drawing-room among the soft lamps and deep shadows she would throw her head back and deliver what seemed to be a witch's incantation.

'Oh that was strong poison, Randal my son,'

'You'll die, you'll die, my sweet, pretty one.'

There was no doubt that Lord Randal was murdered by his 'true love', not, as in some versions, the victim of an injudicious diet. The incident of the hounds swelling before they died haunted me especially, for I loved dogs in those days. After I had heard this ballad – and I repeatedly demanded it – I would go up to bed genuinely but delightfully frightened, and compose myself for sleep by making little pearls from the wax round the edge of my candle.

The dining-room was dark and full of oil paintings. The drawing-room was much cluttered with small tables, draperies, screens and ornaments on carved brackets. It contained two cabinets full of 'curiosities' – fans, snuff boxes, carved nuts, old coins and medals; some of them unremarkable, such as, carefully wadded, encased and labelled, the charred tip of a walking-stick with which some relation had climbed Mount Vesuvius and a lock (unauthenticated) of Wordsworth's hair. Tourists' trophies had not yet become standardised; the presents which my Uncle Alick had brought home from sea were odder and better made than the spoils of a modern cruise and these were all preserved and might be inspected only under supervision on wet days. The most fascinating exhibit in the collection was 'the White Blood', a specimen my grandfather had preserved from a patient dying of some form of acute anaemia. It was kept in a glass phial inside a screw-topped ivory cylinder with some incomprehensible scientific notes in my grandfather's handwriting. The substance had long ceased to be white (if it was ever truly so) and had become congealed and brown. When, years later, after the death of the last of my aunts I came to superintend the disposal of their property I sought vainly for this delight of my childhood.

The house at Midsomer Norton was full of interesting smells, unlike my home, where the windows were always open so that my father's fumes of tobacco and asthma-inhalations and even the scent of my mother's hyacinths which, in their season, flowered in bowls everywhere, never lingered to permeate the rooms. There was no tobacco at Norton, but there was ever present in one part or another the still airs of gas and oil and mould and fruit; in some quarters the house smelled like a neglected church, in others like a populous bazaar. My aunts' dogs smelled more strongly than my mother's and there was an aged and ferocious cockatoo whose tray, before it was cleaned, reeked. The stables still smelled of leather and horses, though my aunts had only a single pony and trap. For some years there was a decaying brougham in the coach-house, highly redolent.

I used also to visit my Raban grandmother at Bishops Hull Vicarage. This too was agreeable; there were the same stable-smells as at Midsomer Norton, there were apricots and figs ripening on the walls, there were objects of Indian workmanship. My step-grandfather had a long white beard and a deep voice which should have been impressive; my step-aunts were companionable and kind, my step-uncle seemed to me a droll fellow (he took eight years to get a pass degree at Cambridge, until after his many failures he at length qualified as a parson and succeeded to the living). But this household never caught my fancy in the same way.

My Waugh aunts had a way of investing all their possessions with an individual character and importance. As Macaulay said contemptuously of Strawberry Hill, 'there was a story about the bell-rope'. In the last years of her life my Aunt Elsie began surreptitiously distributing these possessions (which were not legally hers) to various friends and relations with a certain discernible malice towards those who she thought might value them less exorbitantly.

There was nothing worth very much, but it all belonged to another age which I instinctively, even then, recognised as superior to my own. Most of the furniture at home was old, but it never felt old in its bright new surroundings as did its contemporaries at Midsomer Norton. One, I am sure uncon-scious, imposture made on me in childhood was in regard to a silver reproduction of the bronze bowl found at the Lake Village of Glastonbury. This, I was told, was unique, made specially for my grandfather by Dr Bulleid, the archaeologist who excavated the site. It is a vessel of fine design, but I learned later that it was reproduced in large numbers by the silversmith in Taunton. My aunts, I think, came in the end to regard it as the original; certainly as something of great worth. They always locked it up when they went away, in a little, otherwise empty safe in the smoking-room.

This was no Renishaw or Knole; it was the simple home of a prosperous Victorian country doctor. But a child's mind does not consider sale-room prices nor need great spaces in which to expand. The bric-à-brac in the cabinets, the Sheffield plate, the portraits by nameless artists quickened my childish aesthetic appetite as keenly as would have done any world-famous collection and the narrow corridors stretched before me like ancient galleries. I am sure that I loved my aunts' house because I was instinctively drawn to the ethos I now recognise as mid-Victorian; not, as perhaps psychologists would claim, that I now relish things of that period because they remind me of my aunts.

I was much attached to them and they were unfailingly

indulgent to me. Maiden aunts seem scarcely to exist today; of my own generation I can name less than half a dozen. (I know many unmarried women endowed with nephews and nieces, but these have discarded their maidenheads and found their own independent social circles. 'Maiden aunt' in its true sense should mean one who remained an integral part of the family.) Perhaps they were destroyed by 'Saki' Munro. The deserted mother is now the prevailing type of unattached woman. A generation ago there were maiden aunts in almost every English family and though notoriously ridiculous they exerted for the most part a highly benevolent influence. Miss Hoare of North End was a shining example.

So far as there can be any certainty in a question which so often reveals surprising anomalies, I can assert that my aunts were maidens. The two elder, Connie and Trissie, would have made good wives. Aunt Connie was reputedly a pretty girl and I knew her as a handsome woman; Aunt Trissie was plain but with an agreeable face. Aunt Connie was known to have had suitors, none of whom she found acceptable. Girls in their position met few eligible men. Had they lived in a garrison town or naval base, or had they been sent, like many of my forebears, to India, they would no doubt have been mated. But in the stratified society of North Somerset they were part of a very thin layer, superior to farmers and tradesmen, inferior to the county families. They were seldom asked to the houses where my grandfather shot. Nothing was ever done to introduce them to a larger world, so they remained until their death in the house where they were born, leading busy and cheerful lives.

The youngest, Elsie, my favourite, elected early to be an invalid. In old age she achieved a certain elegance. She was selfish, capricious and sharp tongued and saw to it that she was cosseted. After the second war, when they were left without servants and with much reduced income, my Aunt Connie waited on her with devotion. I remember Aunt Elsie then reclining in a chaise-longue on the vine-covered verandah, her white hair prettily arranged with blue ribbons, in a lace-trimmed jacket, displaying her rings and brooches and toying with the tea things Aunt Connie had brought to her side. She said: 'I try not to feel bitter when I see Connie, much older than me and able to go everywhere and do everything.'

All three women were intelligent. They had not, of course, received any 'higher education'. Before 1914 they travelled a little, never beyond the narrowest tourist limits. Until their last years they were quite comfortably off, deriving their income mainly from the coal mine on the Morgan property at Tylyrcoh. My Aunt Connie sat on the bench when women became eligible as magistrates, and was much distressed by the iniquities there revealed to her. All three had the prudishness proper to maiden aunts, though Aunt Elsie in old age developed a tolerance of very slightly indelicate fiction.

The parish church was the centre of their lives. Aunt Connie was a woman of fervent devotion; indeed her heart stopped at the moment of consecration at an early Holy Communion service. All three had bible classes which met on Sunday afternoons, Aunt Connie of older girls in the dining-room, Aunt Elsie of younger girls in the drawing-room, Aunt Trissie of young men in the library. These began and ended with a hymn and it was noticeable that the singing always began last and finished first in the drawing-room; after a few years the younger girls were amalgamated with the elder and Aunt Elsie spent the afternoon in light reading.

My two girl cousins from Chilcompton (whose parents lived apart) were my constant companions at Midsomer Norton. These Sunday-afternoon classes, since we were excluded from them, fascinated us and we used to spy on them. We were supposed to spend the hour in the smoking-room, but from there a verandah led past the men's privy and gave a covered line of approach to the conservatory (which in my day conserved little except a few ferns and a rocking-chair) from which a coloured glass door opened on the dining-room. It was possible to leave this ajar and so listen with guilty glee to Aunt Connie's simple discourse which would not have held our attention if given from the pulpit. But the more exciting assembly was Aunt Trissie's young miners. These we could observe from the leads over the side door as they clumped up the drive, stiff and shiny in their Sunday best. We knew them as 'bonnies' because a visiting parson had once referred to them infelicitously as 'your bonny lads'. My aunt had greater influence with the bonnies than either vicar or curate. They formed a club, social, athletic, but primarily pious and many of them continued to attend after marriage as grown men. When my aunt died they watched all night in relays at her coffin.

I had other companions besides my cousins, in particular the children of Dr Bulleid, the archaeologist, and a boy of my own age who had had an unusual and, it seemed to me, enviable experience in childhood which was recounted me under the pledge that I should never mention it to him. When his father was serving in India a sepoy had entered the nursery and bloodily murdered his *ayah*. He had been persuaded that it had all been a bad dream (would modern psychologists approve?). I never did question him on the subject, but believed that in his position I would have regarded the adventure as a source of pride.

These and others formed a circle of friends quite distinct from those I knew at Hampstead. There were boisterous little parties several times a week, but all our lives, and mine especially, were much involved in my aunts' multifarious activities. There was always something being 'got up' at Midsomer Norton in which my aunts were the directors and animators. Church bazaars nowadays seem largely to subsist on well-meaning people who purchase ordinary commercial articles and resell them in order to gratify the organisers. Then a number of arts and crafts were practised, sewing, fretwork, wood-carving (at which Aunt Trissie excelled), wickerwork and the adornment of jampots with painted roses. There was a brief vogue for an extinct art called 'pen-painting'; table mats and doyleys were cut out of stiffened muslin and adorned with floral devices in thick quick-drying paint, applied with a broad gold nib. My Aunt Elsie excelled in this exercise, but quickly tired of it. All this was organised and often executed among my aunts' tea things. There were theatricals for the Girls Friendly Society for which costumes, properties and scenery were made and rehearsals held in the house. What is now done in Women's Institutes was then done at home.

Aunt Connie usually had some large work of ecclesiastical embroidery on hand, for she was gently impelling the parish into ritualistic practices. Once there was a whole altar frontal, framed and stencilled in an elaborate design which she laid out in gold thread and later filled with silk. I tried to emulate her, but was discouraged in this girlish pursuit; not, however, before I had acquired some proficiency.

What else do I remember of those long, frequent visits? A series of still-lives of antiquated objects such as I never saw at home: an electric battery, a wire-bound cylinder on a mahogany base, equipped with two brass handles from which by drawing out a rod, an increasingly powerful current could be drawn until the grip became rigid (this had been part of the clinical apparatus of my grandfather, a fad of his time, efficacious, it was believed, in nervous disorders); a magic-lantern; a stereoscope through which one could study in startling relief the scenes of biblical history; an engraved fac-simile of the death warrant of Charles I which I ruined by upsetting a bottle of Indian ink while trying to copy the regicides' signatures; a round table whose top consisted of a single polished fossil – all told, not a big showing of concrete images to represent so potent an influence on a childhood in which, so far as memory testifies, things counted for more than people.

There was much church-going. This never bored me. Sunday evensong was a positive pleasure.

My father's visits became less frequent after his mother's death. Midsomer Norton was a place where he always suffered from asthma. He was by nature a host rather than a guest

and he fretted in other people's houses. We were there together only once, when I was rising eleven. Then, I remember,
he paced about bemoaning the deterioration since his father's
time. There were abundant grounds for his lament. Out-
buildings threatened collapse. The gates of the poultry yard
hung loose on their hinges. The stable-loft, which had been a
special resort and where I had left scratched on the beams a
record of every visit, was pronounced unsafe. Panes were
broken in the hot-houses (no longer heated) and left unmended.
The vines no longer bore fruit.

But none of this decay troubled me. I rather relished it.
Regrets came later when, as my aunts grew older, the interior
of the house grew younger. Late but ineluctable the twentieth
century came seeping in. Plush gave place to chintz, gas to
electric-light; the primitive geyser was superseded; water
came from the main and the pumps rusted; the accumulation of
brackets and occasional tables and china was dispersed; the
walls were stripped of their old papers and painted. The clocks
stopped and their bronze and marble and ormolu cases were
replaced with bright new time-pieces. Aunt Elsie conceived
that stuffed birds and mounted butterflies were no longer
in good taste and had them removed to the 'dark pantry'.
Instead she indulged a liking for deplorable china animals,
which her friends gave her in profusion, comic pre-Disney
puppies and kittens, trios of monkeys covering eyes, mouth
and ears. The postal authorities demanded that the house
should be named – previously the writing-paper bore the simple
heading 'Midsomer Norton, Bath'. She decided whimsically to
call it 'Down-along', and despite Aunt Connie's mild objec-
tions, it was so known at the sorting office, though nowhere
else. (Letters addressed under the old style were always punctually delivered.)

The pony got into the walled garden and died of a surfeit
of unripe apricots which he ate from the tree. The trap disappeared and a Morris two-seater, driven by a 'lady companion',
took its place.

My aunts grew poorer, like all small rentiers, though never approaching penury. The kitchen-garden across the lane was sold and built over. Eventually, after the second war the library and servants' quarters were let as a separate dwelling. I still called often, never staying the night, but driving over for an hour or two. My memories of the final stage are vague, firmly rooted in what I knew during the first fifteen years of my life. After the death of my last aunt, Elsie, who like most invalids lived the longest, the place was sold and converted into offices for the local government.

I have not been back since.

3

Specific treats were rather rare. Those arranged by my father were always on a more lavish scale than my mother's. I did not particularly prefer them, but I recognised them as part of a male, more luxurious style of life. When we went to the theatre with my father we sat in the stalls and lunched before in Soho, eating an unaccustomed number of highly flavoured courses. My mother and I ate in Lyons' tea-shops and queued for the pit. But these were the events of Christmas, one of each yearly.

With my mother I went by bus to museums. Picture galleries did not interest me in childhood. I liked Egyptian mummies, illuminated manuscripts, mediaeval weapons. My father took me to the Tower of London, St Alban's Abbey and such sites. He gave lively explanations of all we saw, put himself on good terms with beefeaters and vergers, tipped liberally, creating a little aura of importance about us that was lacking when my mother and I were out alone together. Mr Roland (of whom later) took his children and me to the Military Tournament at Olympia, where his post at the War Office enabled him to seat us in luxury. Miss Hoare sometimes drove us to the Zoo on Sundays, taking with her a large basket of food for the animals. She knew what each preferred. She knew all the keepers and we were taken behind the cages and allowed to fondle the more docile exhibits.

Once only, in my very early childhood, did the four of us attempt a family holiday at the seaside – I think at Ramsgate. We took a small furnished house, where for the first time in my life we were attended by a manservant, a seedy German who somehow impressed me. I fell down the narrow stairs and cut my eye and was consoled with cherry pie. The experiment was a disaster, I learned later. I was happy enough, but my father detested it and there was no repetition. After that my mother and father always went abroad together in June. Once at least every summer, perhaps more often, she took me to the seaside for two or three days of unclouded delight, usually to Brighton or Westcliff or Broadstairs. We stayed in small private hotels and spent the days on the piers, on sand or on shingle. I never on these expeditions made the acquaintance, or desired it, of other children.

My father belonged to the Savile Club, then in Piccadilly, and he had seats for us there both for King Edward VII's funeral and King George V's coronation. I missed both events, one for measles, one for chickenpox. As I have said, I was very rarely ill. The only serious disturbance of my environment was in the summer of 1912 when I went down with appendicitis and was operated on at home on the kitchen table. It was then considered a rather dangerous affair. My parents were anxious and the régime of the house was disturbed by the presence of a nurse, whom I dubbed 'the Scoundrel', who antagonised family and servants alike. I was kept in ignorance of my condition. Lucy slept in my room the night before the operation. After I had fallen asleep she remembered that various vessels of water, which had been boiled, should have been covered. She went downstairs to do so, and I asked where she had been. She said she had been to 'cover something'. My mother asked her why she did not say that she had left the room for the lavatory. 'I could not tell a lie.' Next morning a strange man, not the family doctor, came into my bedroom and said: 'Now I want you to smell this delicious scent', putting a gauze cone over my face which he drenched in chloroform. It seemed to me a disgusting scent, but the next thing I knew was that I felt very sick and that my legs were strapped to my bed and that I craved water. This was denied me. Instead the Scoundrel swabbed my mouth and tongue with damp cotton-wool. It was the first, and almost the last time, that I have felt really ill. They kept my legs strapped down for a week or ten days. People came with presents and praised my bravery. My idea of bravery was to cut down with a sword hordes of Pathans and Prussians. I did not feel brave at all. I did not know how else I could possibly have behaved, drugged, disembowelled, shackled as I was. I enjoyed a certain sense of importance, but the whole episode was distasteful. During this time I resumed my diary with a lively picture of myself under the knife.

When my scar was healed and my health restored I got out of bed and my feet crumpled under me. The strapping of them had produced a kind of lameness and it was the cure for this disability that for the first time removed me from the close circle of my home and family.

I do not know how my parents heard of the place where I was now sent, a large girls' school in the Thames estuary, then on vacation. The only other inmate was a forlorn little girl named Daffodil, whose father was serving in India. The headmistress had the curious sobriquet of 'Topknot' or something like it. She was in residence. Also a German mistress whom, with all my national prejudice, I abhorred with a vehemence she did little to soften. She taught me a rhyme in German about a poodle who stole the milk, which still, meaningless, echoes in my mind.

For the first time in my life I felt abandoned. We were given Syrup of Figs which griped me. We had some ill-defined liaison with a boys' school where a few ill-conditioned youths also spent their summer holidays. Daffodil and I were uncomprehendingly aware that they had some nasty secret connected with the gate-lodge. Daffodil once wetted her bed and was punished by having her hands bandaged for a day. I had the greatest difficulty in discovering the reason for this ignominy. There was no real unkindness at this place, merely a total lack of sympathy and charm. The large, empty, ugly house weighed heavily. The proximity of the sea, always hitherto a thing of joy, was a bitter irony.

Into this desert there came on a bicycle three times a week a stout and amiable woman with an electric battery to apply to my feet. That and the mud-flats in which at low-water I was sent to paddle for several hours a day, were recommended (in fact successfully) as a means of restoring the use of my feet. To this masseuse I confided my misery in the derelict college. She suggested to my mother that I should come and lodge with her. She had a daughter named Muriel slightly older than myself and a husband whom she supported, an old soldier. The house was in a lonely row surrounded by dykes and salt marsh where on Sundays there congregated parties of disreputable-looking gamblers. Muriel and I were forbidden to approach them. We watched them from afar and, when they dispersed, found the area strewn with torn-up playing-cards. At the end of the row two, as it then seemed, very old spinsters kept a little school to which Muriel and I and three or four other children resorted. The curriculum comprised a great deal of marching round the front parlour to the sound of the piano. For many years afterwards I received Christmas cards from the dames. Muriel from time to time exposed her private parts to me, and I mine to her. She told the other children in the class that I was the son of a millionaire from London.

Muriel's father got mildly drunk most evenings. It made him very jolly. He sang songs and praised me to my face with extravagance. Muriel did not like him, though he built us a platform in an old tree (on which Muriel's exposures took place). When my parents' weekly payment arrived the masseuse went off into town and returned with a barrow laden with odd bits of furniture and ornament. She told me she had bought them. I now realise that they had come out of pawn. They were all manner of objects – a banjo which Muriel's father played, albums of photographs of cantonments in India, a phonograph, china vases and great-coats. The household was extraordinarily Dickensian, an old, new world to me. I was very happy there; so happy that I neglected to write home and received a letter of rebuke from my father. He wrote, or rather dictated, for it was in typescript, what was intended to be a harrowing description of my mother's solicitude for me on the eve of my operation. He recalled the lepers, healed by our Lord, only one of whom had returned to give thanks. I was moved, not to penitence, but intense resentment by this missive.

Soon my feet and ankles recovered their strength and I returned home and this glimpse of another world was occluded.

4

At the age of six, before I went to my first school, I made friends for myself. Walking with Lucy a quarter of a mile from home we watched three children – a boy of my own age, an elder and a younger sister – playing on what seemed a mountain of clay. It had been excavated to lay the road, drains and foundations of what was then a solitary house. Either then or shortly afterwards I was invited to join them and for more than a decade they remained my closest holiday associates. I will call them Roland.

This house with its heap of clay was part of the territory of the Hampstead Garden Suburb. I have mentioned this as being largely inhabited by people of artistic leanings, bearded, knicker-bockered, flannel-shirted, sometimes even sandalled. Mr Roland was not one of these, but a neat, grave, high official in the War Office. He possessed a revolver, an object of limit-less fascination, and a powerful Airedale watch-dog, so remote, ill lighted and rarely patrolled was the district then. (My father had merely a police-whistle, which, like Mr Roland's pistol, was never used.)

The Rolands became my constant companions. We lived in expectation of a German invasion. I do not know what put this idea into our heads. The alarm was not shared by our parents. In 1909 P. G. Wodehouse published *The Swoop*, which describes such an invasion foiled by a boy-scout. None of us certainly ever saw that work. The theme must have been much in the air of the youth of that time. For the defence of the kingdom we converted the clay-heap into a fort, not unlike a real machine-gun post except that we flew the Union Jack from its flagstaff. The clay was easy to work. We dug out the centre and piled ramparts and in covered recesses laid up stores for a siege – bottles of water, a tin of bloater-paste and an armoury of clay missiles. We bound ourselves and one other little boy who, as I remember, always had a somewhat subordinate position, into a patriotic league named The Pistol Troop. A few adults were admitted. Mr Roland was astutely elected 'pay-master', a post which gave us call on his pocket. We drew up a code of laws and ordained savage corporal punishments, which, of course, were never inflicted, for their breach. We also devised ordeals, which we suffered, as tests of courage, walking bare-legged through stinging-nettles, climbing high and difficult trees, signing our names in our blood and so forth. We had some scuffles with roaming bands who attempted to enter our fort, whom we repelled with fists, clay-balls and sticks, but we were not provocative. We were reserving our strength for the Prussian Guard. We were rather priggishly high-minded. 'Honour' was a word often on our lips. Dishonesty, impurity or cruelty would have been inconceivable to us, but we had, I suppose, in that age before Brownies and Wolf Cubs, discovered our own innocent, imaginative version of the street gangs of the slums.

The Pistol Troop flourished for about three years and was never formally disbanded. It was the creation of our home lives. We never mentioned it at our schools, still less sought to recruit new members from that entirely distinct world. In 1912 we produced a magazine which was typed for us by my father's secretary and handsomely bound. My own contribution, a story of hidden treasure, is quite without interest.

After I had been habituated to my new friends for many months Mrs Roland remarked to them that it was sad for me to be an only child. 'Oh, but he isn't,' one of them replied, 'he has a brother at school whom he hates.' This was a distortion of my regard for Alec, but it is true that he held himself aloof from, and greatly superior to, all our doings. He was induced, however, to write a story for the Pistol Troop Magazine. His contribution gave no promise of the tales of passion for which he was later to be known, but was an imitation of Nat Gould, a popular writer of the time, who specialised in misdeeds in racing-stables.

The period when I was closest to the Rolands was the autumn of 1912 when after my operation for appendicitis I spent a happy term at home, doing lessons with them under a governess.

The defence of the realm was far from being our sole concern; we produced a number of plays, written by ourselves and acted in home-made costumes before home-made scenery; nor was I dependent on my friends for all my amusements. I have been told that as a child I was never known to ask 'What shall I do?' I do not remember a minute's boredom and to enumerate my various employments would be to list almost every hobby a small boy can enjoy. I was not particularly talented in drawing, but I drew and painted a great deal, never attempting to portray objects or landscapes, but making graphic decorations and slap-dash battle-scenes in a manner derived from the study of printed books and magazines. Shaw's *Alphabets* (illuminated letters reproduced from mediaeval manuscripts) and a volume of aquatint plates from Froissart's *Chronicle* absorbed much of my attention, but I was equally and uncritically entranced by the pages of *Chums,* where I early learned to recognise the style of the various regular illustrators. I collected practically everything – coins, stamps, fossils, butterflies, beetles, seaweed, wild flowers, 'curiosities' generally. I had a phase of 'chemistry' when with a spirit lamp and

test tubes and assorted bottles, I conducted entirely unregu-
lated and rather dangerous 'experiments' in a garden shed. I
melted lead soldiers and recast the bright metal which formed
below the scum of paint in home-made moulds. For about a
year, off and on, I was obsessed by conjuring and haunted a
shop near Leicester Square whose catalogues offered everything
from pennies, cut across and hinged with rubber, to ornate
cabinets in which ladies could be sawn in two. This catalogue
claimed that a staff of expert conjurers was always on duty and
that behind the shop there was a fully equipped theatre where
prospective customers could see their illusions 'without
obligation to buy'. I never penetrated to that theatre and I
found that the expert staff quickly tired of performing at the
counter for my benefit, but I constructed a number of properties myself – a candle which was a cylinder of paper with a
quarter of an inch of wax and wick, playing-cards which were
made of two cards cut diagonally and backed so that when
exhibited fanwise they could be transformed into a different
hand by closing and reopening them upside down. I must have
proved very tedious to the audiences I was constantly attempting to mystify, particularly as I composed a facetious patter in
imitation of the professionals I sometimes saw at children's
parties. I remember being shocked very nearly to tears at
Midsomer Norton when performing before a party which
included the local doctor. I had borrowed his top hat, from
which I intended to produce handkerchiefs, streamers and
collapsible paper flowers and I asked: 'Now, sir, is there any
hole in this hat?' 'Yes,' he replied, 'the one I put my head in.'

Most of these pursuits, except drawing and acting, dwindled
to an end when I was about twelve.

I had a microscope and an air-gun. I was fascinated by
inscriptions which I attempted to copy in the British Museum
and from the illustrations in Hutchinson's *History of the Nations*.
Apart from the *Children's Encyclopaedia*, which was a joy to me,
there were fewer books of popular culture in my youth than
there are now, or were in mid-Victorian times. Or, if they

existed, they did not come my way. In 1912 my father gave me
a copy of Wallis Budge's grammar of Egyptian hieroglyphics –
a book entirely beyond my capacity.

I wrote a great deal: intermittent diaries and illustrated
stories. These were all imitative of the worst of my reading. It
never occurred to me to emulate the classics to which my father
introduced me early. *Chums* and *The Boys' Friend* were my
models. Only one of my early works, and that the earliest,
shows imagination. It was called *The Curse of the Horse Race* and
is not dated. I think from the evidence of the handwriting it
must have been written in 1910, when I was rising seven. It
begins:

CHAP 1
BETTING
I BET YOU 500 pounds I'le win. The speaker was Rupert a
man of about 25 he had a dark bushy mistarsh and flashing eyes.
I shouldnot trust to much on your horse said Tom for indeed he
had not the sum to spear.

It ends ten pages later:

CHAP IX
HUNG
Then Tom drest himself then Tom took Rupert to the pulies
cort Rupert was hung for killing the pulies man. I hope this story
will be a leson to you never to bet.

No doubt the moral was derived from Lucy, but the tale was
pure fantasy – the men are armed with swords – that bears no
recognisable trace of experience or reading.

Under 'environment' I have included all the memories of
childhood and some of my boyhood as it was lived at home.
School, to which I was gently introduced in September 1910,
was for the following eight years a different world, sometimes
agreeable, more often not, inhabited by a quite different and
rather nastier boy who had no share in the real life of the third
of the year he spent at home.

Chapter Three

MY FATHER

I HAVE MENTIONED my father in the preceding pages, but have so far attempted no description of him. It was only slowly, with growing reason and senses, that I observed him. It is difficult, when one has watched a man for forty years, to recall him precisely at any particular age.

As I have said, in my earliest days I regarded him as an intruder. At the height of the day's pleasure his key would turn in the front door and his voice would rise from the hall: 'Kay! Kay! Where's my wife?' and that was the end of my mother's company for the evening. (My eldest child's first memory of me is of the head and shoulders of a strange, angry man in military uniform, who had arrived on leave the night before at her grandmother's house and now appeared at a window under which she was playing with her cousins, shouting: 'For God's sake, someone take those children to the other lawn.')

Many little boys look on their fathers as heroically strong and skilful; mighty hunters, the masters of machines; not so I. Nor did I ever fear him. He was restless rather than active. His sedentary and cerebral occupations appeared ignominious to me in my early childhood. I should have better respected a soldier or a sailor like my uncles, or a man with some constructive hobby such as carpentry, a handyman; a man, even, who shaved with a cut-throat razor.

He was thirty-seven years old when I was born; in his early forties when I came to take notice of him, and he wrote of that period in his autobiography: 'I must have been the youngest man of my age in London.' I never saw him as anything but old, indeed as decrepit.

63

In childhood I often annoyed him; in early manhood, for a short time, I was the cause of anxiety which bordered on despair; but in general our relationship was social and intermittent, a growing appreciation on my part of his quality and with it a growing pleasure in his company.

In person he was small, of the same height that my brother and I eventually attained, but very much handsomer than either of us. He had large grey eyes, eloquent of kindness and humour, a fine brow and a full head of hair, which changed in imperceptible stages from grey to white. He had been very slight in build, but at about the time of my birth gained weight until in the end he was uncomfortably obese. I remember him as always corpulent. In dress he was conventional and tidy, but though he was noticeable in appearance and noticeably agreeable, he had a genuine conviction of his ugliness. He shunned the camera and, if he caught sight of himself in a glass, would recoil from his reflection crying, in the tones of the ghost in *Hamlet*: 'O horrible! Most horrible' or some similar expression of revulsion.

The illusion of old age was much enhanced by his own utterances. Like his grandfather at Corsley he often adverted to his imminent demise. He always referred to himself as 'incorrigibly Victorian'. Throughout much of the year he was troubled, and sometimes incapacitated, by asthma and bronchitis. He sometimes spoke of this constriction of breath as 'tightness' and once caused surprise by answering an inquiry for his health: 'Better today. I was dreadfully tight all night.'

My earliest memories of him are of his gasping and choking in the grip of this affliction. On those occasions he would cry to heaven for release in a wide variety of quotation. He found great satisfaction in visiting the site of his grave in Hampstead parish churchyard, but his melancholies were brief and quickly relieved. Most of his acquaintance regarded him as exuberantly jovial.

He was by nature sociable and hospitable, but he had no pleasure in large gatherings and no ambition to move among people richer than himself. He did not play cards or chess. He had no interest in any competitive game (except cricket, which, before my time, he played without distinction), but rejoiced and excelled in all paper and acting-games which required spontaneous invention.

He liked to surround himself with a small group whose conversation was general, where full attention could be devoted to his own lively talk. As he grew older and deafer he was happiest with a single companion. He endeared himself easily to the young, won their confidence, drew refreshment from their enthusiasms and enjoyed a series of intimate, but in no way libidinous, associations with young girls, the daughters usually of friends, whom he would meet or correspond with daily, to whom he would address verses and send small presents. Apart from these successive objects of affection most of his acquaintances were subject to genial ridicule.

I think he was a little afraid of Edmund Gosse, the kinsman who had been his mentor when he first came to London. He certainly awaited Gosse's not infrequent visits with agitation and, when bidden to dine at Hanover Terrace, went under protest with much preliminary lamentation. But he invariably returned in the highest spirits, having enjoyed 'a capital evening'.

I held Gosse in disdain. His polished art of pleasing was not effectively exercised on children. I remember him once, when I was, I suppose, eight or nine, greeting me with: 'And where do you carry those bare knees?'

I answered pertly: '*They* carry *me* wherever I want to go.'

'Ah the confidence of youth! To be able to envisage an attainable destination!'

I thought this highly absurd and offensive.

Better judges than I relished Gosse's company. To me he epitomised all that I found ignoble in the profession of letters. He was not, as I soon learned by investigating his quarrel with Churton Collins, a genuine scholar. He had written only one book and that anonymously. His eminence sprang from his sedulous pursuit of the eminent, among whom he was more proud of his intimacy with people of power and fashion than with artists. Unlike Desmond MacCarthy who succeeded to his position, he had little natural amiability or generosity. And his appearance was drab. I was early drawn to panache. I saw Gosse as a Mr Tulkinghorn, the soft-footed, inconspicuous, ill-natured habitué of the great world, and I longed for a demented lady's-maid to make an end of him.

I am certain that my father never did anyone an injury. He was totally free of ambition and envy. Whatever aspirations to literary fame he once indulged had early dissolved among the dreams of youth. He was intensely sensitive to criticism (of which he incurred singularly little) and correspondingly grateful for appreciation from however inconsiderable a source. He was himself prodigal of praise and encouraged more than one young friend to attempt theatrical and artistic careers for which they were not really apt.

He was as munificent as his means allowed, delighting to give. The wish to cause pleasure and the wish for affection were indistinguishable in him. He had no taint of the *goût aristo-cratique de déplaire*. He had no appetite for power, no calculation. He never saved or owed a shilling.

He detested controversy and to him all deliberation smacked of it. When any discussion arose, however amicable, and however little directed against him, he was liable to cry, as though in agony:

> *'Let the long contention cease!*
> *Geese are swans and swans are geese,*
> *Let them have it how they will!*
> *Thou art tired; best be still';*

and to leave the room declaiming behind him in the passage:

> *'They out-talked thee, hiss'd thee, tore thee.*
> *Better men fared thus before thee . . .'*

His decisions, even on matters of some importance, were instantaneous. He answered every letter within an hour or so of receiving it. He answered letters that needed no answer, thanking people who thanked him for a present, so that, when he encountered anyone as punctilious as himself, a correspondence was likely to start which ended only in death.

He was physically brave. Having an irrational abhorrence of all anaesthetics and narcotics he had all his teeth drawn without gas and I remember him one night when warned, falsely as it turned out, that a burglar was lurking in the garden, patrolling it alone with a walking-stick calling: 'Come out, you ruffian, I can see you.' In neither war would he take cover from air-raids.

My father's aesthetic stimuli were primarily verbal. He was not, like his two sons, entirely tuneless, but he had no knowledge or love of music. Painting interested him for its subject. He had a keen enjoyment of sight-seeing both in England and abroad but he valued architecture for its associations with a History which derived mainly from Plutarch, Shakespeare and Scott. He had no itch to get to the truth of a story, frankly preferring its most picturesque form.

He was not a man of strong or consistent opinions.

In politics he would have described himself as a Tory but, since he always inhabited safe Conservative constituencies, did not go to the polls and, apart from the detestation of Northcliffe and Lloyd George which was then common to all civilised men, and a temperate pacificism, he had no political principles. I never heard him refer to any of the controversies of his time. He knew nothing of economics or foreign affairs and was bored by any mention of them. He did not object to imperialism when it took metrical form in the works of Kipling and Henley; nor to Irish nationalism as expressed by the Celtic bards; nor to pessimism in the *Shropshire Lad*: nor to popery when it came to him through Crashaw. The same views in the plain terms of politicians, philosophers or theologians would have been anathema to him. The word was all.

In religion he was a practising Anglican, rejoicing in the texts of the Authorised Version of the Bible and of Cranmer's

Common Prayer. He liked church-going with a preference for colourful and ceremonious services and never missed a Sunday, usually attending whatever place was nearest, irrespective of its theological complexion. Once, at the time when I was born, he had a brief Anglo-Catholic phase and frequented St Augustine's, Kilburn (where I was christened), which was a centre of the movement, but he never took very seriously the doctrines taught there. He made very merry over the experiences of a member of that congregation, a solicitor of his acquaintance who, as a penitential practice, allowed himself to be caned by a curate. In my childhood my father read family prayers every morning. In August 1914 he abandoned this practice on the very curious grounds that it was 'no longer any good'. His complaint against Catholics was their clarity of dogma and I doubt whether he had a genuine intellectual conviction about any element of his creed. He would muse in vaguely platonic terms about the possibilities of immortality. The moral code of his upbringing he accepted without question.

When I was nine years old he gave me Mary Macgregor's *The Story of Rome* (a book which, characteristically, makes Actium the last event in Roman History), inscribing it:

> *All roads, they tell us, lead to Rome;*
> *Yet, Evelyn, stay awhile at home!*
> *Or, if the Roman road invites*
> *To doughty deeds and fearful fights,*
> *Remember, England still is best –*
> *Her heart, her soul, her Faith, her Rest!*

I am not sure what he meant by the capitalized last word. What particular form of insular repose was he commending to his little son? I can only suppose, the grave. But the profession of Englishry is plain enough, as it was in the advice which some ten years later he gave to a school friend of mine who aspired to a literary career: 'With a thorough knowledge of the Bible, Shakespeare and Wisden' (cricket almanac) 'you cannot go far wrong.'

My father's most obvious characteristic was theatricality, but I did not become conscious of this until it was pointed out to me at the age of sixteen by the first adult visitor I introduced into the house; a friend who will be described in detail later. This friend said to me: 'Charming, entirely charming, and acting all the time.' When I consulted her, my mother confirmed this judgement. My eyes were opened and I saw him, whom I had grown up to accept in complete simplicity, as he must always have appeared to others.

From earliest youth, when all he knew of the drama was drawn from the Bristol pantomime, performances by the boys of Downside (where he saw most of the plays of Shakespeare ingeniously rewritten to eliminate the female characters) and schoolroom theatricals, my father was stage-struck. He had a model theatre and wrote plays for his puppets. He found greater scope at Sherborne and Oxford. His failure in Schools – a double third in Mods and Greats – was due to play-going in term and acting during vacations, when he went from house to house with improvised amateur companies. The O.U.D.S. were founded while he was up. He did not join, but he and a group of friends at the House took the Hollywell Music Rooms and performed a skit on Bourchier's *Julius Caesar*, which, like all undergraduate enterprises, reads very flat (cf. Ronald Knox's *Decalogue Symposium*), but was thought at the time highly ingenious. So he went down with only the Newdigate Prize to his credit and when he settled in London digs he attended, usually in the pit, every performance in the town. His health prevented him from attempting the life of a professional actor, but in the days when he was uncertain where his future lay, he more than once attempted collaboration with the friend who had produced *Julius Seesawcar*, my father writing the lyrics and libretto and the friend the music, for light operas which never got nearer to fame than prologues and epilogues for the Old Stagers' productions during Canterbury cricket week. But his zeal for the theatre, tempered by a constitution which made it irksome for him to go out in the evenings, remained until deafness deprived him of this pleasure. He was president of a company of old O.U.D.S. who until 1914 used to stage rather elaborate productions in aid of charity, and always took a part in making up the female players. Later, when the Hampstead Garden Suburb formed a Play and Pageant Union, he was president of that too. In 1918 he acted in a short sketch designed to amuse wounded soldiers in hospital. I remember him throwing himself into the part of one of the Magi in a Christmas play written in verse by a neighbouring clergyman; also into the lead in a farce called *His Excellency the Governor*, produced I am not sure where. That must have been his last appearance in grease-paint behind foot-lights. He always excelled in the charades which were an essential part of our family life, especially at Christmas.

I think he was, by amateur standards, genuinely gifted, but it was in the daily routine of his private life that he acted with the greatest virtuosity. In greeting visitors he was Mr Hardcastle; in deploring the ingratitude of his sons, Lear. Between these two extremes all the more likeable of Dickens's characters provided him with roles which from time to time he undesignedly assumed. Ellen Terry referred to him as 'that dear little Mr Pickwick'. I must not be thought to impute insincerity to him. It was simply that his nature required every thought and emotion to have immediate histrionic expression.

He never sulked. He was mercurial, and a word of humour or appreciation would win him in an instant from the blackest depression. Even in his coughing and wheezing, genuine and distressing as they were, he put his voice into the production, interspersing his bouts with quotations calling on death for release. His sighs would have carried to the back of the gallery at Drury Lane.

He sang softly and often as he moved restlessly about the house. Some of his songs must, I think, have been remembered from the harness-room at Midsomer Norton, such as the dirge which began:

'I'm the ghost of John James Christopher Benjamin Binns.
I was cut off right in the midst of my sins.
I'm only let out for an hour or so
And when the cock begins to crow,
Good-bye John James Christopher Benjamin Binns.'

He also improvised, usually to hymn tunes, in ridicule of his acquaintances and of himself. When despondent he sang to a valse:

'Nobody loves me.
No, nobody loves me.
Nobody cares for me in the least.
Everyone thinks I'm a horrible beast.'

He also talked continually to himself, not muttering in an absent-minded way, but in flamboyant declamation to imaginary audiences. He was never even momentarily straitened financially, but he would not sign a cheque without crying: 'How can I possibly find the money? They will ruin me. They will bring me to a pauper's grave.' He had no ugly rages but frequent explosions of exasperation and was correspondingly extravagant in pleasure, amusement, gratitude and affection. Tears and laughter came easily.

This conjunction in my father of the love of literature and the talent for acting endowed my youth with riches that have fructified throughout my life. He read aloud with precision of tone, authority and variety that I have heard excelled only by Sir John Gielgud. For some eight years of my life for some three or four evenings a week when we were at home, he read to me, my brother and to whatever friends might be in the house, for an hour or more from his own old favourites – most of Shakespeare, most of Dickens, most of Tennyson, much of Browning, Trollope, Swinburne, Matthew Arnold. Often it was pure entertainment; *Vice Versa* or *The Diary of a Nobody*. Sometimes he would read the popular plays of his youth, *The Magistrate, The Gay Lord Quex, School, The Importance of Being Earnest,* standing, stepping about the room and portraying the characters as he had seen them on the stage. Had it not been so well

done, there might have been something ludicrous about the
small, elderly, stout figure impersonating the heroines of
forgotten comedies with such vivacity. In fact he held us
enthralled. But I remember him most fondly as he sat in his
arm-chair under the red-shaded lamp, with a little heap of
volumes on the table beside him; then, excluding himself,
eschewing all gestures or dramatic effects, allowing the melody
of the lines to work its own spell, he would discourse the lyrics
which we soon knew by heart. His choice was not recondite.
Most of his favourite poems were in familiar anthologies or
were the work of the poets of his own generation who had been
his friends; but heard thus, again and again, they assumed new
beauties and significance, as the liturgy does to those who
recite it daily and yearly.

In these recitations of English prose and verse the incompar-
able variety of English vocabulary, the cadences and rhythms
of the language, saturated my young mind, so that I never
thought of English Literature as a school subject, as matter for
analysis and historical arrangement, but as a source of natural
joy. It was a legacy that has not depreciated.

My father lived to be seventy-five and exemplified the lines
in which he often claimed to find consolation:

> *Thank God, that while the nerves decay*
> *And muscles desiccate away,*
> *The brain's the hardiest part of men*
> *And lasts till three score years and ten.*

2

I have attempted to adumbrate my father's domestic character.
I must now write of something much less important to him, his
professional affairs.

In the twelve years after he came down from New College
he established a modest but respectable position in London as
a 'man of letters'.

That category, like the maiden aunt's, is now almost extinct.

It comprised men who liked books and all that concerned them; who enjoyed an easy command and reverence of the English language, which they did much to protect from pollution and misuse. They aimed at something higher than ephemeral journalism, but respected literature too highly to pretend to immortality; they received a severe wigging from Mr Cyril Connolly at the time when he believed that 'the only function of a writer is to produce a masterpiece'. Edmund Gosse was the chief of them. Today that broad, smooth stream has divided; there are the reporters of the popular papers who interview authors rather than review their work; there are the charmers of Television; there are the State-trained professional critics with their harsh jargon and narrow tastes; and there are the impostors who cannot write at all, but travel from one international congress to another discussing the predicament of the writer in the modern world. My father never spoke on the wireless, never had any other preparation for criticism than his own wide reading and genial tastes and never attended a literary congress. He wrote biography, essays, book-reviews, *causeries,* verse (Gilbertian, Tennysonian and in the manner of Austin Dobson); he read manuscripts for publishers, edited new editions of standard works and always replied ungrudgingly and at length to all who applied to him for advice.

In the year before my birth he was offered, and accepted, the post of managing director of Chapman & Hall, at that time an august but somewhat decrepit firm of publishers. From then on this became his main occupation and during my childhood it took him out of the house from 8.30 a.m. until after 6 p.m. He continued to write a weekly review and during the first war, when the *Daily Telegraph* reduced its literary pages, he wrote the longer papers for the quarterlies which comprised his second book of collected essays, *Tradition and Change*; it is a testimony to the integrity of the period that no one, so far as I know, ever questioned the propriety of his thus doubling the role of publisher and critic.

He has left his own account of his work as a publisher,

leaving the impression of a happy, busy life, devoted to duty. At home he constantly complained that he was overworked. 'Driven' was the word he used. 'My dear boy, I'm most damnably driven just now; They've all been at me all day, *driving* me. I don't know where to turn round.'

I think he believed it. He certainly did what had to be done; he never procrastinated. He disliked work and wanted to make a quick end of it.

The firm occupied a house in the neighbourhood of Covent Garden, fronting Henrietta Street, backing on Maiden Lane. My father's room, which was also the board-room, took up most of the first floor. Below him were clerks on high stools, packers, and the men who sold books direct over a counter to the booksellers' boys and sometimes to private customers. Above him were his secretary and the young man in charge of the 'technical' department. My father interviewed all authors, artists, printers, binders, and himself drew up advertisements. He communicated with other parts of the office by whistling down a tube for the office boy. One exotic anomaly was a bearded and monoglot Italian who inhabited a windowless glory-hole half-way up the stairs; he had originally been introduced to make plaster busts of Charles Dickens and could not be dislodged. He did a good deal of spicy cooking there on a little stove.

The annual shareholders' meeting of Chapman & Hall's, which was normally a bland formality, made my father miserable for a week in apprehension of possible criticism. But his hours in the office were not long. He was always there early, before most of his staff. At the outbreak of the first war he took to coming home to luncheon, ostensibly as an economy, leaving his desk at 12.30 and returning to it well after two. In the summer he often left at four and spent an hour or so at Lord's on his way home. In the winter he often dropped in to a neighbouring cinema called the 'Theatre de Luxe'. Most of his huge private correspondence was written in his office. And he never allowed business to interfere with his private life. He

74

refused to have the telephone in his home for fear 'they' might 'drive' him.

Inevitably the majority of his friends were bookish. Many of the Chapman & Hall authors became his friends. There is a whole shelf of books dedicated to him (I use the word in its English, not in its French, sense), some by forgotten writers whom he had advised and helped, but, besides them, by W. W. Jacobs, J. C. Squire, Austin Dobson, E. V. Lucas and others who had no need of encouragement and whom he did not publish. But it never occurred to him to ask anyone to his house or club merely because they were writers or agents; still less to go to parties in pursuit of celebrities who might enrich his list.

One of the most profitable connections of Chapman & Hall's was an American firm of technical publishers for whom they acted in England. He regarded this association as something almost shady, and its representatives as much less worthy of attention than a minor poet. The technical books were unintelligible to him. The visits of these valuable American clients were strictly confined to an exchange of politeness in his office and a swift relegation to the hands of a young man of scientific education whom he regarded as a subordinate rather than a colleague. He never asked to his house the men who had come 3,000 miles to bring him business. By modern standards he would be regarded as negligent, but in his brief office hours he handled alone all the work that is now performed by four or five 'executives', and he was without doubt loved and respected in his trade. When the Publishers' Circle was formed he was elected its first president and it was under his direction that the firm was celebrated in the rhyme:

> *Messrs Chapman & Hall*
> *Swear not at all.*
> *Mr Chapman's yea is yea*
> *And Mr Hall's nay is nay.*

As the literary memoirs of men slightly older than myself

begin to appear, I am delighted again and again to find testimony to his geniality and generosity. There was no one he envied; no one who applied to him, whom he did not encourage; not always sagaciously perhaps, but leaving behind him a trail of gratitude and affection.

3

As a critic my father had the great supporting strength of loving what he loved, deeply. He was quite unmoved by snobbery and incapable of professing to find virtues that were invisible to him, in work that was in the fashion. He knew no German and was not at ease in French. He was saturated in the English literature that is a recognisable descendant of Greek and Latin. In poetry he looked for melody, lucidity and 'ideas'. 'The emotion,' he wrote – rather obscurely for him – 'without which poetry is barren, contains in itself an indirect reference to the mood in which it is evoked, while the poet proceeds from the registration of the emotion to test it by the standard of the universal idea. But it must never be forgotten that the idea is the germ of the poem; that the truth and universality of the idea is the test of the poem's quality; and that, as poetry recedes from the region of ideas into that of emotions, and sinks still further from emotions into moods, it retires more and more from that high vantage ground from whose summit the classic poetry of the age overlooks the manifold activity of the world.'

If I understand him correctly, I suppose that few modern critics would wholly dissent from this opinion.

My father's limitation was the common enough inability to recognise the qualities he loved unless they were presented in familiar forms. He was seldom, if ever, duped by the spurious, but much that was genuine escaped his appreciation. The 'Georgian poets' of Eddie Marsh's anthologies seemed, most of them, to be audacious and incompetent revolutionaries. Mr T. S. Eliot and his côterie he regarded as manifestly absurd.

'Mr Wilfred Gibson', he wrote, 'has evidently thrown aside

in weariness the golden foot-rule of the Augustans . . . Mr Lascelles Abercrombie's blank verse is yet more rough and unmelodious . . . Mr Walter de la Mare, who aims at a simpler form of fantasy than Mr Abercrombie, again and again spoils a dainty fancy by wayward affectations and clumsy inversions . . . a gossamer imagination marred by clumsiness of touch . . . Mr Rupert Brooke has the itch to say a thing in such an arresting fashion as to shock the literary purist into attention even against his will.'

In another essay he wrote: 'What Mr [D.H.] Lawrence's art stands most desperately in need of is a shower bath of vital ideas. At present' (1917) 'his fancy is half asleep upon a foetid hot-bed of moods. It is a vigorous, masculine fancy, but it seems . . . to have been left deserted on a midden. Perhaps some vivifying, ennobling, humane experience will yet help it to save its soul.'

It is not surprising that he was outraged by the *Imagist Anthology* of 1916, for in that volume a preface made high claims to traditional virtues, quoting Milton, Dryden and Arnold as the contributors' predecessors. He wrote: 'The Imagists, we are told, base their poetry upon cadence rather than upon metre and they define cadence as "the sense of perfect balance of flow and rhythm". In this they can hardly claim to be violent innovators; the choruses of Aeschylus are based upon no other principle, nor, for that matter, are the anapaestic splendours of Swinburne.'

Amy Lowell's poem which begins:

> *Bang! Bump! Tong!*
> *Petticoats,*
> *Stockings*
> *Sabots,*
> *Delirium flapping its thigh-bones.*

did not for him convey the tradition of Milton, Dryden or Arnold.

Of Mr T. S. Eliot, little knowing (nor would he have cared

a jot had he known) the great popularity the poet was to achieve before his own death, he wrote: 'It was a classic custom in the family hall, when a feast was at its height, to display a drunken slave among the sons of the household, to the end that they, being ashamed at the ignominious folly of his gesticulations, might determine never to be tempted into such a pitiable condition themselves. The custom has its advantages; for the wisdom of the younger generation was found to be fostered more surely by a single example than by a world of homily and precept.'

This was the function he predicted for the future idol of the academies.

I quote these judgements to show my father's limitations and his staunch loyalty to them. They are not characteristic of him, for his bent was all towards amiability. Only when he saw something which he loved threatened – in this case his conception of English poetry – did he break into indignation. Neologism, journalese, cockney rhymes and false prosody brought out the censor in him. He was happiest when he was able to interpret and applaud, and his general habit of reviewing was to discover, sometimes with difficulty, what the writer was trying to do, and then to acclaim its successful accomplishment. Grateful letters delighted him. 'I think I got to the heart of that book,' he would say. 'The author has written to tell me so.'

He genuinely liked books – quite a rare taste today. I never heard him, as I hear my contemporaries, complain of book reviewing as degrading hack-work. His only complaints were of editors who curtailed his scope. He came to each book, even if it were only the collected sermons of a public school head-master, with a genuine anticipation of pleasure.

He himself wrote, as he did everything, at a deleterious speed. He could turn out regular and quite elegant verse as fast as he could write a letter. In his prose his speaking voice is plainly audible. He never wrote anything discreditable. Nor did he, except very rarely, write anything memorable. His description in his autobiography of his dame-school at Bath is an example of his limited powers most happily exercised. His peer was E. V. Lucas, now, I suppose, as forgotten as he, but in his lifetime better known. Lucas was more productive than my father. His superior physical health and his lack of domesticity led him into far wider social circles. But the tastes and capabilities of the two men were almost identical. They were warm friends and once projected a work in collaboration for which my father failed to fulfil his part. It became *Over Bemerton's*.

My father never, in adult life, aspired higher, nor did he ever repine at his lack of excellence. His primary, overriding, instinctive aim was to make a home.

There were times when I was inclined to regard his achievement as somewhat humdrum. Now I know that the gratitude I owe him for the warm stability he created, which I only dimly apprehended, can best be measured by those less fortunate than myself.

Chapter Four

EDUCATION BEGUN

IN SEPTEMBER 1910, when I was rising seven years of age, I was sent for the first time to school. Three years earlier my brother had gone to a preparatory school in Surrey from which he returned with disquieting reports of cold baths, canes and milk-puddings; it was assumed that I should follow him there in due course. Meanwhile, I was sent to a school in Hampstead named Heath Mount; by the original intention for a term or two, but where, in the event, I gladly remained for the next six years. I was not eager to leave home or experience the austerities of which my brother boasted, and I suffered none of the sharp separation common to boys of my sort.

There were at Heath Mount about sixty boys, more than half of them day-boys. Sometimes for a few weeks, when my parents were abroad, I boarded; normally I followed the road I have described, morning and evening. It was a school of some antiquity, having existed under various headmasters and with varying fortunes since the late eighteenth century. In 1934, still bearing its old name and crest, it moved to Hertfordshire, where it flourishes today. Flats have been built on the Hampstead site.

In my time we occupied the original brick house in Heath Street. It had been added to in the years, but we were rather cramped for space. There were, as I remember it, only four proper form-rooms. Lessons were given in the gymnasium, the dining-room and the headmaster's 'private dining-room'.

It was by general consent the best school in the neighbourhood, but I have never understood by what process it was chosen by parents who lived elsewhere. There were, for example, two brothers who came all the way from the Channel Islands. Why? Heath Mount was not particularly cheap. It was not, like King Alfred's – another Hampstead school which we greatly despised – in any way modern or progressive. It was conventional and by its own standards not notably efficient. Except for gross dunces there was little difficulty in those days about Common Entrance; Heath Mount never, I think, entered a boy for a scholarship; in my time there certainly was none. The cricket-coaching, to which much importance used to be attached, was perfunctory. Nothing was attempted that was not being done better in fifty other schools. But it prospered.

The Headmaster, Mr Granville Grenfell – a name which would seem implausible in fiction – was an old school-fellow of my father's and I was rather a favourite of his. He was the son of an admiral and, though essentially a landsman, affected many of the mannerisms of an old salt, wearing a trim beard and tight-buttoned serge suits; he sharply alternated wrath and explosions of bluff geniality, in a way which might be supposed to derive from the quarter-deck. His study was the repository of texts and crested exercise-books, pencils, a mechanical pencil-sharpener, a pair of skis and a large, framed photograph of Mr Grenfell wearing the insignia of Grand Master of Cere-monies in the United Grand Lodge of England. Perhaps this masonic distinction helped attract pupils. He was a widower and it was believed in the school that somewhere in his quarters was his wife's room, which he had locked and never re-entered since her coffin was carried out. We attempted to identify the window but never succeeded. This death-chamber, real or imagined, fascinated me. I thought of it as of Miss Havisham's bridal room, heavy with dust, festooned in cobwebs and rotting picturesquely.

For my first year at Heath Mount I was under a governess in the bottom form, which was scarcely a part of the school. We did lessons only in the morning and were called for by nannies at 12.30. From my second year onwards I stayed to middle-day dinner and came under men who, at first, made me uneasy and overawed. They were mild enough, but I had never before been shouted at or threatened.

The day began with the school assembled by forms round the walls of the gymnasium; 'toeing the line' under the orders of the prefects, who had a pretty free hand in cuffing us; a boy was posted to watch for the approach of the masters. At the call of *'Cave'* silence fell. Mr Grenfell bounded up the three brass-bound steps and said 'Good morning, gentlemen.' We in chorus cried: 'Good morning, sir.' We then recited the Lord's Prayer (in 1914 the prayer for those in danger on the seas was added to our devotions); any necessary announcements were made and we were dispersed to our classes; except on Saturday mornings, when an alarming ceremony occurred.

Mr Grenfell then appeared with a ledger in which were recorded the results of the masters' meeting on the preceding afternoon. First he read the names of those commended. 'Geoghegan minor, plus three for Latin. Where is Geoghegan minor? Let me see him. Fine boy, Geoghegan minor . . . Mackenzie, plus five for Mathematics *and* French. Keep it up, Mackenzie. I am very pleased with you.'

Then with a dramatic change of tone: 'We will now turn to the other side. What is this I find? *Fletcher*. Fletcher has been idle. Stand out, Fletcher.' Mr Grenfell glared and bristled. Fletcher cringed. 'What does this mean? Idle? We had better understand one another, young man. You do not come here to be idle. And I am going to see that you work. Any idling, Fletcher, and' – with great vehemence and a blow of his fist on the table – 'I'll be down on you like a ton of bricks.' Then he would turn to the assistant masters grouped behind him. 'Keep your eyes on Fletcher, gentlemen. Any more trouble, send him to me, and he knows just what he'll get.'

His rage, I now realise, was simulated, but it was none the less alarming and was enhanced by the swift transition from geniality. I seldom – in fact I think only once – experienced it and then in a mild form, for I was, as I have said, a favourite, but on Saturday mornings there was always the apprehension: that exercise one had done so carelessly last Tuesday, so long ago as it seemed; had it been remembered and recorded against one? Had one been 'put in the book'?

Mr Grenfell very seldom beat anyone and then only for outrageous behaviour; lying and cheating were considered by him and by all of us the extremity of wickedness. When I read the accounts of my contemporaries of the enormities enacted at their preparatory schools by both masters and boys, I admit that Heath Mount had 'a good tone'.

Mr Grenfell never reached the Sixth Form at Sherborne and took a pass degree at Cambridge. He had no pretensions to learning, but he taught geometry in the upper school and, I think, taught it rather well; that is to say he impressed on us the idea of rational argument so that $Q.E.D.$ at the end of a proposition had a real meaning for us. His method of instruction was to line us up on benches before a blackboard. We moved up as we answered a question that had foiled those above us. It became a game of wits, not of memory, to catch the sequence of proof. I had some aptitude in this and enjoyed his lessons. There was a lively excitement in waiting with the correct answer for the question to descend to one, and dismay when it was caught in passage. '. . . Next, next, next, good boy, Stutterford, fine boy, brilliant boy, go top.'

We never got beyond the third book into the mysterious regions of 'proportions' and 'solids' – nor did I do so later. Until I reached the Sixth Form at Lancing and began to 'specialise' I was following the same curriculum as at Heath Mount – quadratic equations, 'roots', 'circles', the constructions and irregularities of Latin and Greek grammar, English and Roman History, French (taught as a dead language), selections from Cicero, Virgil and Ovid, the composition, with liberal assistance from notes, of Latin hexameters and pentameters, a Shakespeare play a term as a 'set book' in 'English'. We did these things more thoroughly in the Upper Fifth at Lancing, but in substance there was little difference between Common Entrance and School Certificate.

Assistant masters came and went. By no means all of them had university degrees. Some liked little boys too little and some too much. According to their tastes they mildly mauled us in the English scholastic way, fondling us in a manner just short of indecency, smacking us and pulling our hair in a manner well short of cruelty. Some could in their turn be tormented. Some were surly and, it seemed, old; some young and facetious; most of them boasted. Then and for many years later prep-school masters were drawn from a heterogeneous and undefinable underworld into which – little did I know it – I was myself destined to descend.

There was a hectoring young man who greatly alarmed me and might have made me very miserable if I had not had the refuge of home to return to every evening.

I remember that I once lost a Latin primer, irrevocably.

'Waugh, where is your grammar?'

'Lost, sir.'

'Nonsense. It can't be lost. It must be somewhere. Find it.'

Next day: 'Waugh, have your found your grammar?'

'No, sir.'

'Have you looked?'

'Yes, sir.'

'Nonsense, if you looked properly you would find it.'

Until after a day or two: 'Don't dare show your face in my class-room until you have found it.'

I returned home in great distress saying that since I could never find the book I must regard myself as expelled. My father asked its title and promised that he would send out his office-boy to purchase a copy. It had not occurred to me that there was any other source of supply than the grim master who had issued it to me. When next day I explained that my father was getting me a new copy and that I should have it by the next lesson, the master was gratifyingly disconcerted. 'You need not have mentioned a little thing like that to your parents.'

Later the parents of another boy wrote to Mr Grenfell and complained of this master's bullying ways. He was reprimanded and at our next lesson displayed an unfamiliar and unbecoming jocularity. We were doing 'comparative adverbs'. 'Tell me,' he said to the boy he had frightened, 'the superlative of *feliciter*.'

'*Felicissime*, sir.' (We were taught what was then known as the 'new pronunciation' in which the 'c's were hard.)

'No. I will not kissy you.'

We all obsequiously laughed, but this demonstration that the ogre was amenable to softer influences stripped him of much of his terrors and at the end of term he made another move on the drab but almost limitless circuit of private education. Masters who were ragged in one school became martinets in transit. Perhaps this disagreeable fellow was revenging on us humiliations he had suffered elsewhere and perhaps wherever he went next he carried his false smile and his joke about *felicissime*.

When one more than normally unsuitable was engaged, Mr Grenfell made an appeal to us for clemency. 'Look here, you fellows, I just want to tell you that Mr So-and-so is leaving at the end of the term. He hasn't been a success here. Now I am appealing to you as gentlemen to play fair with him and behave decently for the next few weeks.'

We day-boys were always aware of the presence of parents, near, benevolent and, in the last resort, authoritative, and the boarders, too, profited vicariously from their protection.

Cases are often reported when enraged fathers or mothers force an entry into the State schools and revenge injustices to their children by chastising the authorities. At Heath Mount we had a gentler but equally efficacious tonic in the lure of our parents' hospitality. The masters were all unmarried. Some lived in the school, others in modest digs. It was agreeable for them to be asked out in the evenings and the younger and soberer were able to dine often in unaccustomed luxury in Fitzjohn's Avenue and Frognal. My father took a part, now and then, in simple style, in this humane system of bribery and it sweetened my school life appreciably.

A normal English boarding-school has one or two days a year – Sports and Concert days – when it has to be on its best behaviour under the cursory inspection of those to whom it owes its life. A day-school is under inspection constantly. It is immune to the grosser scandals. It gives opportunities for a wider culture, but it does little to equip a child for the endurances of adolescence at his public school.

I was quite a clever little boy. Had I gone to one of the preparatory schools which cram for scholarships at Eton or Winchester, I might conceivably have won one. I was quite a brave little boy. Had I been earlier inured to the violence and hardships of school-life, I might have been less forlorn when I met them at the age of thirteen. Meanwhile I was happy enough. School was merely an interruption of the hobbies and affections of home. My father read to me, I consorted with the Roland children, I heard in detail, and without a twinge of envy, the exploits of my brother. I particularly recall autumn evenings when I walked home alone after football down the leafy road amid the scent of bonfires. A high-tea, eggs and fruit, was ready for me in the dining-room, where the curtains were drawn and the fire burnt high. When it was cleared, I did my preparation at the table until the parlour-maid came in to lay dinner.

Lessons seldom distressed me, but I remember an evening when I was in despair, attempting to memorise the principal parts of Latin deponent verbs, in one of those moods which occur at all ages when the mind seems numb. My mother found me near to tears. She knew no Latin, but she devised mnemonics for me, the more absurd the more easily retained. '*Molior*, to contrive,' she said. 'Remember the mole contrives to make a hole.' I have never forgotten it.

My father changed in the bathroom. When he left it I had my bath and went to bed in a room surrounded by whatever possessions captivated me at the moment; my mother heard my prayers. It was a world of privacy and love very unlike the bleak dormitories to which most boys of my age and kind were condemned.

2

My evident happiness at Heath Mount and my mother's pleasure in my company inclined my parents to keep me at home, but the decisive consideration was economic. I was at the age when I should in the normal course have moved to my brother's prep-school when the First World War began. There was an apprehension of imminent financial disaster among most businessmen; in this my father fully shared. Literature of all kinds in fact, good and bad, enjoyed unprecedented popularity, but that was not the general expectation; publishing was regarded as a precarious trade and in August 1914 the *Daily Telegraph*, to which my father looked for a considerable part of his income, abruptly informed contributors who were not regular members of their staff that their services were no longer required.

My father, quick to act as always, wrote to Mr Grenfell to give notice that he might no longer be able to pay my fees (I do not know what other form of education he had in mind for me) and Mr Grenfell answered that, if it should become necessary, he would keep me on free. My father read me this letter with some solemnity, exhorting me that I was thenceforward in honour bound to be an exemplary pupil. As things turned out we were not thrown into penury (though for us, as for most people, money was shorter) and my father never had to take advantage of this kind offer, but it cemented his liking for Mr Grenfell and his sense of loyalty to the school. I had long contracted this liking and this loyalty in a mild fashion, but I do not remember that the gratitude which should have been evoked made me any more industrious or orderly.

The war was at first a keen excitement to me. Travelling to Midsomer Norton immediately after its outbreak I delightedly counted the military guards at the mainline bridges. I followed

87

the retreat from Mons to the Marne and drew countless pictures of German cavalry plunging among English infantry with much blood and gunpowder about. The Pistol Troop had dissolved. Instead of armed resistance the Rolands and I devoted ourselves to raising funds for the Red Cross by collecting and selling empty jam jars. We also cut up linoleum to be used to sole slippers for wounded soldiers.

For a very few weeks my father was caught up in the enthusiasm of the time. He made a recruiting speech at Midsomer Norton; I heard him; in well-turned phrases and absolute sincerity he proclaimed that, if the Kaiser won, the miners of Norton would never again be allowed to play cricket.

He had spent many holidays in the country through which the German army was advancing; each devastated town was familiar to him and he wrote eloquently demanding vengeance. But this was a brief and uncharacteristic phase. The casualty lists sickened him early.

My brother, in his autobiography, has given an admirable account of his return to school in September 1914. At Heath Mount the changes were less dramatic. One or two masters enlisted and, on leaving, were presented with wrist-watches. Two or three boys turned up with names suddenly anglicised – one, unfortunately named Kaiser, appeared as 'Kingsley' – but we did nothing to persecute them. There was a Dutch master whom we believed to be a spy. There were two Belgian refugees whom we earnestly attempted to befriend. The school was admirably free of the kind of malice which, from most accounts, seems to have been rampant elsewhere. Hampstead then as now had a large exotic population. At Heath Mount, inflamed by our reading of mediaeval history, we were divided into Scotch and English factions. Though only a quarter Scotch, I was ardently of their party, and we and the English alike recruited members without reserve from boys whose names proclaimed their alien origin. Our parents differed considerably in wealth also. Some boys on wet days came to school in large motor cars, wrapped in fur rugs, with chauffeurs who leaped out to open the doors for them. Those of us who plodded up in goloshes did not attach the smallest importance, either of respect or resentment, to these superiorities. I think all this was a sign of a genuine 'good tone' in the school.

I joined the Boy Scouts and raised a Heath Mount patrol in one of the local troops. The scouts fell far short of the expectations raised by the books of Baden Powell. I supposed we should be trained in tracking and wood-craft, in disguising the plans of enemy forts in drawings of butterflies; that we should all be inspired by the high sense of honour exemplified by the Pistol Troop. In fact our proceedings were extremely drab. We paraded on Saturday afternoons in the basement of a shop and marched to the Heath. There we divided into opposing forces who with the minimum of reconnaissance engaged in a kind of fencing called 'ankle tapping' in which we sought to hit one another on the foot; being struck we were incapacitated from further adventure, though many boys returned illicitly to the fray. We then adjourned to the Vale of Health, where we purchased tea and cakes from a shop. The tests were cursory. Boys qualified as 'second-class scouts' by bringing billy-cans of already cooked food which they warmed at fires lit with a gross expenditure of matches. The 'gardener's badge' was awarded to anyone who showed half a dozen drawings of flowers. Since our drawing classes at school consisted largely in this exercise, all that was required of us was to submit our drawing-books.

But in the summer holidays of 1915 Mr Roland arranged for his son and me to act as messengers at the War Office. We sat in a smoky den inhabited by an old soldier and from time to time were employed in taking files from one room to another. My ambition was to serve Lord Kitchener. I often passed his door, but was never summoned to his presence. The highest I reached was the Chaplain-General. But Mr Roland took us daily to luncheon at his club; I believed I was genuinely in the King's service; the whole experience was a delight. I believe that we qualified for some medal, but we never received it.

I made friends easily at Heath Mount, but I have lost touch with them. Several were with me at the university, but I have seldom seen them since. Some must be dead, but they have not been given prominent obituaries. None has risen to power; none, I think, is a criminal. None sends begging letters – the most common form of communication between old school-fellows. For all the naval panache of Mr Grenfell I do not see their names in scandals at the Admiralty.

There is a professional photographer (and theatrical designer) who sometimes crosses my path when I go to London. His hair is sparse and his smile wry; his clothes rather flashy. I remember him as a tender and very pretty little boy. The tears on his long eyelashes used to provoke the sadism of youth and my cronies and I tormented him on the excuse that he was reputed to enjoy his music lessons and to hold in sentimental regard the lady who taught him. I am sure he was innocent of these charges. Our persecution went no further than sticking pins into him and we were soundly beaten for doing so.

There was another boy, a particular friend of mine, who came early to grief, falling to his death in a Paris street from the window of a notorious pederast and drug-taker. He was richer and more sophisticated than I. In his early days he had a nanny in attendance at the football field to refresh him at half-time with lemon squash from a thermos flask. He frequented the theatre, kept an album of programmes and knew a great deal about the private lives of actresses.

One Saturday he asked me to luncheon at his home saying casually: 'We might go to a matinée afterwards.' To me, as I have mentioned, a matinée was a rare event, eagerly expected, long remembered. I went to luncheon in high excitement, but when I inquired whether he had got seats he remarked with the same sangfroid that there was really nothing good on which he had not already seen.

It was from this boy that I first heard an obscenity – a very gentle one, but told with conscious guilt under a vow of secrecy. Unlike most schoolboys we were very prudish about the latrines. My doomed friend repeated to me a scatological limerick of the kind which rejoiced eminent Victorians. I was not amused.

He also quickened my curiosity about the processes of reproduction. We had no interest in our own bodies or in the sexual act. It was maternity that puzzled us and, as thousands of other boys and girls used to do before the popularity of biological studies, we searched the scriptures for relevant texts, looking up in the dictionary such words as 'womb' and 'whore' ('a lewd woman'; no help at all). Once, I remember, we looked up 'wail' because I found a reference to a woman 'wailing in childbirth'. Our ignorance remained almost absolute. I attached no significance to the differences of male and female anatomy revealed to me by Muriel.

I in my turn communicated to him the interest in Anglo-Catholicism which captivated me at the age of eleven.

I had regularly attended the services at North End Rooms where Miss Hoare played the harmonium, a village congregation sang the hymns of Moody and Sankey, and lay-preachers and an occasional clergyman from Christ Church, Hampstead, preached a doctrine that would have been equally acceptable in a nonconformist chapel – which was in fact entirely acceptable to Lucy.

When she left, I went to church with my parents, who had taken to frequenting St Jude's, Hampstead Garden Suburb, a fine Lutyens edifice then in the charge of a highly flamboyant clergyman named Basil Bourchier.

He was a man without pretension to doctrinal orthodoxy; a large, florid, lisping man, who was often to be seen in the stalls of London theatres in lay evening-dress. No one could have been more alien to the ideals of Dame Henrietta Barnet and of the general run of the inhabitants of his parish. He was a man of wider claims. His name was constantly in the popular newspapers, giving his wayward opinions on any subject about which he was consulted. He professed an extravagant patriotism and was a friend of Lord Northcliffe and of at least one member of the royal family. He was anathema to the genuine Anglo-Catholics of Graham Street, Margaret Street and St Augustine's, Kilburn. His congregation was not exclusively – nor indeed primarily – local. Personal devotees flocked to him from all parts of London. His sermons were dramatic, topical, irrational and quite without theological content. They would have served, my father remarked – and no stricture was more severe on his lips – as leading articles in the *Daily Mail*.

I have already remarked on the oddity of my father's churchmanship. It would never have occurred to him to take a clergyman as a counsellor or a model. Basil Bourchier he regarded as a rollicking joke and he sat under him with unbroken regularity, never losing his enjoyment of the surprises which the services afforded. My mother was coldly disdainful.

Mr Bourchier was a totally preposterous parson. When he felt festal he decreed a feast, whatever the season or occasion marked on the calendar. He dressed up, he paraded about, lights and incense were carried before him. When the mood took him he improvised his own peculiar ceremonies. Once he presented himself on the chancel steps, vested in a cope and bearing from his own breakfast table a large silver salt-cellar. 'My people,' he announced, 'you are the salt of the earth', and scattered a spoonful on the carpet before us. His service was 'Sung Eucharist', whereas at North End Rooms we had had only matins. Despite all Mr Bourchier's extravagant display I had some glimpse of higher mysteries.

At Midsomer Norton I made friends with a curate of very different character, who died a Catholic. As a young man he was a ritualist whom even my Aunt Connie thought somewhat extreme, but he had the basic principles of the Highchurchmen of the times and a sincere piety. He taught me to serve at the altar. I found deep enjoyment in doing so and there can have been little love of personal ostentation, I think, because the one part of the service which I disliked was the 'confession' which

I was required to pronounce in a loud voice leading the sparse congregation. This always embarrassed me. But I rejoiced in my nearness to the sacred symbols and in the bright early-morning stillness and in a sense of intimacy with what was being enacted.

From now on for a year or more my drawings were no longer of battles but of saints and angels inspired by mediaeval illuminations. I also became intensely curious about church decorations and the degrees of anglicanism – 'Prot, Mod, High, Spiky' – which they represented. It was the time when the undergraduates of Ronald Knox's circle used to bicycle round the countryside engaged, half humorously, half devoutly, in just such inquries. Somehow I caught the infection; at Mid-somer Norton my cousins at Chilcompton joined in these expeditions; in London my friend who had told me the dirty limerick. The Roland children did not share this interest, which marked the first division in what had until then been a life of fully shared activity.

In the night-nursery I made a shrine by my bed, three brackets of diminishing size, one above the other, each hung with a kind of little frontal. On these I arranged brass candle-sticks and flower vases and statues of saints which I bought at a religious emporium lately opened in Golders Green. These were of white plaster. I attempted to enliven them with water-colours, but the paint quickly exfoliated. Statues coloured in the factory, which I greatly admired, were beyond my means. I burned little cones of incense on a brass ashtray before these images.

I was much impressed by Newman's *Dream of Gerontius*, which found its way into the house in an edition illustrated in the *art nouveau*, and in emulation composed a deplorable poem in the metre of Hiawatha, named *The World to Come*, describing the experiences of the soul immediately after death. The manuscript was shown to a friend of my father's who had a printing-press on which he did much fine work. He conceived the kindly idea of producing some copies on hand-made paper and binding them for my father's birthday. They were distributed within the family. I do not know how many were made or how many survive, but the existence of this work is shameful to me.

I began at this time to express the intention of becoming a parson. My mother, who had seen a great deal of the drearier side of clerical life in her childhood, was unsympathetic, as she was to all this phase of churchiness. She no longer heard my evening prayers when I began to recite long devotions from a pious book. It was the first time when she had been unwilling to share a hobby with me.

Is 'hobby', I wonder, the right word? Almost everything was absurd in these activities but, *sub specie aeternitatis*, how much is not absurd in adult pieties? God speaks in many voices and manifests himself in countless shapes. Was I living in a world of my own imagination or was I in some faint contact with an objective reality? It would be ungracious and ungrateful to dismiss as pure fancy these intimations of truths which I was more soberly, but still most imperfectly, to grasp in later years.

My ecclesiological interests did not exclude others. I edited a school magazine called *The Cynic*, which my father's secretary typed and multiplied for us. It was flippant rather than cynical; the few jokes that are now intelligible seem very feeble. I collected 'war relics' – bits of shrapnel, shell cases, a German helmet, brought back from the front. There was, I believe, a market for them at Victoria Station, where soldiers returning on leave could provide themselves with acceptable souvenirs. But after the first few months the war had little interest for me. I accepted it as a condition of life. Scarcity of food was not felt in the first years. An anti-aircraft gun was posted at the Whitestone Pond and made a great noise when Zeppelins were overhead. No bomb fell within a mile of us, but the alarms were agreeable occasions when I was brought down from bed and regaled with an uncovenanted picnic. I was quite unconscious of danger, which was indeed negligible. On summer nights we sat in the garden, sometimes seeing the thin silver rod of the enemy caught in converging search-lights. On a splendid occasion I saw one brought down, sinking very slowly in brilliant flame, and joined those who were cheering in the road outside.

My father gave up taking in *Punch* because he disliked its style of light-hearted patriotism. His own heart grew heavier as the names appeared among the dead of boys whom a year before he had watched play cricket at Sherborne and entertained to dinner at the Digby. My mother spent all her days as a V.A.D. in a hospital at Highgate. My father, when most men of his age were acting as Special Constables or packing parcels for prisoners of war, declined to take any part. He managed his business with its depleted staff, he wrote literary criticism and watched with foreboding the *impasse* on the Western Front into which it seemed my brother must eventually be drawn.

His interest in Sherborne remained obsessive. The names of all my brother's contemporaries and their peculiarities were as familiar to me as the boys at Heath Mount. Cricket scores were received by telegram. My brother, as he has graphically described in his autobiography, got into a number of scrapes at school which culminated in his expulsion. This I never knew until I came to read his account of them. My father was anything but secretive; Alec's misdemeanours must have been constantly in his thoughts. He never mentioned them in my presence. When from time to time I heard echoes of scandal, I indignantly repudiated them. Alec appeared in khaki, first in the Inns of Court O.T.C. then as a cadet at Sandhurst. The poetry readings took on a new poignancy on Sunday evenings as they filled the time when he was waiting to take his leave-train back to camp. He had a particular relish at that time for the English lyric poets of the nineties; their dying cadences were always the prelude to his departure (on which my father accompanied him as far as the London terminus) so that when I read them now the picture they bring to mind is not of feverish eyes and wispy beards over the absinthe of the Café Royal but of puttees, heavy boots and a sturdy young soldier with a cup of cocoa under the rosy lights of the book-room at home.

3

Both my father and my brother have written accounts of the sensation and bitterness aroused by the publication of *The Loom of Youth*, my brother's first novel, an undisguisedly autobiographical work describing his schooldays with a realism that was then unusual. There were controversies in some papers and for my father many broken friendships. Its effect on me was that Sherborne was now barred to me. As soon as the book was accepted by its publisher, before it appeared, a new school had to be found for me in a hurry. Choice was limited by the lack of notice. My mother would have liked to keep me at home and send me to Westminster or St Paul's or the University College School in Hampstead, but these would have seemed unnatural to my father and with a minimum of deliberation his choice fell on Lancing, which he had never seen and with which he had no associations.

It is one of the Woodard foundations, designed originally to inculcate Highchurchmanship, especially in the education of the sons of the clergy, and it was this reputation which, in my phase of piety, decided him.

It was characteristic of him that, the decision being made, it was put into immediate execution. I took the Common Entrance exam in the Easter term, passed-in rather low, and went to Lancing next term.

I went, as I remember it, with no misgivings. All my reading of school-stories and all I had heard spoken at home made me regard going to a public school as an advance into a wider world of opportunity and adventure. I should have been ashamed to remain a day-boy all my life. It was not then, as it is now, the universal custom to send boys to school for the first time at the beginning of the school year in September, but it was more usual. As things turned out it was unfortunate that I went when I did. I was the unconscious victim of my father's instinct to push every affair on to completion. I would have been happier had I stayed another term at Heath Mount, but I bore no grudge for the precipitancy of my dispatch.

Nor is 'dispatch' the right word. My father took me to Lancing. We travelled down together by train on May 9th, 1917, a black day in my calendar – literally, for I carried one in my pocket on which I marked off the days of the term, some blacker than others according to my fortunes, surrounding the page with a border of chains.

It was a cold, damp spring. We changed trains at Brighton, arrived at Shoreham in the early afternoon and took a taxi to the school.

Nowadays the district is rather populous. It was not so then. The River Adur at low-water revealed empty mud flats; on one side lay a hutted army camp, on the other a field occasionally used by aeroplanes; eastward the sea-shore ran desolate to the suburbs of Brighton; westward to Worthing, broken only by the hamlets of Lancing and Sompting, pasture and arable fields running down to the edge of the shingle; and across the sky, as my father reminded me, ran 'the line of the downs, so noble and so bare'.

It was a countryside much painted and hymned in Edwardian and Georgian days, its valleys graced by little Norman churches, its heights almost treeless, close-cropped, scattered with dewponds, sheep-folds and isolated, bleak farmsteads. Our taxi turned across the timber bridge of Old Shoreham and we came into full view of the college buildings imposed on the horizon.

Then, and often subsequently, my father remarked on the contrast with Sherborne. There the school had grown up round the mediaeval abbey, incorporating monastic buildings; the Houses were domestic dwellings presided over by masters' wives, scattered among shopping streets; the place was served by a good hotel and a main line station. The school was never wholly separated from the slow-moving private lives of a mellow west-country market town. Lancing was monastic, indeed, and mediaeval in the full sense of the English Gothic revival; solitary, all of a piece, spread over a series of terraces sliced out of a spur of the downs. We had been sent some photographs of the buildings, but they had failed to prepare us for the dramatic dominance of the chapel which filled the scene before us. Mr Woodard had paid dear for his choice of site. The foundations, it was said, lay deeper below ground than the chalk groining above. He intended all his schools to be a reaffirmation of the Anglican Faith and Lancing chapel was to be the culminating monument of his design, proclaiming his purpose in the clearest tones. The great building was unfinished, but the east end which confronted us gave no evidence of the ruinlike, temporarily abandoned areas which lay behind. The glass seen from outside was greenish as though enclosing an aquarium. Visiting preachers not infrequently compared the apse to the prow of a ship. I know no more spectacular post-Reformation ecclesiastical building in the kingdom.

The great nave grew larger as we came up the private road. The porter's lodge was a temporary shed. Here we stopped. I had been put in the Headmaster's House (a choice which all who enjoyed it, regarded as conferring particular superiority over those in other Houses). It was there that the porter directed my father and myself.

The Rev. Henry Bowlby was then Headmaster. He was a contemporary of my father's at Oxford, a tall, lean man, distinctly handsome except when the keen winds of the place caught and encrimsoned his narrow nose. He walked with a limp, but in youth had got his blue, in a bad year, for hurdling. A fair scholar with an old-fashioned habit of introducing not very recondite classical allusions into his speech and letters, he had no particular interest in education. He hoped to become a bishop. This was not an inordinate ambition. He was a bishop's son and had followed a course – chaplain to the Archbishop of York, assistant master at Eton – which should have led to this elevation. A headmastership was the normal next stage to the bench. In 1917 he had been at Lancing for eight years and it was during my time under him that he must have realised that he had been passed over. I heard it said later that he was not greatly revered at Eton, where he had made himself rather ridiculous by his courtship of the more illustrious fathers and by flirtations with the prettier mothers and sisters. Of that aspect of him, if it existed, we saw nothing. We imitated him of course – he was the only man I have known who clearly sounded the 'Ts' in 'apostle' and 'epistle' – but we held him in some awe and he remained aloof from us, never dissembling the opinion, to which we all assented, that Lancing was a less important place than Eton. His outstanding gift was in the choice of subordinates. We were very fortunate in almost all the masters he appointed.

Mrs Bowlby was a kind, silly woman with a peculiar proclivity for *gaffes* which, repeated and exaggerated, formed part of the lore of the school. It may be that this weakness of hers counted against her husband when he was considered for preferment. She gave us tea that afternoon in her drawing-room and said nothing more memorable than that it was a 'patriotic' tea; we could eat with a good conscience because none of the cakes contained flour; some were made of potatoes, some of rice.

This theme of famine, which was to assume large importance in the next eighteen months, was almost new to me. As a treat before going to school I had been taken to hear Harry Lauder, the Scotch music-hall comedian, who after his songs had addressed us on the subject. 'When you cut yourself another slice of bread,' he had declaimed, 'look at the knife. There's blood on it. The blood of a British soldier you have stabbed in the back.' The papers were full of warnings that only voluntary self-denial could save the country from the shame we had so much derided in the Germans, State control of food, but neither at home nor at Heath Mount had there been any shortages. It was in 1917 that the submarine blockade became effective. Adolescents were not as tenderly treated by the rationing authorities of the first war as of the second; my introduction to public-school life coincided with my first experience of hunger. Mrs Bowlby's patriotic fare was the best I was to enjoy until the summer holidays.

The time for my father's departure soon came; I parted from him without a pang. I believed I was at the beginning of a new and exciting phase of life. I was conducted from the Headmaster's private house to the House-tutor's room.

The reader unfamiliar with the Lancing of the time may require some explanation of this office. The Headmaster read House Prayers on Sunday evenings and sometimes made a round of the dormitories, like a general officer inspecting troops, stopping capriciously to address an unwelcome inquiry or a pleasantry to one or other of us, as he passed down the ranks. That was the full extent of his personal care for us. All other matters were left to the House-tutor. There were four House-tutors during my time in Head's. It was a post always given to the assistant master next in line for a House, so that, despite our assumption of superiority, we were really at some disadvantage with boys in other Houses, who remained all their schooldays under the same man of known idiosyncrasy. English boys resent change and are happiest with the familiar, even when odious or ludicrous, and, as I have suggested, Mr Bowlby normally chose a very good sort of Housemaster.

The House-tutor to whom I was introduced was an extremely agreeable young man; especially agreeable to a new-comer. His name was Dick Harris. His brother owned a preparatory school at Worthing named St Ronan's, many of whose boys came on to Lancing. Dick later inherited the school when his brother prematurely died, and sustained its prosperity. He was at his best with the young. Older boys inclined to patronise him, but there could hardly have been found any-one more reassuring to meet at the beginning of a new and exciting phase. He was, though I did not know it, due to leave for the army at the end of the term. He used Christian names to boys – a custom far from established in 1917. I found myself under him not only in Head's but in school, where I was placed in the Middle Fourth, his form. Such vestiges of happiness as I enjoyed during my first term were entirely due to Dick Harris.

It was characteristic of Dick that one Sunday evening, when he had a House of his own, he read Leigh Hunt's *Abou Ben Adhem* as a homily; characteristic of his kindness and immaturity.

He was not large in person, but neat and springy; a Cambridge soccer blue, with light, clear eyes and light clear skin, a frank and friendly manner. It was still an hour or two before the official time of arrival. Dick lent me a book – *The Iron Pirate* by Max Pemberton – and showed me into the empty House Room, where a table was set apart for 'new men'. There I sat alone for what seemed an age. In the last eighteen months I had become precocious in my choice of reading. I had the free run of my father's books and read voraciously without guidance and with far from perfect comprehension. My favourite books were Malory's *Morte d'Arthur* and Compton Mackenzie's *Sinister Street*. *The Iron Pirate* did not command my attention. I gazed about me at the long room furnished with an oak settle beside an empty fireplace, with lockers on one wall, tables and benches, framed photographs of athletic groups, some silver cups in a glass case, a notice-board already bearing a number of lists and orders which I was too shy to examine in detail. Gothic windows gave on the masters' garden, and a frieze of Gothic script read '*Qui diligit Deum diligit et fratrem suum*'. The place was newly scrubbed and dampish.

At length two boys appeared and said: 'O God. Same old House Room'; 'Same old smell'; they glanced at me with cold disdain and turned to the notice-board. 'Same old dormitory.' 'They've moved that tick Barnsley into Lower Ante-room.' 'Malcomson's head of Upper Head's.' They then read with consternation a new sumptuary rule: from then on food-parcels were forbidden, also an institution unknown to me described as 'Settle tea'. The Grub Shop would sell only fruit.

These two were the first of a noisy incursion. The school train had arrived at Shoreham and the two taxis went back and forth to the station bringing loads of half a dozen boys and their hand bags. About forty-five boys shared the House Room. When they had reported to Dick they stamped round the notice-board, declaiming with varying degrees of disgust the two promotions and the drastic ban on grub which had so alarmed the first-comers. All ignored my existence. I had been given some highly mysterious hints on leaving Mr Grenfell of the danger of too friendly approaches from older boys. The warning seemed singularly inappropriate to my condition.

At length I was joined at the 'new men's table' by a large-headed, soft-spoken boy of my own age – Fulford minor. As his suffix denoted he had an elder brother in the school. He enjoyed the further advantage of coming from St Ronan's. I think it probable that I was more conscious than he of these superiorities. Since then Mr Roger Fulford has written and edited a number of highly enjoyable historical works. He has often stood for Parliament and has prosperously divided a romantic loyalty between Liberalism and Royalty. He was then the only boy out of three hundred and fifty with whom it was permissible to associate. Two years later he and I became cronies, but at that time I would not have chosen him as a friend, nor he me, had any choice been possible.

It was the custom at Lancing that during one's first three weeks an 'underschool', as Lower boys were dubbed, was deputed to take charge of one and instruct one in the habits of the place. In theory – though I do not remember it ever put into practice – any punishment incurred during this time was visited on him. The code inculcated was elaborate, trivial but nor particularly irksome, and related chiefly to dress and to the places where one might set the feet. Costume was entirely subfusc for the first two years; then coloured socks were permissible; in the Sixth Form coloured ties. For the first year hands must be kept from the trouser pockets, for the second year they could be inserted but with the jacket raised, not drawn back. A two-year man might link arms with a one-year man, not vice versa. Grass, in which the grounds abounded, was in general forbidden territory; every plot was the preserve of some privileged caste, the most sacred being the Lower Quad, where only school prefects might tread. All this, and much else of the same kind, was explained to me. At the same time I was 'heard' the form of House prayers which had to be known by heart. On the third Sunday of term one stood on a table in the House Room and sang a song, after which one was an initiated member of the tribe and subject to fagging and beating. All these details of deportment I acquired without difficulty or question. They formed a very small part of the novelties of school life.

During those first three weeks I learned my way about the school buildings. These comprised, essentially, two large, cloistered quadrangles. The Houses were on opposing sides of this plan. Each had its own House Room, dormitories and changing-rooms, but there was no element of domesticity. The Headmaster's wife, living apart, had no business with our welfare. Housemasters were all unmarried, about half of them clergymen, and we ate in common in a dining-hall, the masters on a dais as in a university college, the Houses segregated only by their separate tables. The buildings were of flint. An ancient and obsolescent Sussex craft had been kept alive for two generations in their construction. Experts often came to study the perfection of the south wall of the dining-hall. The tracery of windows and arches was of less durable matter – a local stone which the fierce, salt gales constantly corroded. An old mason and his apprentice had life-long employment in restoring the decay. Gas was the lighting throughout. At this stage of that war there was a partial black-out in coastal areas, so that after dark the place was deeply gloomy. Shadowy, faceless couples perambulated the cloisters during the quarter of an hour's break between hall and evening-school. The chapel was lighted by burners over the masters' pews in the side-aisles; the

roof of the nave was lost in the evening and a curious kaleidoscope of shadows played round our feet as we came in and out.

Each house had its matron; in our case the former nanny
of the Bowlby children, an admirable, diminutive woman who
gave us self-esteem by addressing us as 'Mr', as distinct from
the matrons of other Houses who called their patients by their
surnames without prefix. Apart from them there were no
women in the place except 'skivvies', the unseen maids who
made our beds, emptied the slops and, I suppose, took a hand
in the kitchens and sculleries in the area behind the hall and the
chapel; a strange waste land forbidden to all except the band
who used it for practice. There lay the foundations and first
walls and arches of the abandoned tower, the ammunition store,
and an assemblage of impenetrable sheds clouded by steam
and smoke where ghastly stews were concocted and muddy
clothes boiled. I never learned where the skivvies slept or
went for amusement. Only one master was recognised as
married; a clergyman who lived within bicycling distance and –
as was regarded as equally eccentric – grew his own curiously
smelling tobacco in a glass frame. We never met his wife. It is
possible that some of the masters on the 'Modern Side' may
also have been other than celibate, but these constituted a distinct and lower order, never appointed to posts of authority
or influence. We did not inquire into their privacies. The
exclusion of feminine influence and domestic life was absolute.
We never entered a human dwelling or saw a shop; to a boy
like myself coming straight from home, the experience was
chilling.

At the time of writing I revisited Lancing after an interval
of forty years and wandered about with a few tremors of nos-
talgia. The place has grown considerably and unlike those
schools and colleges where poverty has demanded a com-
promise with modern tricks of construction, the new buildings
are all in the style and materials of the original nucleus. The
corbels, plain in my time, above the Hall stairs have been
prettily carved. Rock-gardening has horribly appeared on the

grass slopes, which I was so often conscribed to mow, beside the steps of the Lower Quad. The interior walls of the chapel were spotted with a miscellany of pictures. The House Room has been furnished with stalls, one to each boy, in imitation of the 'toys' of Winchester. Boys no longer wore black coats. J. M. Neale's collection of theological works had disappeared from the library. The rock-gardenery and the pictures in chapel provoked no protest or lamentation of the kind normal in old boys. The startling change since my day was in the environs. Little red houses were everywhere, some of them on the school property. The austere isolation deliberately sought by the founder has, for good or ill – I dare say for good – been entirely lost.

I saw a small boy running on the gravel margin of the Lower Quad and as I came into the Upper Quad I saw something which would have been still less conceivable in my boyhood. A car drove through the tower gateway and halted outside what was the entrance to Old's and Saunderson's Houses, and from it emerged a young mother with two pretty children who proceeded to collect a scooter propped against the wall.

The monastery has been dissolved. Suburbia had entered and established itself.

In Hall we were waited on by youths who also lived in but enjoyed privileges denied to us such as the use of bicycles and tobacco. There was also a strange body of 'bootmen', old, illiterate, misshapen, who lived in lightless dens under Great School, smelling of blacking and shag. Morning and evening they emerged, pushing baskets full of dirty and clean boots, muttering to themselves as they stumbled along. They can have had no recreation of any kind. There was no inn within range of their faltering steps. Apart from those of the skivvies, the waiters and the bootmen all menial tasks were done by 'underschools' and done under rigid discipline, the results closely scrutinised and any imperfection punished with the cane.

Almost all discipline in the House was in the hands of the prefects and House-captains; the head of the House alone could beat and three strokes was the regular punishment. Graver crimes were punished by the school prefects in their common-room. There was seldom any injustice. Indeed a code of sharp legality prevailed. The Housemaster beat for offences reported to him from the form-rooms by other masters. Most boys during their first two years got beaten at least once a term.

During my first term an Irish boy named Fitzgerald started an insurance company. The premium was a shilling and claims were paid at the rate of threepence a stroke. Fitzgerald had studied the actuarial form and was thought to be sure of a profit. Fulford and I were induced to subscribe and it was remarked that this was rather sharp of Fitzgerald as lawlessness was considered bad form among new boys, who normally got through their first term without punishment. The enterprise was ruined in dramatic circumstances.

The dormitory of the youngest boys was named Upper Head's. We went to bed at 8.45 and it was the duty of the senior boy to turn out the lights at 9. After lights out all speech and movement was forbidden and it was this boy's unenviable task to enforce the rules. I had no intimation that the head of our dormitory was disliked or that he had committed any outrage, but one evening at about half-term there was a sudden concerted attack on him. Fulford and I stood by our beds uncomprehending and aghast while the rest flung themselves on the head, punching him and hitting him with belts and slippers. Eventually he fought his way clear of the *mêlée*, out of the dormitory, through the changing-room, still pursued by blows, and down the turret stair that led to Dick Harris's quarters. Panting and triumphant, his attackers awaited the outcome. Within five minutes Dick arrived with some canes. No investigation was held. He simply said: 'I'm going to beat the lot of you. Come into the changing room one at a time in House order.' One of the conspirators said: 'The new men had nothing to do with it, sir.' 'Can't go into that now.'

Next day Fitzgerald paid out nearly £3 and declared himself bankrupt. The victim of mob violence was moved into another dormitory and a senior boy was put in charge of us for the rest of the term. I never learned what provoked the assault. Even Fulford, who was so much more in the know than I, could not explain it. Nothing like it occurred again anywhere during my time at Lancing. It was an episode quite out of character with the place.

I was grateful to Dick for including me in the common punishment. It gave me a slight sense of kinship, where before I had been totally alien. For I was not at all popular then or at any time in my first two years.

Friendlessness was at first inevitable in the rigid segregations and stratification of seniority by which I found myself isolated. Odium was personal and something quite new to me. For thirteen years I had met only people who seemed disposed to like me. Experience has taught me that not everyone takes to me at first sight (or on closer acquaintance), but I am still mildly surprised by rebuffs, such is the confidence which a happy childhood founds.

At Lancing the antipathy was mutual. I did not at all relish the continual proximity of these large, loud youths. I was too old, indeed at exactly the worst age, to accept cheerfully the sudden loss of all privacy. I was a fastidious little boy. For a long time the latrines so disgusted me that I dreaded using them. At Heath Mount, as I have mentioned, we were peculiarly reticent in this matter. At Lancing the four Houses which comprised the Lower Quad shared what was known as 'the Groves' – a name which often excited amusement in chapel when the kings of Israel and Juda were alternately commended for cutting down the groves and reprobated for restoring them. These Groves were a white-washed yard divided by a double row of tarred urinals. On either side were two covered rows of latrines, one for the Upper, the other for the Lower, School, both inadequate in number and to my delicate senses appallingly exposed. They had no doors and were built over a deep open

drain which was periodically, but not often, sluiced and disinfected. After breakfast this place was a social centre for the
exchange of gossip; it was the closest communication we had
with the other Houses. In order to secure a seat one had to
book one from its occupant. There were cries of: 'After you';
'I've got second off of these three'; 'I'll take third off'. I was
shy of addressing any of these strangers at any time; in that
posture I found it quite impossible. One could go to the
Groves during school hours at the cost of writing twenty-five
lines. I found this preferable.

The food in Hall would have provoked mutiny in a mid-
Victorian poor-house and it grew steadily worse until the end
of the war. In happier times it was supplemented from the
Grub Shop and by hampers from home. In 1917–18 it afforded
a bare subsistence without any pretence to please. There was,
I recall, a horrible substance named 'Honey-Sugar', a sort of
sweetened cheeselike matter, the by-product of heaven knows
what chemical ingenuity, which appeared twice a week at
supper in cardboard pots. There was milkless cocoa and small
pats of margarine and limitless bread. At midday dinner there
was usually a stew consisting chiefly of swedes and potatoes in
their skins. Perhaps the table-manners were an unconscious
protest against this prison diet. Clean cloths were laid on Sunday; by Tuesday they were filthy. Boys from perfectly civilised
homes seemed to glory in savagery and it was this more than the
wretched stuff they slopped about which disgusted me. Exceptionally accomplished boys were able to flick pats of margarine
from their knives to the high oak rafters overhead, where they
stuck all the winter until released by the summer heat they fell,
plomp, on the tables below.

We each had a weekly bath in the evening. That was bliss.
But it was also compulsory to bath every afternoon except
Sunday. There were two baths to each dormitory. There was
seldom enough hot water to afford a change. In the winter
terms after football one waited one's turn to immerse oneself
in tepid mud. As we waited our turn, climbed in and out of

the muck and rubbed ourselves with towels which, like the table-cloths, were clean on Sunday and filthy by Tuesday, I boggled at the contact of all these naked bodies and no doubt my repugnance communicated itself.

I was not only prudish but priggish. It was common for small, clever boys to gain favour with larger, stupid ones by doing their exercises for them in preparation. This I refused to do on the grounds that it was dishonest. A better-informed conscience would have recognised compliance as being not only more prudent but also more charitable. My scruple did not endear me.

I find it quite impossible to identify myself with the lonely schoolboy of this chill time. All I remember is inconsistent. I was, for example, morbidly afraid of being in any way conspicuous. It was the function of the head of the House Room to distribute letters. I received rather more than most and once or twice they were tossed to me with a slight asperity: 'Another one for Waugh.' This was enough for me to ask my father to write less often although his letters were a delight to me. On the other hand I defied convention by kneeling at the *incarnatus* in the creed at Holy Communion. This had been my habit at St Jude's. It was not done at Lancing. During my first term I remained standing with the others. During my first holidays I suffered remorse, as though I had betrayed my convictions. During my second term and for some terms afterwards until it no longer seemed important, I did kneel; at first with trepidation, but no one ever commented on this singularity. If there was no great devotion at Lancing there was a respect for religion. It would have been thought bad form to mock another's piety and there were in fact a number of pious boys who never incurred unpopularity on those grounds.

I did not admire the other boys. I did not want to be like them. But, in contradiction, I wanted to be one of them. I had no aspirations to excel, still less to lead; I simply longed to remain myself and yet be accepted as one of this distasteful mob. I cannot explain it, but I think that was what I felt.

Perhaps I may have exaggerated the dislike in which I was held, but I do know that on Sunday afternoons, when the House Room was put out of bounds for two hours and we were sent out to the downs in our straw hats and black coats, I often found myself walking alone or obliged to make a rendezvous with some equally unpopular boy in another House.

The most bitter of these experiences occurred early in my first term, on Ascension Day. This was a whole holiday, the only one in the year. It was a feast I had not hitherto commemorated. I overheard a good deal of talk about what would happen on that day, but nothing prepared me for the event. After morning chapel the whole school dispersed. Those who had parents or friends in the district were taken to Brighton or Worthing. Others walked to Bramber, where there were riverside tea-gardens, a ruined castle and a repository of stuffed animals, the hobby of an inn-keeper, arranged in *tableaux* – rats playing cards and drinking wine in a den raided by other rats clothed as policemen, and so forth; a two-headed sheep and other monstrosities which I came to enjoy in later years. That first year I knew no one and had nowhere to go. The whole place was emptied as though by plague. Inquiry elicited the information that there was no dinner that day. The steward gave me some slices of bread and a ghastly kind of sausage meat. Rain came on. The House Room, as on Sundays, was locked. The library was out of bounds to me. I wandered out with my damp packet of food and after a time took shelter among the trees called Lancing Ring, ate a little and, for the first and last time for many years, wept. It was with comfort that late that afternoon I heard the noisy return of the holiday-makers.

I have brought up my children to make a special intention at the Ascension Mass for all desolate little boys.

Except on Sundays leisure was scant. Games, which were called 'Clubs', and the Corps took up every afternoon. The Corps was detested and I think few associated games with pleasure. They were a source of intense competition, anxiety and recrimination to those who excelled; of boredom and discomfort to those who were bad at them.

Cricket was an exception. Those who played well seemed to enjoy themselves. They wore pretty colours and enjoyed great prestige, but no reproach attached to the duffers. Those who played good cricket were recognised as possessing a peculiar and enviable aptitude, but it was not disgraceful to spend long tedious afternoons in the Third League. Failure at other sports was contemptible. 'Wrecks' was the Lancing word for such unfortunates. I was not a total wreck. At football, boxing, swimming and the half-mile I eventually got into my House team. But I was not good enough in my first year to attract any notice. I never enjoyed competition and was glad to escape without ignominy.

On match days those not in the team had to watch and applaud, in summer lying out on rugs on the bank and clapping, in winter standing on the touch-lines cheering. This was the universal custom of the period. Nowadays in most schools more imagination is said to be shown. There was some relaxation towards the end of my time at Lancing, but during my first two years there was absolutely no form of recreation other than Clubs.

I remember during my first term watching a first eleven match (perforce with Fulford minor). The batsman of a visiting team drove straight to where we sat. A large boy despaired of fielding it and fell into a trot. The ball ran more slowly, mounted the bank and came to a stop on our rug. More adroit boys in these circumstances rejoiced to throw in. Fulford and I sat gazing at the sacred, scarlet object, afraid to touch it. The sweating and furious personage thundered up on his nailed, buckskin boots and was obliged to retrieve it himself from beside our bag of cherries. 'You little ticks,' he said; 'you'll pay for this.' For the rest of the afternoon and all that evening we lived in fear of retribution. In fact we heard no more of the matter.

The best hours of my first year were spent in the library, in chapel and in school.

The library was a peaceful place, well stocked. It was open to us for an hour in the evening on half holidays and Sundays. Conversation was subdued. We could take books out and return them and we could sit and read. I spent most of my time there turning over the plates of the 'Art' books, in particular a set of volumes called the *Bible in Art* which reproduced paintings of every period illustrative of the scriptural narratives. Thus I learned dimly to recognise the characteristics of the various schools. My preference then, and now, was for the Quattrocento and the Pre-Raphaelites, with deviations, since corrected, towards Bouguereau and Puvis de Chavannes. Rubens and Rembrandt seemed very ugly.

In school I was at first under Dick Harris, who read to us and made us learn poems much more modern than those my father had introduced to me – Flecker, Rupert Brooke, Ralph Hodgson, all Eddie Marsh's young protégés. But, alas, I had been placed too low. I was effortlessly top of the weekly order and was promoted at half-term to the Upper Fourth, where again I was always top but in less congenial surroundings. I think my Common Entrance papers must have been given cursory attention. At the end of that term I got a double remove into the Upper School, where I found myself in the same stage of education as in the First Form at Heath Mount.

We went to chapel morning and evening every day and three times on Sundays. I have heard the complaint that this was excessive. I never found it so even when I had become an avowed agnostic. The diction of the Anglican services and of the Authorised Version of the Bible never failed to charm me. For all their reputation of Highchurchmanship the services were not ritualistic, nor was the doctrine touched by the Romanism then current in the world of Ronald Knox. The clergy were surpliced, not vested. Two candles stood on the altar. There was no incense used; none of the extravagances of Mr Basil Bourchier. All was ordered in the spirit of the Tractarians.

Morning and evening chapels gave refuge from the surrounding loneliness; contact with home and with Midsomer Norton rather than with Heaven. On Sunday evenings the names were read of old boys killed in action during the week. There was seldom, if ever, a Sunday without its necrology. The chapel was approached by a passage in which their photographs were hung in ever-extending lines. I had not known them, but we were all conscious of these presences. It was not uncommon for preachers to refer to the sacrifices which were being made for our benefit. This did not seem humbug. It is said that an exhortation of this kind now rouses derision. It was not so in 1917.

The music in chapel was, I believe, very good. Had I been differently constituted, it might have been an additional solace to me. The organist, Brent-Smith, had a reputation beyond the school. On Sunday evenings there were anthems with pretty treble solos, followed, for those who cared to stay, by organ recitals. Visitors came from outside to hear them, but I preferred to go to the House Room, where in evening-school we were allowed to read books approved by the authorities as 'literature', a distinction conferred on all books more than fifty years of age.

Term dragged on. 'Red-letter' Saints' Days were '*Veniam*' days when leave could be had twice a term to go out with parents or friends. I knew no one in the district and was barely accessible to a day's visit from London, so I stayed back, lonely as on any Sunday. At length when the end was in sight and trunks had appeared in the dormitories I was felled by an insupportable blow, symptoms of mumps too manifest to be disguised. The first fortnight of my first holidays was spent in the sanatorium – with Fulford minor.

The woman in charge, named Sister Babcock, did nothing to mitigate our sorrow. She was by nature ill-tempered and was especially irate on this occasion of having her own holidays curtailed. (She had a heavy moustache. A Russian boy was birched for presenting her with a razor; his father presented an ikon to the chapel, the sole extraneous ornament to its severe grandeur.) After a few days we were out of bed but in quarantine. I was sent a cold chicken from home which was stolen and eaten by Sister Babcock's cat. Sister Babcock apologised for the outrage with poor grace and shouted at the ward-maid who had left open the larder door: 'Don't beat my cat; beat yourself.'

Home, when after weeks of yearning I regained it, was no less dear to me than ever, but it was less joyful. My brother had been posted to the front; the battle of Passchendaele was in progress – if the phrase can be used of that notorious operation – and huge casualty lists appeared daily. My parents were in perpetual anxiety for his safety. Moreover, my father was agitated by alternations of distress and exultation at the reception of the *Loom of Youth* and deeply hurt by the alienation of many old Sherborne friendships. My mother walked to and from the hospital in Highgate for her tours of duty as a V.A.D. I often walked with her, but she was away from the house for many hours a day. I was never bored or lonely at home, but that holidays, and for many holidays to come, my happiness began to wane as soon as the half-way stage was reached and gave place to growing melancholy and dread which quite over-cast any pleasures that might be arranged for my last days.

My second term was one of black misery. There was no spice of adventure in returning; merely odious familiarity. I was now in the Classical Lower Fifth, it is true, and under the chaplain, an emaciated young clergyman named Mr Howitt, a holy, musical man, gentle and enthusiastic; he had come to Lancing, it was said, to recuperate after breaking his health in a slum parish; the hours in school with him were always agreeable. Also, Dick Harris had left a final benefaction by appointing me 'library underschool'. This relieved me of all routine house-fagging. The duties were to replace the books in the shelves and to make out lists of those due for return. They carried the inestimable privilege of access to the library at all times. These were two mitigations. Apart from them all changes were for the worse. Dick Harris had been replaced as

House-tutor by an elderly walrus-moustached man who had hitherto taught German. He was quite ineffectual and the whole management of the House was taken out of his hands by the House-captains, martinets who in peace-time would still have been subordinates and were too young for office. There was an exceptionally large incursion of new boys among whom later I made many friends, but for their first two terms inflexible convention forbade all intercourse with them. There was still only Fulford with whom I could consort. Food was scarcer; the waiters had disappeared, absorbed in some kind of war-service and there was now a roster of boys to wait at table; not only the underschools but all except the highest. This added to the gloom of those barbarous meals, for those who served their superiors were harried and chidden; when superior served inferior he slammed and splashed the dishes about with violent disdain. When cold set in, it was piercing. The Corps had hitherto been a mild infliction; as a small squad of recruits we had paraded under the band-master and gone through the elements of drill. Now we were drafted into companies. One half-holiday a week was given up to a uniform-parade, for which we had to prepare with brasso, blanco and boot polish. The rifles had been designed for men six feet tall; they seemed an intolerable incumbrance. Potato digging was added to our patriotic duties.

Wind, rain and darkness possessed the place as we scurried to early school. Chilblains swelled and burst. I urgently besought my father to remove me. He counselled endurance.

I do not seek to harrow with these mild austerities the reader who has vicariously supped full with the horrors of the concentration camp. I merely assert that *I* was harrowed. I had lived too softly for my first thirteen years.

My brother and thousands like him, not five years my senior, were wintering in the trenches in conditions immeasurably more severe. These were dismal years for half the world. I believe it was the most dismal period in history for an English schoolboy.

There are many well-known accounts of bullying and flogging in the schools of the early nineteenth century, but one can glimpse through them a rude humanity and variety that was lacking to us then. Boys, eighty years earlier, roamed the countryside, tippled ale and, when they were not roasting fags, roasted snared pheasants over the open fires; they fought one another and sometimes locked out the masters. Except for the unique, unexplained riot in Upper Head's, everything was grimly correct at Lancing in 1917 and 1918.

I have heard it said that when, in the last century, criminals were removed from the squalor and corruption of the old gaols and confined in the modern houses of correction prescribed for them by the humane, many went out of their minds. An analogous process transformed English schools at the same period. The system worked well under men and boys of goodwill, imagination and enthusiasm in a time of plenty and bright prospects. These were temporarily lacking at Lancing. The boys in authority were too young, the masters too old. Everything was of necessity a makeshift – the clothes we wore, the food we ate, the books we worked with, the masters who should have taught us. We were cold, shabby and hungry in the ethos, not of free Sparta, but of some beleaguered, enervated and forgotten garrison.

4

I returned home for Christmas to find a new member of the household. This was no surprise. I had been kept informed of the change by letter, but whether or no I had met the newcomer before, I cannot now remember. I certainly knew a great deal about her. She was Barbara Jacobs, to whom my brother had become engaged after a brief courtship which he has described in detail in his own autobiography. She was less than three years my senior, a soft, drooping girl, lethargic but capable of being roused both to strenuous activity and to gaiety. I think I acted as an animator to her. I heard it remarked that when I was about she was less liable to lapse into reverie.

She had a gentle sense of the absurd in all around her. Her hair was bobbed; she wore low-heeled shoes and was mildly artistic in dress; never *outrée*, but unconventional in eschewing hats and gloves and sunshades, and adorning herself with crude jewellery of beaten silver and copper, enamel, semi-precious stones and amber, that was made by a bearded crank in Berkhamsted. She had many admirers, but I never thought her particularly beautiful or attractive (I was given to insignificant romantic attachments to girls of my own age). I liked her very much and enjoyed her company. She must have enjoyed mine, for, until my brother's return from the army, she spent the holidays with us as my companion in the house where she had originally come merely in order to attend lectures at a ladies' college in Regent's Park.

Barbara requires more than passing mention in a chapter attempting to describe my education. She was well educated and well read, but the knowledge she had acquired and the names she revered seldom coincided with anything I had been taught. Her experiences and upbringing had been entirely different from mine; her tastes, her reading, her opinions were in some respects antithetical, in others complementary. She was an agnostic, a socialist and a feminist. Until I met her, maiden-aunts and Anglican clergy had been in the ascendant; in Barbara I met the new age. I did not surrender to it without reserve, but I was stimulated by the encounter. My father always assumed (as I do now) that anything new was likely to be nasty. Barbara found a specific charm in modernity. She did not pursue novelty; she was no butterfly of fashion flitting from vorticism to dadaism. She was, rather, subversive by tradition, a spaniel lolloping dreamily along at her mother's heels. I argued sturdily with her but I picked up many of her arguments, which I reproduced next term in my essays, with the result that Mr Howitt in my report made a rebuke which I have seldom incurred in my later years: 'He must learn to "approve those things that are excellent", not merely those that are ultra-modern.'

Barbara's original aspiration in coming to London had been to enter the Slade School of Art, not because she had any aptitude for drawing but because at that time the institution had a peculiar lustre of emancipation. Her father discerned her motive and forbade her entry. The school in Regent's Park was for girls only and had no Bohemian taint. I never knew what she was studying there. It provided a convenient escape from a turbulent home.

She was the eldest of the large family of an ill-assorted couple.

Her father, W. W. Jacobs, was a writer who in his middle years developed an exquisite precision of narrative. He was at the height of his power and reputation when I came to observe him, but I was not impressed. His stories had been read aloud at Heath Mount; I did not regard them as 'literature'; they were 'prep-school stuff'; nor did his children take any pride in his achievements. They were taught to see him as a niggardly breadwinner. Lately he has come to the notice of serious students of fiction. I doubt whether he often raises laughter among the young as he used.

In person he was wan, skinny, sharp-faced, with watery eyes. Like many humorists he gave scant evidence of humour in private intercourse. In losing the accents of Wapping he had lost most of his voice and spoke through the side of his thin lips in furtive, almost criminal tones, disconcerting in a man of transcendent, indeed of tedious, respectability. He was a secular puritan, one of those 'who have not got the Faith and will not have the fun', and all his opinions were those of Lord Northcliffe. But concealed behind this drab façade, invisible to my boyish eye, there lurked a pure artist.

His wife, much younger than he, was an earnest and effusive Welshwoman who had done time for breaking windows as a suffragette; a 'new woman' of the kind depicted by H. G. Wells, who had, in fact, portrayed her as one of his heroines. She had fine eyes, generous impulses, eager responses to suffering and injustice, and was at the core a booby.

The two were in continual, furious conflict on every subject, more especially that of the education of their children. Memory may have multiplied a few occasions; I have a general impression of Mrs Jacobs constantly arriving at our house with one child or another which she was in process of kidnapping from the school chosen by its father and secreting in some more progressive establishment.

They lived on the outskirts of Berkhamsted in a large modern house named Beechcroft. Jacobs was one of the best-paid short-story writers of the time, but their prosperity brought little comfort, for Mrs Jacobs regarded it as derogatory to the status of woman to attend to the management of the home. Distinctions of sex were for her and for those who thought like her as invidious then as distinctions of race and colour became to the generation of her grandchildren. Even motherhood was regarded as a kind of colonialism in which the female was exploited for the male's profit. In a better-ordered world William Wymark would have suffered the pangs of childbirth.

In all the family rows the children sided with their mother. Barbara, when she first came to live with us, accepted all her opinions. Only when, a year or two later, Mrs Jacobs abandoned politics for theosophy, did Barbara begin to suspect her of fallibility.

I made many visits to Beechcroft during the next two years and members of the Jacobs family often came to us. They began to supplant the Rolands as the friends of my holidays.

During this time there was in Berkhamsted a boy of my own age who was later to become an honoured friend. Graham Greene was the son of the headmaster of the local school, which the elder of the Jacobs boys attended. His father and Jacobs knew one another, but in all the parties I attended in Berkhamsted I never met him. There is nothing remarkable in this except for one fact which should interest those who investigate the raw material of a novelist's work and its transmogrification in the mind.

I think it likely that I put on some airs before young Jacobs, contrasting the severe life of a boarding-school with his softness as a day-boy. Somehow these boastings must have spread at Berkhamsted School. Graham Greene himself is unaware of the process. But again and again in his novels, when he wishes to portray a seedy character who nurtures a pathetic loyalty to a minor public school, he attributes this emotion to Lancing. I am the only old boy of Lancing whom he has known well. Neither he nor I see any likeness between myself and these sad fictions. Something young Jacobs said may at second or third hand have engendered them.

In the Jacobs household there was a second sister, a dark, handsome girl, slightly younger than I, with whom my terms of friendship were quite different from those with Barbara. She did not attempt to teach me, but looked up to me with gratifying respect. There was a large, galleried music-room at Beechcroft with a slippery oak floor often lent for local dances. Here a children's game of undefined rules was played in the dark. The ostensible object was for one party to crawl through the ranks of the other to a goal on the further side. Here on the polished oak floor she and I would seek one another, grapple and, while the younger players squealed in the excitement of arrest and escape, would silently cling and roll together. We maintained a pretence of conflict. There was no kissing, merely rapturous minutes of close embrace. No mention of our intimacy was ever made between us. But after the game, when the lights came on, we would exchange glances of complicity and it was always either she or I who proposed 'the dark game'.

With Barbara there was never a hint of physical contact. I found in her the kind of friend I lacked at Lancing. Together we explored London, of which neither of us had any knowledge. We spent whole days in unplanned expeditions, boarding buses at random and leaving them as fancy took us. To the modern Londoner, who stands long in the queue and then creeps through blank fuming chasms of concrete and masonry in a cushioned, enclosed saloon, it must seem bizarre that a happier generation followed these routes for pleasure. In those days buses stopped on demand, but the young took pride in leaping on and off them at speed. From their open decks there was a wide prospect over the low skyline. In sun and rain (against which a tarpaulin was hitched to the back of the seat giving some protection) Barbara and I learned the topography of a city that still abounded in idiosyncrasies.

We did little specific sight-seeing – my taste in architecture was still for the mediaeval – but we visited many galleries and exhibitions of painting. Neither of us had any comprehension of the post-impressionists, but Barbara had a sympathy for them, feeling that they belonged to her period. There are cases of aesthetic conversion when eyes accustomed to traditional styles are accorded a revelation, and find beauty and significance in what has previously seemed ugly and chaotic. I have never had that experience. I admired the worst of what Barbara showed me – the war paintings of C. R. W. Nevinson for instance. I was immediately at ease among Mestrovic's woodcarvings, but the appreciation I professed of the Futurists (whose *Manifesto* I studied) was spurious. Barbara communicated to me something of her own belief that exciting events were afoot. At the age of fourteen I wrote an essay which was published in a magazine named *Drawing*. It was entitled *The Defence of Cubism*. I have preserved no copy. It must have been utterly fatuous, for I knew nothing whatever of the theory of the movement and had seen very few of its products. In my excitement at seeing it printed I attempted to make what I took to be a Cubist drawing and sent it to the editor of *Drawing* with the suggestion that it should be reproduced in his next issue. That was the end of my career as an apologist for Picasso. The drawing was promptly returned to me with the note that my contribution was not regarded as an 'article', as I had described it, but as a 'letter'.

Before this rebuff Barbara and I had covered the walls of the former day-nursery with what we took to be cubist paintings

– that is to say, we reduced our figures to angles and flat planes. Mark Gertler was shown them. Hard put to find an amiable comment, he remarked that there was originality in the way in which we had combined so many various pigments – enamel, oil paint, blacking and poster-paint.

I soon resumed my attempts to counterfeit thirteenth-century manuscripts and to draw like Beardsley.

In the vacancies of the adolescent mind mutually contradictory principles make easy neighbours. From Beardsley there was no great distance to Eric Gill, for whose wood-cuts I developed an abiding love. I had no interest in his teaching, preferring Samuel Butler's *Notebooks*, to which Barbara introduced me, as a source of wisdom. I had not read much Ruskin, but I had in some way imbibed most of his opinions; nevertheless I respectfully studied works that would have been anathema to him, and my mind was divided by the knowledge that all that was most admired in modern painting was being done in defiance of his canon. I halted between two opinions and thought it more showy to express the new. Barbara, in fact, made an aesthetic hypocrite of me. It was many years before I would freely confess that the Paris school and all that derived from it were abhorrent to me. Perhaps it was Economics that Barbara read in Regent's Park. She was better informed on the subject than most girls of the time. I was totally ignorant of it and, picking up some of the jargon from her, for some years intermittently pretended to be a socialist. (At other times I advocated the restoration of the Stuarts, anarchism and the rule of a hereditary caste.) My motive was the wish to shock of which Barbara was entirely innocent. She, the professed agnostic, was full of charity, compassion for the poor (of whom she knew little; far less than my mother), faith in the perfectibility of human nature and a longing for social equality; I, the professed Christian, merely scorned industrial and commercial capitalists and relished the arguments that proved them villains.

The Easter holidays were darkened by the report that my brother was 'missing' in the Ludendorf offensive. Barbara remained tranquil, while my father was tormented by anxiety. Presently there was a telegram announcing that he was a prisoner. My father, even at the moment of victory, was haunted by the fear that the Germans would massacre their prisoners. Barbara, to whom the Russian revolution had been exhilarating, was confident that German militarism was destroyed for ever and that a Utopia would emerge.

Chapter Five

EDUCATION CONCLUDED

WHEN THE ARMISTICE was signed I was idling in the Classical Middle Fifth under an exceedingly dull form master. The
event was boisterously celebrated. There was a cancellation of
all impending punishments, a *Te Deum* in chapel, a bonfire,
spontaneous processions, cheering, ringing of bells. Certain
unidentified revellers went too far, I forget in what direction.
I think they did violence to the fire-engine or threw something
on the bonfire that should not have been burnt; perhaps they
did both by putting the fire-engine to the flames. I cannot
remember; but I do vividly remember the rhetorical performance of Mr Bowlby, who, addressing us in Hall, denounced 'a
dingy trick. I repeat a dingy trick.' At that moment his eye
alighted on an uncouth youth who was smirking at a table
near him. 'But Barnes laughs. Thank you, Barnes. Now we
know Barnes's ideals.' He then expatiated on the ignominy of
the outrage introducing as the refrain of each reprobation:
'But Barnes laughs.'

It was an admirable performance.

My brother was home by Christmas and that holidays were
the most joyous of my life. I returned to Lancing to find Dick
Harris back at his post as House-tutor. With him were a hand-
ful of other young masters – notably J. F. Roxburgh, about
whom in its place I shall have much to say – who came back to
civil life with zest.

When Lord Curzon moving the victory address to the Crown
in the House of Lords quoted: 'The world's great age begins
anew', he was expressing the sentiment of the country which

found echoes in the flinty walls of Lancing. From then on both the amenities and the interests of school were increasingly enriched.

Gluttony, the master-passion of boyhood, reasserted its sway. No subsequent experiences of the *haute-cuisine* or the vintage can rival the gross, innocent delight in the commonplace confections that now began to reappear. The Grub Shop, which hitherto had offered an irregular and meagre supply of fruit and oat-cakes was now replete with 'whipped-cream walnuts', 'cream slices', ices and every kind of bun and chocolate. Our appetites were bounded only by our purses. Most Lower boys had £1 a term pocket money and it was soon exhausted. While it lasted, we gorged. For two-thirds of the school the 'Grubber' and the 'play-boxes' where we kept food sent from home were the only sources of gourmandising. For the upper third of the school there was a variety of entertainment. The lowest was the 'settle-tea' on Sundays for the seniors of the House Room. These were provided by each member in turn, with ostentatious rivalry. They began with crumpets, eight or more a head, dripping with butter. From there we swiftly passed to cake, pastry and, in season, strawberries and cream, until at six we tottered into chapel taut and stupefied with eating. The House-captains had tea daily in their own room served by fags; as became their dignity they were more moderate. Between these were 'the pits', the half-dozen or so boys with private studies. There we had some pretensions to be epicures. Little pots of *foie gras* and caviar occasionally came from London and we were as nice in the brewing of tea as a circle of maiden ladies. There was then a shop on the north side of Piccadilly which offered a dozen or more varieties of China tea. We subscribed for quarter-pound packets and tasted them with reverence, discoursing on their qualities as later we were to talk of wine. We were scrupulous about filling the pot with steam and allowing the leaf to open before adding boiling water. We eschewed milk and sugar. But when the rites had been performed and the delicacies consumed we fell back on stuffing ourselves with the same fare as the Settle. Fullness was all.

School-life in 1919 broadened into happier prospects.

But one product of peace was an interruption in the normal (or rather abnormal) rate of promotion. Boys who were doing well stayed on, as they had done before the war, until they were nineteen. Only those who would not have been promoted, left early. Thus there was formed, in Head's House particularly, a body of retarded irresponsibles. The first step to official position was 'the Settle'; the top eight boys in the House Room who enjoyed certain privileges and authority, above whom were 'the pits', and the six House-captains (of whom one, and sometimes two, were school prefects). My friends and I found ourselves for a year blocked in our advance to these eminences and well content to be so. In this essentially subversive stratum – we were, in the language of the day, 'Bolshies' – the leaders were Fulford and I and Rupert Fremlin, a delightful mercurial fellow, whose father we wrongly believed to have been eaten by a tiger. His alternations of exuberance and depression – 'Fremlin's "states" ' – later became settled in melancholy. He was with us at the university and died very young in West Africa.

After two terms Dick Harris was removed from Head's and given a House of his own. We regarded the change as a personal bereavement and did not like his successor, whom we thought sly. He was, I think, rather more devious than was suitable to his profession. He had a genuine concern in, and some understanding of, our character and was full of goodwill towards us. But he seemed capricious and inquisitive. We called him 'Pussy-foot' and 'Super-spy'. Many passages in my diary record with pride our ruthless rebuffs to his overtures of friendship. As will appear, I soon had ample reason to be grateful to him, but we were as pettish as a girls' school at the loss of Dick and I withheld confidence and affection.

He was succeeded in my last year by a stubborn young clergyman with whom I was always at loggerheads.

It would be tedious to follow in detail the various stages of advancement in my last three years at Lancing. The record I have in the diary mentioned above. This was kept almost daily at school, but less regularly at home, from September 1919 to December 1921 in a series of paper-covered exercise books which were known as 'blue note books'. When I left school I had them bound and seldom looked at them until I did so lately for the purpose of this autobiography. I found them painful reading. Most adolescent diaries are naïve, trite and pretentious; mine lamentably so. The cover of each section bears a quotation: 'A tale told by a madman full of wind and fury, signifying nothing'; 'We play out our days as we play cards'; 'I have lived, I shall say, so much since then', and so forth, but the shame of re-reading springs from deeper sources. If what I wrote was a true account of myself, I was conceited, heartless and cautiously malevolent. I should like to believe that even in this private journal I was dissembling a more generous nature; that I absurdly thought cynicism and malice the marks of maturity. I pray it may be so. But the damning evidence is there, in sentence after sentence on page after page, of consistent caddishness. I feel no identity with the boy who wrote it. I believe I was a warm-hearted child. I know that as a man my affections, though narrow, are strong and constant. The adolescent who reveals himself in these pages seems not only cold but quite lacking in sincerity. This may have been in part the result of a peculiar intellectual fermentation which developed in us at the time.

As we grew older we began to enlist friends in other houses, two of whom have made their careers in politics; one was Tom Driberg, some time chairman of the Labour Party, then a reserved, precise classicist, a thin, sallow boy with old-fashioned steel-rimmed spectacles and an obsessive interest in the Anglo-Catholicism which I was shedding.

The other we called 'Preters' because in his first term, when asked if he were interested in politics, he had answered 'pre-ternaturally so'. He came to Lancing more than two years late, having previously been at Dartmouth. There was in 1919 a considerable number of ex-cadets whose lives were sharply interrupted at the age of sixteen by the reduction of the navy. Their nautical education did not fit them for the curriculum of the public schools and their age was anomalous in the established order of seniority. Two or three came to Lancing and contrived to adjust themselves tactfully to their difficult circumstances; not so Preters, who was flamboyant from the first. He was highly intelligent and, compared with most of us, highly sophisticated, and he descended on Lancing as Psmith, in P. G. Wodehouse's *Mike*, descended on Sedleigh. He was in Dick Harris's House and he scandalized us, who had a cult for Dick, by describing him as 'essentially a good-hearted fellow'. He affected, out of mockery, a superb pomposity of manner and vocabulary which in later life became habitual. At the age of sixteen it was highly diverting. He has since been prominent as a Conservative in both Houses of Parliament. When I first knew him he professed socialism, atheism, pacifism and hedonism.

At meetings of the Debating Society the upper school were allowed to attend but only the Sixth might speak. Preters proposed the formation of a society for the Upper Fifths. He needed support from boys of more established position in the school, solicited Fulford and myself and overcame our conventional suspicions. Our excited discussions expanded and ramified into a society we called 'the Dilettanti', a name of my choosing. It appears first in my diary as 'Dilletantes' then as 'Dilettantes'; finally in correct form.

There thrived a political group run by Preters, a literary group run by Fulford and an art group run by myself. Dick Harris acted as sponsor and secured us permission to use various rooms for our meetings, which we organized entirely by ourselves. We opened membership to the whole Upper School and were obliged to scrutinise the mass of applicants. Some joined, or sought to join, all three groups. The craze lasted for a year, during which time almost every leisure hour was spent in lecturing and heckling one another, in debates, in committee-meetings and in elections.

Once or twice we invited visitors to address us, but that was not the prime object of our association. We did not wish to learn, but to talk. Among the more loquacious of us it was the fad to speak against our convictions. Anyone, we argued, can plead a cause in which he sympathises; it took a clever fellow to find arguments for the enemy. Ronald Knox in *A Spiritual Aeneid* records that as an undergraduate he 'acquired the unenviable reputation for defending the indefensible'.

'I have once,' he writes, 'owing to a shortage of speakers opened and opposed the same motion . . . A serious consequence of this continual talking before audiences greedy of originality is the extraordinary distaste for the obvious with which it indoctrinates the mind. You learn, in approaching any subject, to search at once for the point that is new, original, eccentric, not for the plain truth.'

There is an obvious absurdity in comparing our group of schoolboys with the undergraduate wits of the golden age of the university, but we did, in fact, suffer from just the ill which Knox diagnoses.

In the role of iconoclast which I assumed, I fascinated and dominated a boy of my own age in another House, who had previously enjoyed all the enthusiasms proper to his condition. I set out to ridicule his loyalties, particularly his devotion to myself, which secretly I rather relished. He was warmly confidential; I patronising and sardonic. He addressed an ode to me which had a certain affinity to *Hymns Ancient and Modern*:

> *You have broken all my idols,*
> *Given me fresh creeds to keep.*
> *You have waked me from my dreaming,*
> *Shattered by sweet, careless sleep.*
> *Some are born to high endeavours.*
> *For them much easier lies the way.*
> *To me 'tis dark, unknown forbidding.*
> *Guide me lest I go astray.*

It concluded:

For you I've given up all that I cherish,
Curses I find now where once friendship grew.
Give me then freely of your knowledge.
Be fair, my friend, 'tis all I ask of you.

I copied this into my diary with the comment: 'It is rather embarrassing to have so large an influence which works out in such a bad poem.'

I do not believe that I ever called down curses on this devotee's head. Some of his former associates in his House may have looked askance at him. He was a natural hero-worshipper and in a year or two transferred his homage to (Sir) J. C. Squire, who encouraged his interest in cricket, introduced him to whisky, and was altogether a kinder and more fortifying mentor than I.

No doubt these intellectual activities were as good a way as any for employing the superfluous energy of a boy's seventeenth year. In spite of them my friends and I were able to render ourselves obnoxious in other ways.

I have mentioned above that we were known as 'Bolshies'. What I find repugnant in reading my account of our outrage is the impression that they were not high-spirited or courageous but full of malice and calculation.

In Head's House we made life unbearable for anyone who incurred our displeasure. We were not bullies in the old-fashioned sense of ill-treating the weak. Towards our juniors we showed a kind of feudal benevolence. But we hunted as a small pack to bring down our equals and immediate superiors.

At school it is not prowess which is coveted but popularity. There was a boy in the Army Class, a sturdy long-distance runner who was promoted over us to the Settle and to be head of the dormitory. He was not a very likeable boy. I believe he later committed suicide. He might well have done so at Lancing, for we exercised every ingenuity to humiliate him within the bounds of law. We called him 'Dungy', for no good reason. Once this large, desperate youth approached me by dark in the cloisters and said: 'If you'll stop calling me

"Dungy" I'll do anything you like. I'll publicly kick *anyone* in another House.' I replied: 'Oh, go and kick yourself, Dungy.'

There was a rather corpulent boy whom we named 'Buttocks'. He put on airs about his superior wealth. In order to chasten him Fulford and I composed a song in the form of 'The Ram of Derbyshire' which celebrated his large posterior, his gluttony, his affectation of shaving before he need and other personal traits. One term, on the third Sunday when new boys were required to stand on the House Room table and sing, Fulford and I leaped up and before the whole House and the wretched 'Buttocks', sang this song. He now belongs to the same club as myself in London. We do not bandy reminiscences.

There were frequent small shifts in the kaleidoscope of personal importance, but in the House my friends and I practically controlled the founts of popularity and capriciously stopped them or let them flow. In all these nasty manoeuvres there lay hidden the fear that I myself might at any moment fall from favour and become, as I had been in my first year, the object of contempt.

In school we demonstrated our contempt for 'stinks' and our resentment that we, on the classical side, should be required to study them once or twice a week. Scientists were regarded as a socially inferior race and we treated our masters in these subjects superciliously. We also had much innocent fun in causing explosions in the laboratories. These men tried to make a fetish of the weights in the glass-enclosed scales. We were forbidden to touch them with our fingers lest we corrupted their accuracy. We used to heat them on bunsen-burners and drop them sizzling into beakers of cold water.

But the main object of our offensive was the O.T.C. We pretended that we were inspired by high motives of pacifism. In fact the choice of target was chiefly the immunity it provided from severe punishment. One of us, malingering off parade, could not restrain himself from throwing a cake of soap from a changing-room window at the commanding officer inspecting the companies in the quad below. He got birched because he had committed the offence as a civilian, but for crimes in uniform the only punishment which could be imposed in the orderly room was a defaulters' parade, which could itself be rendered farcical.

Once our whole platoon fell in, each with one boot scrupulously polished and the other muddy. Always we drilled with ostentatious incompetence, dropping rifles, turning right instead of left, making the movement of forming fours odd and even numbers together, and so forth. On field days we either hid from action or advanced immediately at the 'enemy' so that we were 'killed' at the first moment of battle.

When, route-marching, we were exhorted to sing, we ignored the ballads sanctified by the infantry of the World War and loped along out of step droning the American ditty:

> *'I didn't raise my boy to be a soldier.*
> *I brought him up to be my pride and joy.*
> *Who dares to put a rifle on his shoulder*
> *To shoot another mother's darling boy?'*

We were not unique. At other public schools at this time there were contemporaries behaving in much the same way. At Eton there was a platoon which paraded in horn-rimmed spectacles and numbered off: ' . . . ten, Knave, Queen, King.' We did nothing as stylish as this, but we outraged local tradition. Lancing took a particular pride in the Corps, which before and during the war had been outstandingly smart. It was one of the ways in which the smaller public schools could assert superiority over those they could not compete with at cricket or in scholarship, just as in the Corps itself boys without other distinction could by zeal achieve positions of authority. That indeed was one of the points of military training that were emphasised by its apologists. We merely despised the 'Corps-maniacs' and regarded their stripes as further evidence of the fatuity of the institution. (The other argument was that it fitted us for immediate commissions in time of war. Before the next war that was changed. When eventually I came to serve, no one asked me whether or no I had Certificate A, nor would anything I could have learned as a schoolboy have been any use to me in the army of 1939.)

The climax of Head's House anti-militarism came in March 1921. I was then seventeen years old and in the Upper Sixth. I had a 'pit' and was a likely candidate for the next promotion to House-captain. It was the term in which the competitions were held for the House shield. Normally the Houses were split into two companies with the platoons in each drawn from two Houses. For the competition Head's House came together as a single unit. We were formidably delinquent. Reprimands on parade and in the orderly room were part of our normal week. Now we were addressed by our House-tutor, the stubborn young clergyman whom I have mentioned above, and threatened that there would be no promotion for anyone who did not exert himself in the Corps.

This reasonable proposition disconcerted me, for I was not, as I pretended, free from ambition. This covert self-seeking, more than the cruelty to individual boys – odious as that was – constitutes the 'caddishness' which I found revealed in my diary. While affecting to despise all forms of 'Clubs' I was secretly eager to get what colours I could (boxing, swimming and the 220 yards were my most likely sports). Also I wanted to be a House-captain, not, I may say in justice to my former self, from any appetite for authority, but because there were school offices I coveted, such as the editorship of the magazine and presidency of the debating society, which were held by House-captains only.

We discussed our House-tutor's challenge in the 'pits'. There was a party strongly in favour of increased disorder. Capitulation would have been dishonourable. I disingenuously proposed what should be our final and best rag.

It was the custom at Lancing when a cup passed from one House to another to hold a 'jerry-run'. The defeated House congregated in their House Room and applauded while the captain of the winning team entered and was formally presented with the trophy. He was then lifted shoulder high by his own House assembled outside and carried at speed with wild cheering round the cloisters to his own House. My proposal was that Head's should win the shield, thus demonstrating that anyone could excel at this ignoble competition, and that we should then ignore it and take no part in its transference. My colleagues and I then called a meeting of the House – an unprecedented performance – explained the scheme and took a unanimous vote in its favour. From then on for the remaining week before the competition the House was in a fever of military zeal. Manuals, hitherto ignored, were studied. Equipment was buffed. Prizes were awarded for individual smartness among the Lower boys. The authorities were uneasy about these ostentatious activities. They knew that we had held a meeting of the House, but did not know what had been said. It was clear that this meeting, and not the House-tutor's exhortation, had started the transformation.

I composed and circulated an Order of the Day: 'It is more than ever vitally necessary for the honour of the House that we should win the Platoon Shield. We have the Houser's promise and are confident. Trust in God and stand steady in the ranks.'

How far did I delude myself that this was not a face-saving manoeuvre to achieve my ambitions? To judge from my diary, completely. We had a craven respect for legality, based on the stern discipline of the school. On the eve of the competition I went to the Head of the School and asked for an opinion as to whether a 'jerry-run' was a compulsory event. He said there was no precedent, that he could not prejudice a hypothetical case, but that he thought we should be within the law.

On the day our platoon was in the lead in turnout and squad-drill. When it came to open order the worst section was picked – we suspected, falsely I am now sure, as a premeditated device of the authorities. That section lost us the shield. Head's was placed third in the final score. I expressed bitter chagrin in my diary. A day or two later I was summoned by my House-tutor and given the choice of accepting a Housecaptaincy or leaving. He seemed in doubt as to my preference. I accepted and for the next two terms was segregated from my former cronies. Preters quoted Browning's *Lost Leader* to me and then devoted himself to the study of military law in order to discover, as he succeeded in doing, the correct form in which he could discharge himself from service.

Apart from general malevolence and particular cruelty, we were not vicious. Public opinion was against sex, which was spoken of as 'filth'. It was the subject of endless, tedious jokes but not of boasting. Whatever indulgences there may have been were kept private. Many senior boys, on the other hand, were infatuated with one or other of their juniors and played a restoration comedy of assignations, secret correspondence and complacent chaperones. I was susceptible to the prettiness of some fifteen-year-olds, but never fell victim to the grand passions which inflamed and tortured most of my friends (to whom I acted as astringent confidant).

Public opinion condemned smoking except in the summer term. In the autumn and the early spring one was supposed to be in training for one thing or another and tobacco was reputed to be deleterious. In my last summer there were some pleasant late-afternoon sessions behind the chapel where we consumed, without inhaling the smoke, sweet-smelling gold- and silk-tipped Levantine cigarettes.

There was no fetish about drinking. Housemasters quite often gave punch or cup to their House-captains, though they could never offer them a cigarette. On my last Ascension Day, very different from my first, I went out with a friend who had borrowed a motor car. He got very drunk at luncheon in Chichester and drove round and round the market cross shouting to passers-by that we were looking for the alms houses. No one interfered. He drove later into a country lane and slept in the hedgerow until dinner-time.

On gambling the authorities were evasive. It was forbidden but connived at to some extent. Sweepstakes on the five-mile cross-country run were always held. A request for official permission was greeted with: 'Don't let me know anything about it.' This was unsatisfactory, as the organisers ran the risk that some martinet might invoke the law.

Permission to play bridge in the 'pits' was given and then withdrawn.

In my last summer I took to going out after lights-out with a prefect in another House and walking down to the sea. These expeditions were entirely innocent. The object was simply to get clear of the school for an hour or two. It was like landing during a brief stop in a sea-voyage and walking the public gardens of a strange port. News of this reached my father in a roundabout way and provoked a rhetorical reprimand.

Your mother and I had a sickening shock when we learned this evening that you are making a practice of escaping from the House and going down to the sea-shore at night. It is years since we heard anything that has so disturbed us. That you, a House captain, in the confidence of your leaders, should play such a rotten and contemptible game. It is unworthy of the name of Waugh . . .

I cannot threaten my own sons. I can only appeal to them. When Alec told me this sort of thing was going on at Sherborne, I asked him for his word of honour that he would never do it. He gave me that word and he kept it. I appeal to you to send me by first post your honourable assurance that never again will . . . you do anything so fatuously foolish to endanger your own future . . . I cannot have a son of mine betraying his trust and be privy to his conduct . . .

There were many such paragraphs. I wondered at the time how anyone at Sherborne could have walked to the seaside and supposed the temptations of a town different from those of the downs and the shingle. I thought my father was making a great ado about nothing. As I have mentioned above, it had been kept from me that my brother had been expelled from school. I did not know the circumstances until he published his autobiography forty years later. My father, I now realise, was in fear that I should repeat his history.

2

My last two terms at Lancing were occupied with school work. I caused my father pleasure by writing the Prize Poem; the subject set was an incident from Malory to be composed in Spenserean stanzas. It was characteristic of me at that period that I chose, not a story of heroism or romance, but the nostalgic disillusioned musing of Sir Bedivere after the death of Arthur; I also won the English Literature Prize, but my prime concern was with the Oxford scholarship for which Preters and I were sitting in December. We now made nuisances of ourselves by our exorbitant claims on the Sixth Form History master – an indolent, humorous clergyman, who we did not think was extending himself fully in coaching us. We read hard during term and in the intervening holidays. For some weeks Preters and I took rooms at Birchington and kept a severe time-table. Even so I was rather wayward in reading and instead of pursuing the topics normally set in the examination would find myself interested in inessentials.

My father's hope was that, like him, I should go to New College. Two or three other colleges were in the same group, among them Hertford. When the time came to fill up the application form, I found that the senior Hertford scholarship was considerably the most valuable. My father was not well off – worse off in fact, like most men of his position, than he had been ten years before. I knew that, unlike Preters's father, he would find the financial emolument very convenient. I knew, too, I was not up to a New College scholarship (indeed this examination was regarded by the masters at Lancing as a trial run). The motive of the very strenuous work I did in my last six months was primarily the wish to leave school at the earliest possible date. Both these considerations prompted me to an act which was to make a great difference to my university life. I put down the Hertford scholarship as my first preference.

Boredom with school, now that I had divorced myself from the bolshevists, was very strong. Most men in their memoirs speak of their last privileged terms at school as a golden age. I was free of the whole place, could walk in the various enclosures and across the lawns which had hitherto been forbidden. I could wear a bow-tie. I was exempt from almost all rules. But I had no relish for such things. Instead I formed a 'Corpse Club' of those who were weary of life. We wore black ties, a black tassel in our button-holes and wrote on mourning notepaper. I held the chief office as 'Undertaker' and the election of a member was notified in the form: *'The Undertaker finds a mournful pleasure in announcing the interment of the late Mr . . .'*

My last editorial in the school magazine was a preposterous manifesto of disillusionment.

What will the young men of 1922 be? [I wrote] They will be, above all things, clear-sighted, they will have no use for phrases or shadows . . . And because they are clear-sighted, they will not be revolutionaries and they will not be poets and they will not be mystics; there will be much that they will lose, but all they have will be real. And they will be reticent, too, the youngest generation . . . Middle-aged observers will find it hard to see their soul. But they will have – and this is their justification – a very full sense of humour, which will keep them from 'the commission of all sins, or nearly all, save those that are worth committing'. They will watch themselves with, probably, a greater egotism than did the young men of the nineties, but it will be with a cynical smile and often with a laugh. It is a queer world which the old men have left them and they will have few ideals and illusions to console them when they 'get to feeling old'. They will not be a happy generation.

I was just eighteen when I wrote this, from which I have omitted some painful literary flourishes. It may have corresponded to the mood of the moment. It was totally false as a prediction of my own future or that of my contemporaries.

The scholarship exam was a week of pure euphoria. Preters and I were the only two candidates from Lancing. We had a week-end at home, met at Paddington and travelled to Oxford together. We stayed at the Mitre – the first time that I had stayed in an hotel on my own – and arrived to find a heap of visiting-cards and invitations from old boys who had preceded us. We were entertained to every meal and taken to the theatre and to a debate in the Union. Preters was attempting only New College and had little hope of success, but he fortified himself with a preparation of strychnine, which he claimed acted as a stimulant to the brain. (Later, when he took a first in his Final Schools, he was visited by a hairdresser in his rooms and shampooed between papers.)

I followed the advice to extend myself on a very few questions and disregard those that would expose ignorance.

In the General Paper I wrote copiously about the Pre-Raphaelites and Arthur Symons's *Life of Beardsley*. In the *viva* a polite New College don exposed my lack of information on eighteenth-century agriculture. But I was confident I had done well. We took an illicit extra day off from school. Five days later the results reached Lancing. I had won the Hertford Scholarship and was now free to leave; to do so, moreover, amid congratulations.

To sum up my schooling:

My knowledge of English literature derived chiefly from my home. Most of my hours in the form room for ten years had been spent on Latin and Greek, History and Mathematics. Today I remember no Greek. I have never read Latin for pleasure and should now be hard put to it to compose a simple epitaph. But I do not regret my superficial classical studies. I believe that the conventional defence of them is valid; that only by them can a boy fully understand that a sentence is a logical construction and that words have basic inalienable meanings, departure from which is either conscious metaphor or inexcusable vulgarity. Those who have not been so taught – most Americans and most women – unless they are guided by some rare genius, betray their deprivation. The old-fashioned test of an English sentence – will it translate? – still stands after we have lost the trick of translation.

Those who passed through the Sixth at Lancing might spell atrociously, for our written work was seldom read and then only to criticise style or meaning; spelling was regarded as too elementary for attention. Those of us who 'specialised' in History had a vague conspectus of the succession of events in the Mediterranean from the time of Pericles, a rather more detailed knowledge of English History from the time of Henry VII, and of European History from the War of the Austrian Succession to the battle of Sedan. We could translate literary French unseen, but spoke it with outrageous accents and without knowledge of idiom. In verse the classical metres had been well drummed into us – 'drummed' is the right word. The syllables and rhythms resounding into our ears were to deafen us to modern verse which followed different patterns. We were completely ignorant of Geography and all the natural sciences. In Mathematics we had advanced scarcely at all since we left our preparatory schools. Our general information was of the kind that makes *The Times* cross-word puzzle soluble.

My education, it seems to me, was the preparation for one trade only; that of an English prose writer. It is a matter of surprise that so few of us availed ourselves of it.

Chapter Six

A BRIEF HISTORY OF MY
RELIGIOUS OPINIONS

ON 18TH JUNE 1921 I wrote in my diary: 'In the last few
weeks I have ceased to be a Christian. I have realised that for
the last two terms at least I have been an atheist in all except
the courage to admit it myself.'

This seems to me one of the few candid entries in a document
replete with affectation.

As I have mentioned, I was, when I went to Lancing, if
not genuinely devout, a particularly church-loving boy. I had
aspirations to becoming a parson. I enjoyed the chapel services
and the more ritualistic worship I attended in the holidays.
That interest passed never to return. When, later, I became a
Catholic it was not for the attraction of the ceremonies and I
have never taken a special interest in their details. As I became
bored with Lancing, I became bored with the chapel which,
more than in most schools, was embedded in our curriculum.

More than a year before I had composed some verses that
were wholly false in sentiment. Their origin was the observa-
tion that a play might be made with the words 'tedium' and
'Te Deum'. I worked this simple pun into the following
deplorable invocation:

O God, who blessed the chapel's height and founded it on chalk and flint,
Canst not thou hear the coin debased that's loudly jingled in thy mint
Or hear the long, mute, listless prayers, our prayerless lips are forced to raise?
Accept, for 'tis our widow's mite, this plainsong tedium of praise.
The coin they give us rings untrue; it swells the purse but leaves us poor.
It will not pay th' incessants tolls that wait beyond the chapel door.

When we are hungry, tired, oppressed; it will not stay our failing health.
Then help us, God, lest in that hour we lose all hope of future wealth.
So if on judgement day I stand, a broken abject, hungry, cold,
Remember in thy timeless love who turned to copper thy pure gold.
Remember all and say of me: 'They paid their score in lead and tin.
They gave thee nothing; thou has brought thyself. Poor servant enter in.'

There was, I am sure, no sincerity in any of this. I had no apprehensions about the final judgement nor special resentment against the clerical masters. Some time later I describe a Confirmation service as 'grotesque'. 'I have never noticed', I wrote, 'how menacing it is before. Some small frightened children taking a lot of oaths they'll never keep with a dressed-up coloured thing [the bishop] like a Dulac figure and gloomy, threatening masters and provosts all round.'

This was stark nonsense. The confirmation candidates were not frightened and I knew it. All I meant was that I was losing my taste for everything ecclesiastical. But in my last two years at Lancing I was eager to dispute the intellectual foundations of Christianity and I now think it odd that in a place so dominated by religion we should have been given so many hours of instruction in the Greek of the New Testament and the history of the Church of England, and practically none in apologetics. In the Dilettanti and the various societies which prospered among us, we were continually debating that: 'This House does not believe in the immortality of the soul'; 'This House believes the age of institutional religion is over'; 'This House cannot reconcile divine omniscience with human freewill' and so forth. All the humdrum doubts were raised and left unanswered. We were encouraged to 'think for ourselves' and our thoughts in most cases turned into negations. There was no question of secretly conning illicit, subversive books. They were pressed upon us. I can think of three occasions when I was nudged into infidelity by those set over me.

During the war many university dons went to teach in public schools in order to set free younger men for the army. We had two at Lancing; one an aged physicist of high distinction who made pathetic and ineffectual attempts to make himself heard by the howling mob of urchins before him; the other, a bright young clergyman, later to become a bishop, the 'brilliant Arcturus' of Ronald Knox's *Absolute and Abitof-hell*. Both in his divinity classes and in the pulpit this eloquent and learned young man introduced to us the then popular speculations of Dr Schweitzer. 'Did Jesus,' he questioned, 'know he was God? Did he know it from the first or was he persuaded of it in his last year on earth? Did he expect to die on the cross or to be rescued by angels?' Such problems were entirely new to us; we were left to suggest our solutions and encouraged to be unorthodox.

Another influence was *Loose Ends* by Arnold Lunn. This was read aloud to us by our House-tutor. It recorded, in the form of fiction, the arguments between two schoolboys in which the atheist, as I remember, always made the better case. 'What did God send his son for? Why didn't he come himself?' seemed a cogent point. Arnold Lunn was himself an atheist at the time of writing and his manner of reasoning was such as to be particularly acceptable to boys of sixteen.

The third case was one which the authorities could not have foreseen. Pope's *Essay on Man* was the set book for the English Literature prize. The study of it led me to a cursory acquaintance with the philosophy of Leibnitz; from him I skipped easily to the Enlightenment, whose exponents seemed eminently acceptable.

Mine was not a unique case. I think at least half the Upper Sixth in my time were avowed agnostics or atheists. And no antidote was ever offered us. I do not remember ever being urged to read a book of Christian philosophy.

I suffered no sense of loss in discarding the creed of my upbringing; still less of exhilaration. My diary is full of pagan gloom and the consideration of suicide. There was, however, a question of propriety. I was one of the boys appointed a sacristan. One Saturday evening Driberg and I were doing something in the sanctuary to prepare it for next day when I revealed to him my discovery that there was no God. In that case, he remarked, I had no business to be handling the altar cloth. I made an appointment with the chaplain, whom I particularly liked and respected, to discuss the matter with him. When I came to his room another master was sitting smoking with him. I was obliged to explain my predicament before this third person. Adolescent doubts are very tedious to the mature; I was genially assured that it was quite in order for an atheist to act as sacristan.

Chapter Seven

TWO MENTORS

I HAVE RESERVED for a separate chapter the description of
two characters who were equal and opposite influences on my
adolescence; one a secret man, the other of some renown;
Francis Crease and J. F. Roxburgh.

I met Francis Crease in December 1919 in circumstances that
need some explanation.

Since I first learned to write and studied Shaw's *Alphabets*
in my father's library I had maintained an interest in illuminated
manuscripts. In 1919, as part of the general renaissance promoted by the young masters who returned from the army,
there was for the first time a school art competition. For this
I entered an illuminated prayer which I had made during the
holidays, and was awarded first prize by the architect Detmar
Blow, who came to judge it. It was an unpopular choice, but
from then on I became associated at Lancing with this hobby,
that had long occupied part of my time at home.

In the summer of 1917 my father and mother visited Ditchling and I joined them there for a few days.

As I write I find an advertisement in the newspaper:
'Exclusive Ditchling. 8 miles Brighton and University of
Sussex. Doctor will consider offers over £7,000 for 4 bedroom
house.' In 1917 Ditchling was exclusive but in a very different
way. The little village under the downs knew nothing of
Brighton. I doubt if any house there cost £700. Eric Gill was
the first settler; a small group of Catholic craftsmen formed
round him, who lived by the rule of the Third Order of St
Dominic. Then came others who were not of his faith or of his
austere rule of life. My father's host, a London printer, drank

to excess and professed agnosticism. In a year or two the place became too populous and too much publicised for Gill and he removed with all his household, but among the later, non-Catholic immigrants one was in complete harmony with the Gill community; Edward Johnston, the scribe.

I was fourteen and Johnston was forty-five when I was taken to see him. He received me with exquisite charm and demonstrated how to cut a turkey-quill into a chisel-pointed pen and there and then wrote a few words for me on the title-page of his book in what is now called his 'foundational' hand.

Eric Gill recorded: 'The first time I saw him [Johnston] writing, and saw the writing that came as he wrote, I had that thrill and tremble of the heart which otherwise I can only remember having had when first I touched her [his wife's] body or saw her hair down for the first time.' I, too, had something of this experience. The art of the scribe is sometimes considered spinsterish. The sweep and precision of Johnston's strokes were as virile as a bull-fighter's and left me breathless. But I had not the patience to follow his teaching. It was the decoration of initials and borders that attracted me; the script seemed a tedious adjunct. And since it was the drawing of the thirteenth century which I emulated, I continued to use the stiff 'black-letter' hand of the period, skimping even that and using the steel, obliquely cut nibs which artists' suppliers had taken to selling to those too lazy to cut their own pens. It was a work of this kind that won me the prize at Lancing.

In December 1919, after a boxing competition (in which I had been beaten), I was summoned by my House-tutor to show my prize work to a visitor. The man I found in his room, incongruously seated among lists and canes, was one already familiar to me by sight.

His appearance in the side-aisles at Sunday chapels, where he came for the music, had already caught my attention. He was of middle age, middle height, plumpish, with the pink and white complexion often found in nuns, with a high nose. His dress was the rural-aesthetic of the period, soft tweeds, cloaks, silk shirts and ties of the kind which later became familiar to me at Hall Bros in the High at Oxford. His gait was delicate, almost mincing. He spoke, I found, in soft tones which in moments of amusement rose shrilly. Today he would be identified as an obvious homosexual. I believe he was entirely without sexual interests.

I do not know how my House-tutor came to know him. He had some acquaintance with the school and although, as I have said, without immoral proclivities, showed a distinct interest in the better-looking boys. On our first meeting in my House-tutor's room there was restraint on all our parts.

Mr Crease, it appeared, was an amateur scribe who also made black and white decorations, none of them for reproduction. He was partly an invalid and lived nearby in a farm on the farther side of Steepdown. My House-tutor suggested that he might be willing to give me some encouragement.

The entry in my diary states: 'After change I had to go and be shown off to an illuminator friend of ——'s. He was most contemptuous over my script but praised the illumination. Apparently if one is ever going to do good work one has to give one's whole life to it.'

I was sure that I did not want to devote my entire life to script, but I was fascinated by the man and by the opportunity he offered for an escape from the régime of the school.

Without solicitation from me my House-tutor – the man we ungratefully dubbed 'super-spy' and 'pussy-foot' – arranged the matter. It was an act not only of kindness but of some courage, for Mr Crease's singular appearance had already been noted by other House-masters and his influence suspected. Early next term I was given permission to visit him on one half-holiday a week and these became golden hours for me.

He had rooms, which he had furnished himself and where the woman of the house cooked for him, in Lychpole Farm on the estate of the neighbouring squire named Tristram, with whom he had an undefined connection, either of friendship or kinship. The distance across the downs was some four miles.

Sometimes I walked, sometimes my House-tutor gave me a lift on the back of a motorbicycle. I first visited him on January 28th, 1920, when, having lost my way in the mist, I at length found him sitting before his fire working on a piece of embroidery. I noted that evening in my diary that he was 'very effeminate and decadent and cultured and affected and nice'. He showed me some of his work, of which I recorded: 'I don't admire his script awfully but he can undoubtedly teach me a lot of technique.'

Next day I came for my first lesson. He had a work-table carefully arranged with the tools of his art. He made me sit down and write a few words for him, threw up his eyes and hands and exclaimed: 'You come to me wearing socks of the most vulgar colours and you have just written the most beautiful E since the Book of Kells.'

I wrote of our meeting: 'He is not as affected as he struck me at first. Very well bred and very individualist. He is most my ideal of a true dilettante of anyone I have yet met. He is a great student of character and claims to be able to sum anyone up by intuition at first sight. I think he rather likes me. I could gather practically nothing of his life, he learns all he can without giving anything out. His secretiveness is his only bad quality as far as I can see. All I can gather of him is that his career has been spoiled by ill health and that he was in some rather distinguished post at Oxford.'

Mr Crease retained his mystery to the last. Certainly he never held any academic post. He had little formal education. I think he had been some kind of companion-secretary-almoner to a rich American who held an honorary fellowship at Corpus, and in his company met most of the university and collected some fine china and silver. He sometimes hinted that he had at one time been attached to some Anglican fraternity (perhaps the Cowley Fathers). He had an income adequate to his simple needs, perhaps an allowance from the Tristrams, perhaps from the American savant. When he found his 'down-land cloister', as he called his rooms at Lychpole, too austere he took refuge in their absence at the Tristrams' unromantic but well-found house, Sompting Abbotts.

For a year I was entirely captivated by Mr Crease. It may seem odd that I, who so despised the lack of heroic qualities in Edmund Gosse and so resented what I took for duplicity in my House-tutor, should thus delight in a neuter, evasive, hypochondriacal recluse whose work, as I remarked at first sight of it, did not impress me. There was nothing about Mr Crease's script or decorations of Edward Johnston's authority. He wrote somewhat in the Celtic style in large, wide-spaced, fanciful characters. His decorative panels were in the tradition of Beardsley and Walter Crane, from whose influence I was then emerging. Nor was script an obsession with me. By winning that prize I had in the eyes of authority been wedded to the craft. I was indulgently given permission to practise it instead of reading 'literature' in third-evening school. But it was one of a dozen interests and it required more discipline and devotion than I was ready to give it. The time spent at the desk at Lychpole, whether under Mr Crease's extravagant praise or, often, peevish criticism (alternations stemming from my host's mood rather than from the quality of my exercises) tended to be irksome. What I relished was the succeeding session of hot scones, Crown Derby cups and conversation. I was proud of having made an adult friend for myself to whom from time to time I could introduce fellow Dilettanti who I thought would be appreciative of his subtle character. Even Preters succumbed to his charm, but I soon found difficulties among House-masters less enterprising than mine, who gave as their reason for withholding permission to visit Lychpole that Mr Crease was not known to the boys' parents.

In order to establish my own claims I invited Mr Crease to stay at my home during the first holidays of our friendship. His response was characteristic. First I asked him face to face. He demurred. I asked my mother to write to him and was delighted on my next visit to see an envelope on his chimney-piece addressed in her hand. I sat and wrote my lines of script.

Presently tea-time came and I sat opposite the missive with the familiar writing and postmark. Still he said nothing. At length, without hesitation, I said: 'I see my mother has written to you.'

With a kind of arch rebuke he said: 'Yes. She has written to *me*. I shall reply in good time.'

I did not then at all conceive the doubts and hesitations that might afflict a man of his age and temperament at the prospect of subjecting himself to an unknown milieu. My father had written the preface for a book of poems by one of Alec's Sandhurst friends who had died of Spanish flu in the first days of peace. The poet had been a frequent visitor at home and, in attempting to present his character as the antithesis of the decadents of his own youth, my father had, with his habitual exaggeration, given a picture of our domestic life as peculiarly robust; our activities being paper games and charades, our main interest county cricket. This work fell into Mr Crease's hands and greatly alarmed him. Moreover, there was the question of expense. He wrote to me on this subject with great delicacy, saying that I might have formed a false impression of his means (I had; he clearly was under no necessity to support himself; he had chosen his retreat for spiritual and aesthetic rather than for economic motives. His wardrobe was extensive and his possessions enviable); that he was very poor and that the expense of a visit to London might prove insupportable, if he were to move about, as I was proposing, to various museums and galleries. When I next came to see him I said: 'About paying; of course, my father will see to everything.' He exclaimed in agony which, I think, was only partly simulated: 'Oh, my dear Evelyn, you are so *direct*.'

But eventually he did come to stay; the first of many visits. My father treated him kindly if somewhat derisively; my mother solicitously. Then and later he took to his bed rather often. When he was strong enough, we went together to many art exhibitions, museums and High Church ceremonies. I carried an ebony cane with a silver top in the fashion of the time and he spoke of it as my crook, of himself as my sheep whom I led through the wilderness of London.

I recorded in my diary only one curious incident of his visit.
Mr Crease had some business with the incumbent of one of the
city churches. We sought him out one afternoon, Mr Crease
having made an appointment with him at his vicarage, and were
told he was in church. It was dark and wet. The old church
was quite empty, but we saw a light under the vestry door and
there found a portly, yellow-faced clergyman seated in a high
chair, comatose, and, as I supposed, either drunk or drugged.
He spoke to us incoherently and fell again into a stupor.

We left him and returned to Hampstead by tube, Francis
Crease wrapping himself in his magic cloak of secrecy. We never
spoke of the meeting. Next day he took me to luncheon with a
Conservative Member of Parliament at the St Stephen's Club.
A day or two later he left to stay with an earl's daughter in
Earl's Court. The macabre visit to the City did not tarnish his
glitter in my eyes, but rather enhanced it.

Our first and to some extent decisive rift was over quite
another matter. He went abroad for a month and very kindly
arranged that I should still continue my visits to Lychpole and
do my exercises at his desk, on which he laid out certain
materials for my use, among them a knife for cutting quills.
It was a modern instrument of the kind sold at artists' colour-
men. Crease had another which I used when he was there – a
very delicate blade of some antiquity, which reposed in a
leather case. This I sought and found hidden in a drawer. Then
followed a disaster from folk-myth. I took the forbidden tool
and it immediately shattered under my hand. I was disconcerted
but unconscious of the doom I had incurred. I wrote to Crease
that evening mentioning the mishap among other trivial
matters. His reply came in ten days. The knife, he said, was
unique and irreplaceable. I had had no business to touch it.
He had put out what was necessary for me. His drawers were
entirely private. Without that knife he would never be able to
write again. I must at once collect the broken pieces and the
handle and send them by registered post to the best firm in

Sheffield to see whether anything could be done. But he was sure nothing was possible. I had betrayed his trust and ruined his life as a scribe.

I was radically shocked, not so much by his magnification of his loss as by his imputation to me of presumption and curiosity. By the next post another letter came saying that the first had been written in momentary vexation; that I must not think him unkind; that I was still to use Lychpole as a refuge in his absence and that he looked forward to seeing me again in the autumn. But the wound did not heal. I did as I was bid with the knife and in due course it returned with a new, manifestly inferior blade. When Crease returned, I continued to visit him though no longer to ply the quill. He remained a friend for many years; when our paths diverged he still frequented my home to be cosseted by my mother. But after the incident of the broken blade the old glad, confident morning light never shone on our friendship.

The curious thing is that he never did practise again as a scribe. He made some increasingly original designs – there was room for increase there – but his penmanship ceased when I broke his knife. He adverted to it once, much later, half whimsically, half seriously. 'I told you I should never be able to write again.'

Some eight years after our first meeting Crease issued in a fine folio thirty-four of his decorative designs privately printed, for which at his request I provided a preface. As was appropriate to the task I evinced a stronger enthusiasm than I then felt.

Only one man [I wrote] could have suitably undertaken to write a preface for this collection of temperate and exalted designs; that is John Ruskin . . . The qualities for its just appreciation are exactly that fineness of perception and equipoise of sense that [he] possessed . . . He would have risen exuberantly to these designs . . . which belong to no period; they are the outcome of no particular school or training but of an individual sensibility patiently concerned with the beauty of natural form and in intimate com-

munion with other minds of the same temper, whether in their
period they showed themselves in the profuse invention of luxurious
textiles or in the austere incision of gems. They are Northern rather
than Mediterranean, more of Chartres than of Rome, but often,
particularly in the later designs, leaving a faintly discernible frag-
rance of the East as of a spiced wind borne to alien hills or of the
Magi at some Flemish Nativity.

Through the kindness of a friend a copy of this volume,
which I had not seen for more than thirty years, recently
came into my hands and I read these words and the many
more of the same kind without much shame. I was twenty-
three when I wrote them – the age of pomposity – and I
owed Mr Crease an abiding debt of gratitude which I attempted to particularise in the latter part of the essay. I described our early associations much as I have done above and
caused some offence to my father by suggesting that until I met
Mr Crease I had lived among philistines. My father rightly
thought that my youth had been lapped about in poetry.

In writing [I continued], once the barest respect has been paid
to the determining structure of the letter, the pen is free to flourish
and elaborate as it will. In the control of these often minute varia-
tions of form, in the direction of serifs, the spacing and poising
of shapes, the sense of historical propriety, there is scope for every
talent required in the building of a cathedral

but it was in revealing the beauties of nature to me that Mr
Crease had given me most.

Ruskin started his pupils with a lichened twig or spray of ivy
to teach them the alphabet [Did he?]; Mr Crease started me with
the alphabet and led me to the lichened twig and to the singularly
lovely irises that grew in the garden at Sompting Abbotts . . . He
used to walk back with me sometimes as far as the turn of the
Roman ditch round Steep Down where Lancing Ring suddenly
comes into view, I eagerly questioning him about architecture or
aesthetics or Limoges enamel or Maiolica, he trying to turn me to
the beauty of the evening on the downs.

After one of these meetings he wrote to me (in March 1920):

This evening while you were in Chapel was one of extraordinary splendour and I wished you also might have been touched by it. For myself, the shadows of the prison house have fallen long ago, but now and again some shape of beauty lifts the shadow for a time. It is so much easier to feel one could write 'Resentment Poems' [The title of a book of verse by my brother] than 'Songs of Exuberance'; I hope it may never be so with you.

What I have in mind is the hope that you, like so many others of intelligence, may not run after definitions of Art and Beauty and the like, feeling the definition and failing to feel the Beauty itself as it approaches on an evening like this evening. I can think of an Oxford friend at this moment who feels nature described in a sonnet and sitting in his arm-chair, but seems to fail in the open air. And again I remember a Don at Oxford learned in Greek gems telling me how all the other Dons would be interested in curious knowledge and facts about any gem, but its beauty always, or nearly always escaped them . . .

No Flemish painter of the seventeenth century or English school of the nineteenth could hope to convey more than a suggestion of the visionary splendour of this evening . . . I wish you could have seen the flight of the gulls in the fields on the left of the Ring, against the softer greys and greens, blues and rose colour; hundreds of them suddenly took their way home to the sea in one long stream following each other and changing colour in the sunlight and making sad music as a prelude to the coming symphony of colour.'

I was an obdurate pupil in this matter. For most of my life I found greater joy in the works of man than of nature, until quite late, and now it is revulsion from the works of man that has constricted, rather than an approach to nature that has enlarged, me.

I have few letters of Crease's. Most of them, characteristically, end with an injunction to secrecy. 'Do not let So-and-so see this'; 'Be sure you do not leave this epistle about'.

There was a lesson other than aesthetic which he tried to inculcate. He had read some of the mystical writers and achieved a certain detachment from the world. He had no personal ambitions for fame. At Lancing, though it was a specifically religious foundation, it was never seriously questioned that power of one sort or another was the proper aim of life. Success meant riches or reputation or authority. 'I always feel,' Crease wrote, 'that those passing through Lancing have had all I never had – but it seems sad that somehow or other it so often leads to the Hotel Metropole at Brighton as an Ideal and not to the Truth which makes you free.'

One evening after a meeting in which I had lamented, in normal adolescent fashion, the lack of purpose in my life, he wrote:

What you ask today to have, no one has completely and indeed many of the best only have sufficient light for the day or the nearest duty. You will not be humble – humility seldom appeals to youth – but nothing less will do . . . You must have sufficient light to know of the day of small things that surround you when you are at School or at home. If you despise them darkness will come not light. It is only by doing them that more light will come that is any true light. Success and conceit close the windows. You *have* more light than most, far more. What is the matter is impatience nothing more or less – I can be as direct as you sometimes and you don't like it so much in others as in yourself – but it is good for you. You want a friend who is a thorn in the flesh not an echo. I shall disappoint you in many things – Alas! that it must be so – but in this I will not disappoint you.

I was in sore need of such an admonition. I was in a receptive state. I have often wondered whether my subsequent life would have been very different if at this age I had come into touch with a real, disciplined, religious contemplative.

At about the time I left school Mr Crease found that the winters at Lychpole were too severe and that the farmer's wife tired of taking care of him. He moved with all his possessions to a cottage at Marston, a village, then secluded, on the other side of Mesopotamia from Oxford, where I sometimes visited him, and Preters, on his way to seek worldly counsel from John Buchan at Elsfield, would pause for spiritual counsel.

Several years later my mother received a distraught letter from him. He had been involved in an unpleasant incident. When returning from early church he had been falsely identified as a clergyman wanted by the police on charges of unnatural vice and had been taken in charge and questioned. For a man of his highly nervous temper it was a disaster. My mother took him in and comforted him, but he declared he would never be able to go to church anywhere again. Nor, I believe, did he. It was the incident of the pen-knife grossly enlarged.

Later he lived in Bath. When I was in the army I received a letter from his landlord telling me that he had died there.

2

Much of the strength and virtue of the public school system was drawn from unambitious men of the kind celebrated in the dedicatory verses to Stalky & Co; 'men of little showing'; men of moderate learning, often with private means, who found refreshment in the company of the young and were content to settle for a lifetime in the scene of their own youth, preserving its continuity, corresponding with old boys all over the world, guarding their fading photographs in their rooms, gaining affection and respect as a familiar institution, remembering faces and dates and scores, becoming in a small world notable characters. There were several such men at Lancing; J. F. Roxburgh was not of them; his brilliant passage lasted an interrupted decade.

He was thirty-one years old when he returned to Lancing from the army.

He was then a House-master, and the boys in his House knew him best. He treated them with great solicitude and on at least one occasion gave a place there to a boy who was being expelled from another. Instead of the perfunctory termly report – 'Conduct in House satisfactory' – he wrote a long private letter to each parent. He had a tall standing desk in his room, designed to avert drowsiness, and spent many hours at it when the rest of the school were asleep, completing the correspondence for which his day's activities gave him no time, on writing-paper of the highest quality embossed for himself.

Boys not in his House, until they reached the Sixth Form, saw little but his outward appearance and that was impressive; tall, broad, lean, slightly stooping; a fine brow, full hair, a face alive with intelligence and humour; a dandy whose numerous suits and ties we studied with respect. He had a panache of the kind to which adolescents were specially susceptible. Even in academic dress he was sometimes showy. Once a term he went up to Communion and then he wore the gown of the Sorbonne with the air of an advocate in a drawing by Daumier. Perhaps this was an assertion of continental laicism, for he did not profess the Tractarian beliefs on which the school was founded. He was reticent about his scepticism, occasionally insinuating a doubt at the Debating Society – 'When you speak of survival after death, what precisely do you think survives – physical appearance, character, intellect, memory, affection? How can these things exist without the body which we know disappears?' – common enough questions which we were of an age to consider but to which he never suggested an answer. It was generally thought that he doubted the existence of the entire supernatural order. In this, as in other characteristics, he might have been cast as an eighteenth-century Anglican bishop. Perhaps he would have described himself as a stoic. It is significant that when he created Stowe School he chose that appellation for its alumni. He was certainly a moralist with a stern disapproval of waste and frivolity.

He worked unremittingly. The hours he spent in the form-room would be regarded by a modern schoolmaster as a heavy day's work. In addition to that he had his House; he was an officer in the O.T.C., he was the energiser, if not the founder, of all the school's societies – the Shakespeare Reading Society,

Modern Play Reading, the Debating Society; he also reviewed books for weekly magazines. He observed scrupulous courtesy to the Headmaster and to the many colleagues who were officially his superiors, but he was, in my days, consciously pre-eminent. His religious position alone set him apart from the spirit of the school. It was evident that he was destined for greater importance. His appointment during my last term as the first Headmaster of Stowe surprised no one.

Always, in whatever he did, was the panache. While other masters reproduced their blurred exam papers with various deficient devices of jelly or stencil, J.F. had his elegantly printed. Every year he set a 'General Paper' to (I think) the Sixth and the Upper Fifths. These would not seem remarkable in the age of Intelligence Tests and of the competitions in the weekly newspapers. Forty-five years ago, when J.F. instituted them, they were, as far as I know, entirely original – half game, half examination, in which the sitter was able to display whatever he had of ingenuity or knowledge.

Everything about J.F. was calculated to impress. His voice was sonorous and, in him, attractive; less so when imitated – and many of us sought to imitate it with the result that we developed a 'hot-potato' enunciation of which I still sometimes discern a tang among my old schoolfellows. To hear him declaiming: '*Nox est perpetua, una, dormienda*' or '*Toute une mer immense où fuyaient les galères*', or 'Jousted in Aspramont or Montalban, Damasco or Marocco or Trebisond' – not, as my father read poetry with a subtle cadence, but like a great negro stamping out a tribal rhythm – was to set up reverberations in the adolescent head which a lifetime does not suffice to silence.

His humour was often expressed in the tricks condemned by Fowler as 'pedantic' and 'polysyllabic', but with J.F. these were never stale repetitions. They were fresh, ingenious and genuinely funny. Our boyish attempts to emulate him were less happy.

His entry into his form-room was always a moment of exhilaration. He never seemed weary. When some masters, especially in early school, were content to sit as invigilators while their sleepy forms turned the pages of textbooks, or at the best to dictate notes from yellowing sheafs, J.F. appeared always jaunty and fresh as a leading actor on the boards, in the limelight, commanding complete attention. He never gave the impression of performing a routine task. I think he found the spectacle of us positively stimulating.

I gave up Greek when I reached the Sixth Form and, as a result, never experienced what were his most exact dealings with his classical specialists. The history set went to him for Latin and French and for an hour a week when he took the whole Upper Sixth, classical and modern together, in what were called 'general' subjects. These might be anything from Greek sculpture to some recently published book on politics which had caught his fancy. Sometimes he would be spontaneous in his choice. I remember, as an example, how one morning after we had sung in chapel Cowper's 'God moves in a mysterious way', he treated us to an examination of the mixture of metaphors in that hymn.

'A mine is a hole from which you extract something or else an explosive weapon. In neither case would you "treasure up" anything in it. And how, if his footsteps are on the sea, does God get into his mine? Is the "never failing skill" something God put there or found there? What is the use of the skill if it lies in "unfathomable depths"? If his "designs" are "treasured up" they are presumably not put into practice. How then does he "work his sovereign will"?' and so on.

Before the publication of Fowler's *Modern English Usage* J.F. was inculcating in almost the same terms precision of grammar and contempt of cliché.

We were required to write a weekly 'paragraph' (as he called it); a single sheet of about two hundred and fifty words, on the most diverse subjects. He would return them to us sometimes without comment, conveying by his silence that he had been bored, sometimes with praise or, taking up a point, with debate. The most pejorative expression was: 'Excellent journalism, my dear fellow', by which he meant trite in thought, colloquial in expression and aiming for effect by smartness and overstatement. He referred, as did Fowler, to the work of the leader-writer, not of the reporter. The lively description of an event always pleased him.

Once I tried to score off J.F.

As part of his general diffusion of culture he gave us a lecture on Praed, with readings from some of his *vers de société*, holding him up to mild ridicule as the type of a decadent period. I do not know what determined his subject that morning. Perhaps he had lately had a reprint for review. It so happened that, through my father's reading aloud, I was rather more familiar than J.F. with the poet. In my next 'paragraph' I contrived, quite aptly, to introduce some five or six quotations from verses of Praed which J.F. had not read to us. I awaited the result with curiosity. My 'paragraph' was returned to me with the comment in J.F.'s writing: '*A mere orgy of dittography.*'

J.F. did not at all approve of Mr Crease. I was present when they met in my House-tutor's room when he said: 'The Sage of Lychpole, I presume' with apparent geniality, but he would not allow boys in his House to go to Mr Crease's. Mr Crease, as I have said, was effeminate in appearance and manner; J.F. was markedly virile, but it was he who was the homosexual. Most good schoolmasters – and, I suppose, schoolmistresses also – are homosexual by inclination – how else could they endure their work? – but their interest is diffused and unacknowledged. J.F.'s passions ran deep. I do not think he ever gave them physical release with any of his pupils, but as distinct from the general, romantic pleasure of association with the young, common to the best of his colleagues, he certainly fell in love with individual boys. I was not one of them. I was small and quite pretty in a cherubic way. His tastes were more classical than rococo – 'Greek love' as the phrase was used by innocent scholars and clergymen before the Wilde trial – and he was then ardently attached to a golden-haired Hyacinthus.

He gave this boy a motorbicycle from which he was immediately thrown and much disfigured, but J.F.'s love remained constant until the friend's death in early middle age.

J.F.'s interest in me was professional. He thought he discerned in me potentialities worth cultivating. Indeed I have a letter of his written in 1921, in which he says: 'If you use what the gods have given you, you will do as much as any single person I can think of to shape the course of your own generation.' Alas, my subsequent career disappointed him. I am not sure what he meant by 'shaping the course of my own generation' – As Prime Minister? As a great headmaster like himself? As Editor of *The Times*? Whatever it was, I did not do it. I believe that he deplored my writing and what he heard of my conduct. He was a Scotchman and believed in success as something desirable, measurable and attainable only by toil and virtue.

I saw nothing of him after my first year at Oxford, by which time he was engrossed in his work at Stowe. A suggestion I made in my last year that he should give me employment there was sharply and justly rebuffed. But the four terms of his favour were honeyed. I was always in awe of him so that he was, in a sense, the courtier and I the courted as he sought to draw me into his confidence. He, alone among Lancing masters, kept a 'pit' for himself where he could retire from the House-masters' room in which he was at anyone's call. Before I had any official position in the school – that is to say before I had any claims to notice – I was asked to tea with him in this minute, almost secret, retreat – an enormous honour rarely accorded, and noted with respect by the prefects. I remember that as the clock struck half past five he said: 'How delightful. We have nothing to do until chapel but eat éclairs and talk about poetry.' And I remember with shame that I counted the éclairs – six, to occupy half an hour. I ate two éclairs a minute in those days. I had little to say about poetry, and I do not remember what he said, but I went into chapel less swollen than most senior boys on a Sunday evening but giddy with the sense of having been in communion with the Most High.

Mr Crease was there in the side aisle in his cape and soft cravat. He seemed diminished. I did not exactly turn coat, but I knew that Mr Crease and J.F. were opposites and at about that time I transferred my allegiance to the more forceful and flamboyant person. I do not yet know which of the lessons these two sought to teach me was the more valuable nor to whom I have proved more faithful.

I had one further letter from J.F. in July 1930, to welcome me to his London club to which I had just been elected. I had by then had some success as a novelist. He began: 'My dear Waugh (you are now so eminent that I dare not use your christian name as I once did)' and ended 'I hope that I shall run against you before long and renew an association which I once valued very much'. He avoided saying whether my 'eminence' was deserved. He was, I think, simply acknowledging the unexpressed estrangement and preparing the ground for a possible encounter in the club.

In fact we never met, there or elsewhere. Six weeks after he wrote this letter I was received in the Catholic Church. He must have regarded this as the betrayal of all he had tried to inculcate.

Chapter Eight

NEVER A PALINODE

In his autobiography my father wrote plaintively: 'I was a week late at my dame-school; at Sherborne I began my time in the summer, instead of in the autumn, when the new generation commonly arrives; and now, at Oxford, I was in the least lucky case of all, for the freshmen of 1885 were well established in work and friendship before I made my belated appearance and it took me all the rest of my first year to recover lost ground.'

It is curious that, alive as he was to the disadvantages of his own experience, he should have set me on precisely the same road. I have mentioned above the bitter, avoidable loneliness of my first terms at Lancing. Now in January 1922 he decided to send me at once to Oxford in the by-term. I was eager enough to go and my father was showing his habitual impatience to get a task finished; in this case my education. He was growing weary of the routine at Chapman and Hall's and looked forward to retirement. He believed (a delusion as things turned out) that when I had my degree I should be off his hands and he so much the nearer to leisure or to less exacting work.

The original plan had been that, if I won a scholarship, I should go for nine months to France to get some command of the language. It has been my life-long impediment that I never did this. But I do not regret my premature matriculation. It sent me into the university as a lone explorer.

Many men were content to confine their interests and friendships to their colleges. I do not know if I should have been so, if I had come up at the normal time. As things were, I had little choice but to rove.

Hertford was a respectable but rather dreary little college. When Mr Bowlby announced my scholarship to the school, he described it in a phrase which, by reason of its combination of patronage with grammatical infelicity, amused my father intensely, as 'a very rising college'. If I can believe my children, it has not yet risen to a higher position than it enjoyed in my time. There was then no scholar of importance among the dons; among the undergraduates, no member of the Bullingdon, no President of the Union or of the O.U.D.S., no Blue; the boat never came near the head of the river. There was at the time a generally recognised order of precedence among the colleges. Hertford came half-way up, on a par with Oriel and Exeter. Of my immediate contemporaries there, one became an ambassador, one a bishop, one a Dominion Chief Justice, one a film actor, one a popular composer, one a Q.C. I do not know of any other notables.

The advantages were a good kitchen and a unique system by which term was kept merely by residence; there were neither roll-calls nor chapels as there were at other colleges, to take one early from bed on cold mornings. In order to hold a scholarship one had to be a member of the Church of England, in the sense of belonging to no other. I never attended chapel.

Hertford was also agreeably free both from the schoolboyish 'college spirit' which was the bane of many small colleges and of the hooliganism which on occasion broke out against the eccentrics in the larger; though it is true that both these defects were exemplified when at a 'freshers' blind' – the last, I believe, to be held – a tipsy white colonial invaded my room demanding belligerently what I 'did for the college'. I replied that I drank for it and the colonial's friends removed him before any violence occurred. No one was ever debagged or had his rooms wrecked or his oak screwed up. It was a tolerant, civilised place in which to lead whatever kind of life appealed to one.

The buildings are nondescript, befitting their history. Since the early Middle Ages they had successively housed a Hall, a College, a Hall again, until finally re-established as a

College and endowed by the first Lord Revelstoke in 1874. The front on Cat Street, it has often been remarked, looks like a bank. But those who adventure beyond the lodge find a medley of odd constructions. There are ancient but unremarkable buildings in the front quad and a chapel and hall in Jackson's French renaissance manner. Its peculiarity is the 'Bridge of Sighs' leading over New College Lane to the new buildings. There are no gardens. Since my time the charming mediaeval octagon bookshop at the corner has been restored out of recognition and incorporated in the new buildings.

A government department would no doubt have condemned the place for use as a penal institution, on the grounds of danger from fire and lack of hygiene. It was the period between the hip-bath and the bath-room proper. When men in the main quad wished to bath, they had to cross the 'Bridge of Sighs' and penetrate the steamy cellars of the new buildings. There were some privies hidden behind the chapel. Scouts brought us small jugs of shaving-water every morning and emptied chamber-pots in our rooms twice daily.

During my first term I lived unobtrusively. There were some old Lancing boys at Hertford but none, except one named Machin, whom I knew well. Rupert Fremlin and Max Mallowan (now a Professor of Archaeology) from the Headmaster's House at Lancing, were near by in New College and Preters was in digs being coached for the scholarship he won at the next entry. I began by frequenting New College. I received calls from various senior men whose parents had some connection with mine. These were returned – we had engraved visiting cards in those days – and there the acquaintance ended.

Public-spirited senior men in Hertford asked freshmen to tea, usually with the aim of enlisting them in philanthropic and evangelistic work among hop-pickers or at the Hertford mission in South London, or in the League of Nations' Union. I did not find much in common with these.

My first rooms were modest. As a scholar I was entitled to live my three years in college, but, arriving late, I found the only set available were in the oldest building, that looked out on New College Lane. They were over the J.C.R. buttery in which teas were prepared and my chief memory of the staircase is of the rattle of dish-covers on foggy afternoons and the smell of anchovy-toast and honey buns as the scouts filled their trays.

I followed the routine of the college. We had luncheon – normally, 'commons' of bread, cheese and beer; delicious little fresh-baked loaves, wedges of well-chosen, well-kept, English cheeses, bitter ale drawn from the cask in silver tankards – and tea in our rooms. Most men dined in hall most evenings, where the food was good and cheap. We had to pay for five dinners a week whether we ate them or not. In my later terms, when I had acquired extravagant tastes and a circle of friends in other colleges, I wasted much money on the inferior cuisine of the George. At first I followed the custom of dining in, gowned and in subfusc clothes. There were certain formalities. Scholars sat at a separate table and the senior scholars said grace. 'Sconcing' – a fine in the shape of a huge silver basin of beer exacted for such offences as quoting a foreign language, mentioning a woman's name or wearing incorrect dress – was done often and with much ceremony. If a man were able, as few were (certainly not I) to 'floor the sconce', i.e. drink it all off without drawing breath, the cost was divided among all at table. Normally the sconce passed from hand to hand and any inadvertence in its employment or of the napkin which accompanied it, was punished by a further sconce. The custom was not observed in all colleges and has now, I learn, become obsolete everywhere.

I was entirely happy in a subdued fashion during these first two terms, doing all that freshmen traditionally did, purchasing a cigarette box carved with the college arms and the popular printed panorama of the *Towers and Spires of Oxford*; learning to smoke a pipe; getting drunk for the first time; walking and bicycling about the surrounding villages; making an un-remarkable maiden speech at the Union; doing enough work to satisfy the examiners in History Previous. But all the time it seemed to me that there was a quintessential Oxford which I knew and loved from afar and intended to find.

My imagination was aglow with literary associations. I had by heart, and in fact quoted in my scholarship essay, Matthew Arnold's apostrophe of the 'Adorable dreamer'.

Quiller-Couch's '*Alma Mater*' was one of my favourite poems. I was steeped in *Zuleika Dobson* and the second volume of *Sinister Street* and had read all the Oxford novels that came into my hands, from *Verdant Green* to *Patchwork*. Belloc and Flecker had hymned the place:

> *Balliol made me, Balliol fed me,*
> *Whatever I had she gave me again;*
> *And the best of Balliol loved and led me,*
> *God be with you, Balliol men.*

and

> *Proud and godly kings had built her, long ago,*
> *With her towers and tombs and statues all arow,*
> *With her fair and floral air and the love that lingers there,*
> *And the streets where the great men go.*

Cambridge may have engendered greater poets but, surely(?), fewer poems of homage to herself.

I had a clear preconception of the place and I suffered very small disillusionment.

> *Know you her secret none can utter?*
> *Hers of the Book the tripled Crown?*

It is not given to all her sons either to seek or find this secret, but it was very near the surface in 1922.

Oxford then was very much closer to my father's (and, indeed, my great-grandfather's) university than to my children's. There was no feverish competition for admittance; indeed Pembroke harboured Hugh Lygon and certain other aristocratic refugees from the examination system, who had not even taken Responsions. The town was still isolated among streams and meadows. Its buildings proudly displayed their grey and gold, crumbling ashlar, now condemned by the pundits as 'leprous' and renovated at prodigious cost. Its only suburb comprised the Ruskinian villas and well-kept gardens round the Woodstock and Banbury Roads. The motor works at Cowley existed, but were far from sight or sound of the university. During term tourists were few. The surrounding woods and hills were those the Scholar Gypsy haunted and could be reached on foot in the middle of the road. We walked up the tow-path and practised sortilege at Binsey, as we believed our predecessors had done. In the quiet streets predatory shop-keepers waited on the university and tempted the young into debts that were seldom repudiated. At Canterbury Gate and in the Broad hansom-cabs and open victorias were for hire. Bicycles and clergymen abounded and clergymen on bicycles were, with the cattle coming to market, the only hazards of traffic. I doubt if there were thirty cars in the university owned by dons or undergraduates. Telephones were never used. Correspondence was on crested cards delivered by college messengers on bicycles.

It was a male community. Undergraduettes lived in purdah. Except during Eights Week girls were very rarely to be seen in the men's colleges. The proctors retained, and in my day on one occasion at least asserted, their right to expel beyond the university limits independent women who were thought to be a temptation. The late train from Paddington was by tradition known as 'the fornicator', but it was not much frequented for that purpose. Most men were well content to live in a society as confined as it had been before the coming of the railway and to indulge in light flirtations during the vacation and deep friendships during the term.

At the time of writing the senior lecturer in forensic psycho-logy at London University has delivered a report on young criminals. 'We read,' he says, 'much about delinquent areas and delinquent subcultures but less about why the delinquent does not have a girl friend like most of his non-delinquent

168

contemporaries', and he goes on to reveal that forty-six per cent of borstal boys had no experience of heterosexual intercourse. I am sure that fewer than ten per cent of my contemporaries had what Dr Gibbens means by 'girl friends'. Some had made a single, pleasureless adventure with a prostitute abroad. Few had any serious interest in women, but, as far as I know, only one has been to prison (motoring trouble) and very few have developed into homosexuals.

We were in some respects more sophisticated than our successors, but in others barely adolescent.

In a novel I wrote many years later I compared the comparatively new, century-old, but ostensibly time-honoured, system of English public school education to the manufacture of port. 'It was,' I wrote, 'like the spirit they mix with the pure grape of the Douro, heady stuff full of dark ingredients; it at once enriched and retarded the whole process of adolescence as the spirit checks the fermentation of the wine, renders it undrinkable, so that it must lie in the dark, year in, year out, until it is brought up at last fit for the table.'

Those of my contemporaries who were bored at Oxford were mostly of foreign origin or had been oddly educated. Hubert Duggan, who later became one of my closest friends, was part American, part Irish-Argentine. He languished at the House without feminine company and went into the Household Cavalry after two terms complaining of damp sheets and an immature society.

Mr Peter Quennell, whom I have met since from time to time, had been at a day-school. He, too, despaired of the place. To me it was a Kingdom of Cokayne and I believe that I was especially fortunate in my generation.

The mid-1920s were a St Luke's or, as some say, Indian, summer. The traditional life of the university ceased abruptly in 1914; many thought, never to be restored. After the war came the generation of ex-soldiers, two or three years older than normal undergraduates and timelessly older in experience. These had gone down or else were studiously sequestered in digs by the time I came up and the colleges were repossessed by the young.

After my time there were jazz, cocktail parties, a constant coming and going to London, new smart slang and the cult of the rich; soon to be succeeded by the cult of the proletariat. But for a single lustrum we lived and spoke very much as our predecessors had done ten years before. When I read their records (as I did in some detail when I was writing *The Life of Ronald Knox*) I recognised a kinship that I miss in those of our successors.

Some of us were sharply conscious of those legendary figures who, almost to a man, were wiped out in the First World War. We were often reproachfully reminded, particularly by the college servants, of how impoverished and subdued we were in comparison with those great men. It seems that now, after the second war, my contemporaries are regarded with a mixture of envy and reprobation, as libertines and wastrels.

I lately came upon a magazine article compiled from the answers of elderly dons to the question: 'Have undergraduates deteriorated?'

From New College the verdict was: 'The men have gained somewhat in sobriety and are more careful of their money.' From Merton: 'Undergraduates are becoming more and more heterogeneous. Many of the good homes where university education was a tradition have become impoverished. An increasing number come from homes with no such tradition – poorer men, with help and with utilitarian views, wishing to better their worldly prospects.' From University: 'There are (I believe) about twice as many undergraduates in residence now as were in residence thirty years ago. Then the majority were Pass men. The proportion of mere loafers now is very small. The advent of Colonial, American and foreign students has stimulated the intellectual interests of undergraduates.' From Wadham: 'The modern undergraduate is more virtuous because he is poorer; more intellectual because he has to work harder and competition is more severe; better physically because more temperate.'

The date of this article (in the *Strand Magazine*) is 1911.

2

From the first I regarded Oxford as a place to be inhabited and enjoyed for itself, not as the preparation for anywhere else. And I entered it as though through that mythical stream where Alexander the Great rejuvenated his cavalry; whose waters were sought in the Bahamas by Ponce de Leon.

In my last two terms at Lancing I was studious and aloof, affecting world-weary cynicism. The editorial of the *Lancing College Magazine* which I have quoted above, expresses that era of the Corpse Club. At Oxford I was reborn in full youth. My absurdities were those of exuberance and naïvety, not of spurious sophistication. I wanted to do everything and know everyone, not with any ambition to insinuate myself into fashionable London or make influential friends who would prosper any future career, nor to cut a figure among the intellectuals which would attract the notice of the hierarchy of Bloomsbury. I did not even look outside the university limits to the salons of Lady Ottoline Morrele at Garsington or Lady Keeble on Boars' Hill. My interests were as narrow as the ancient walls. I wanted to taste everything Oxford could offer and consume as much as I could hold.

I abandoned my diary on the day I left school and have no source for the following years except an inexact memory. I think it must have been towards the end of my second term that I began to develop my indiscriminate *bonhomie*. In my third term I had large rooms on the ground floor of the front quad and these were seldom empty. I had passed my preliminary exam; final schools seemed far distant. I regarded my scholarship as a reward for work done, not as the earnest of work to come. My ambitions, so far as they were formed, were artistic. But there was a prevalent illusion that a man of parts could idle for eight terms and at the end sit up with black coffee and master the required subjects in a few weeks. It was, I believe, the legend of F. E. Smith (Lord Birkenhead) which thus bedevilled us. We had to the full his capacity for pleasure but not for concentration. Most of my associates, including many who have been highly successful in later life, went down with bad degrees or with none at all.

Such reading as I did was done in the vacations with an eye on the beginning-of-term college 'collections'. From my third term onwards I was subject to admonitions which became increasingly authoritative and threatening. I did not wish to be sent down and I was just able until my Finals to keep the hostile critics at a distance. I had faint interest in History as it was taught. Sometimes an historical character would catch my imagination, but most of the curriculum seemed to have been designed to show that the British parliamentary system at the turn of the century was the consummation of human wisdom and that the affairs of other countries were significant so far as they showed an approach to this ideal. This delusion was fortified by my unconsidered choice of my 'special subject'. I might, for example, have read about the Italian cities of the renaissance, which would certainly have fascinated me. Instead, when asked by my tutor what I wished to read, I could remember the name of only one of these 'special subjects'; Representative Government. Nothing could have been drearier to me than the peculiarities of the various democratic constitutions of the world and no one was to blame except myself for directing me towards them.

I was not at all singular in this indifference to work. At least half of the undergraduates were sent to Oxford simply as a place to grow up in. Some concerned themselves with rowing or cricket, some with acting and speech-making, some with pure pleasure. I knew everything about my friends' political and religious opinions, their love affairs, finances, homes, families, their tastes in food and clothes and drink, but would have thought it indelicate to inquire what school they were reading. English Literature was for women and foreigners; a new, disreputable school named Modern Greats (now dubbed P.P.E.) was for 'publicists and politicians'. Classical Mods and Greats was still pre-eminent in esteem; next to them Modern History and Law and Theology. Mathematicians were respected but were thought to be out of their proper milieu; they should have been at Cambridge. There was said to be a laboratory somewhere beyond Keble, but I never met anyone who dabbled there. No Fellow of Hertford, when I went up, had any connection with the Natural Sciences.

I never came to any considered decision to give up work. Intermittently my conscience or a particularly menacing interview with the college authorities would make me open a book or attend a lecture, but I had no heart to continue long.

It may be that I was unfortunate in the dons of my college, who, compared with J. F. Roxburgh, did not captivate the imagination.

I did not meet the first head of my college. He had taken to his bed before I came up and early in my first term I was called by my scout, Bateson, a man of deep, habitual melancholy, with the words: 'Half past seven and the Principal's dead.' He was succeeded by a blue-faced wizened Scotch baronet with whom I had only official and sour relations. Most of the dons at Hertford then were a modest lot, as befitted their abilities. One was outstanding, less for his deep learning than for his peculiarities of character.

C. R. M. F. Cruttwell was Dean and senior History tutor. Later he became Principal and died insane. He had written me a cordial letter of congratulation and welcome when I was elected scholar and I was called to his rooms on my second evening in college. I had met very few dons and was disposed to think highly of them as of remote hierarchs. Cruttwell's appearance was not prepossessing. He was tall, almost loutish, with the face of a petulant baby. He smoked a pipe which was usually attached to his blubber-lips by a thread of slime. As he removed the stem, waving it to emphasise his indistinct speech, this glittering connection extended until finally it broke leaving a dribble on his chin. When he spoke to me I found myself so distracted by the speculation of how far this line could be attentuated that I was often inattentive to his words.

He was, I now recognise, a wreck of the war in which he had served gallantly. No doubt a modern doctor would have named, even if he could not cure, his various neuroses. It was as though he had never cleaned himself of the muck of the trenches. His conspectus of history was narrowed to the few miles of the Low Countries where he had fought, and the ultimate, unattainable frontier towards which he had gazed through his periscope over the barbed wire. He was obsessed by the Rhine and it was the first, sharp difference between us that I was ignorant of its course.

He had a kind of rough geniality which found expression in coarse soldiers' language and quickly gave place to a frustrated pugnacity. He had been a fellow of All Souls before 1914 and must then have been a young man of more polished manners, for he was of perfectly respectable origins; but all were blown and gassed away in two years' fighting. As Dean of the college he seemed often to fancy himself in command of a recalcitrant platoon. He had binges like a subaltern on leave, got grossly drunk when he dined out and was sometimes to be seen as St Mary's struck midnight, feeling his way blindly round the railings of the Radcliffe Camera believing them to be those of the college. When crapulous, as he normally was when conducting college business, he fell into violent rages. He was a misogynist to such an extreme degree that he refused to have women at his lectures. The college porter had instructions to repel them. If one slipped in, he drove her out, crimson faced, by his obscenities. He had one associate, whom he referred to as 'that little hack', a Platonist and fellow infantryman. Sometimes he and this friend played lawn-tennis; more often they went for long silent walks together.

Cruttwell had political ambitions and intrigued clumsily but assiduously for the Conservative nomination for the university seat, which at that time was regarded as safe. In this he succeeded, but when it came to the polls he was voted down for a light-hearted independent.

Altogether he was not at all the kind of don for whom I had been prepared by stories of Jowett.

In my first two terms I saw little of him. My ignorance of Rhenish geography could have been corrected, but there was an antipathy between us that went deeper. After the 'freshers' blind' in my third term, during which, in common with at least a third of the college, I had been conspicuously drunk, he attempted to give me advice, saying he knew that, having come up in a by-term, I was at a disadvantage, and warning me that I had not chosen the best way of ingratiating myself with the college. He was undoubtedly attempting to show kindness. I was feeling the ill effects of my debauch and, instead of responding generously to him, I became fatuously haughty, saying I regretted my excesses but that (as was true) they had not been committed with any wish for popularity. I added that I was quite indifferent to college opinion.

I think it was then that our mutual dislike became incurable.

I had just begun reading with him for my final schools. After a very few sessions he fell into such frenzies of exasperation that for a time he refused to see me at all and I was left without tutoring of any kind. This blissful period ended by my being handed over to a gentle, newly elected fellow who preserved the politeness which I had supposed was universal. But I did not learn very much from him.

At the beginning of my third year, struck by conscience and a momentary restlessness and knowing I was doing no good at my books, I wrote to my father asking to be taken away and sent to Paris to enjoy the full life of *Trilby*. He told me I must first get my degree. This reasonable verdict gave me the sense that, as far as my schools went, I was in Oxford under protest. I perversely regarded it as the *laissez-passer* to a life of pure pleasure.

We kept early hours. The gates shut at nine o'clock, after which no member of the college could go out nor any visitor come in. There was a small fine for returning after eleven and a list of late comers submitted to the Dean. After midnight the only means of entry was by climbing. Both the possible routes into Hertford, one through the garden of All Souls, the other from Hell Passage and over the roof immediately past the Dean's windows, were tricky for drunks and I do not think I used either more than a dozen times.

Congenial company could be found in Hertford; in particular Terence Greenidge, a second-year man I soon took up with. He had much to commend him to the authorities. He was the orphan son of a don and the ward of the Bursar. Like Cruttwell he was a Rugbeian. He was an enthusiastic Greats man and he ran with some success on the Iffley track. But he had certain eccentricities which separated him from the conventional elite of the J.C.R. Dining Club. He was given to declaiming Greek choruses loudly, late at night, in the quad. Although wildly unkempt in his person he was a stickler for tidiness and stuffed his pockets with wastepaper from the gutters. There was a wicket-gate leading to the kitchens from the front quad. Terence, who had rooms near by, appointed himself its keeper. The scouts would open it and go down to collect their trays. Out would pop Terence and shut it. The laden scouts ascended and perforce went back, left their trays, reopened the gate and returned for them. Out popped Terence again as soon as their backs were turned, to bar their way. They made official complaints. Terence with apparent candour denied any knowledge of the incidents. Eventually, until Terence went into digs, they had to post a sentry at meal-times.

He also indulged a mild kleptomania, collecting from the O.U.D.S., the Union and other men's rooms trifles which took his fancy – hair-brushes, keys, nail-scissors, ink-pots. These he would secrete in orderly little nests, often behind books in the library. On one occasion he took all the college keys from the porter's lodge and kept them hidden for some days.

When the film *The Enemies of Women* appeared in Oxford it exercised a peculiar fascination over him. He sat through it again and again, 'identifying' himself (as the modern jargon has it) with Lionel Barrymore, whom he in no way resembled. He had a short black jacket made with astrakhan collar and cuffs. Lord Beauchamp (no prude), calling unexpectedly on his elder son, Elmley, at his rooms in Magdalen, surprised Terence there so garbed and, concluding that Elmley had got into an undesirable set, took him down for two terms.

Terence had a special felicity in inventing sobriquets and permanent epithets – 'Baldhead who writes for the papers' (my brother Alec); 'Midnight Badger' (the night porter), to distinguish him from a namesake among the college servants; 'Philbrick the Flagellant'; 'Subman' (for a mild man at Worcester who wore pince-nez and was elected President of the Union); 'Hotlunch' (for Preters, who complained of the prevalence of cold food at midday); 'Mr Tristram, who makes polite conversation at breakfast'. These and countless others were spontaneously generated and for the time consecrated by use. They do not now scintillate, but all formed part of the lore of many of my contemporaries.

It was Terence who first imaginatively imputed to Cruttwell sexual connection with dogs and purchased a stuffed one in a junk-shop in Walton Street, which we set in the quad as an allurement for him on his return from dining in All Souls. For the same reason we used rather often to bark under Cruttwell's windows at night.

Unlike Lord Beauchamp, my mother took an immediate fancy to Terence, who appealed to her as a waif, and he spent much of his vacations at my home. My father, normally hospitable to all my friends, was less welcoming. Returning weary from his office, he did not enjoy being drawn into disputes about Hegel and Kant, authors of whom he had long forgotten what little he ever knew. There were times when Terence stayed with us without my father's knowledge. He would keep his room until my father left the house, then come down to breakfast; he would be out or in hiding between the hours of six p.m. and ten to re-emerge when my father went punctually to bed. Sometimes he was betrayed by the smell of his tobacco. 'You've had that boy here again,' my father would say, gasping with the onset of asthma, provoked more by the thought of Terence than by the evidence of his presence.

The rooms from which Terence made his sorties against the kitchen wicket-gate were the only double set in college. These, during my first year, he shared with a singularly dissimilar man, James Parkes, now an Anglican clergyman learned and influential in Jewish affairs, already much concerned with what may be called undergraduate public life. Parkes was one of the last of the ex-service men; he would normally have been in digs. It was in order to remain in college, conveniently for his many committees, that he shared with Terence. He was a man of rugged appearance who, Terence maintained, had been the model for the bronze statue which stands as the war-memorial in Paddington Station. Lunching with this pair I first met the then President of the Union and the editor of *The Isis*. Neither was particularly formidable (both, if I remember rightly, Welshmen) but I was impressed at finding myself among these public figures and I took advantage of the acquaintance to contribute to *The Isis* and to speak at the Union.

When Terence's obsession with Lionel Barrymore subsided, he became an addict of Dostoevsky. It was his gift to devote himself with enthusiasm to whatever interested him. Later he acquired a cinema camera and made burlesque films into which we were all dragooned.

When Parkes went down in my second year Terence and I formed the nucleus of a coterie which we used to call 'the Hertford underworld'. Tony Bushell, who later became a film actor, and my Lancing friend, P. F. Machin, were of us. We used, unless any of us was giving a luncheon party or going to one, to have our commons together in my rooms. This soon developed into my keeping open house for men from other colleges; sometimes as many as a dozen collected; Terence dubbed these assemblies 'offal'. We drank large quantities of beer and made a good deal of noise. Few of us could sing. We used to recite verse in unison.

Later more formal luncheon parties occupied an increasing part of my life. In my second and third years I gave, I think, four or five a term and attended countless others. Few, if any, colleges sanctioned private dinner parties. At Hertford certainly they could only be given by special permission of the bursar and then for a good reason, but luncheons for four or five were a matter of arrangement with one's scout and the chef. The food was abundant and highly decorated. In winter the staple drink was mulled claret followed by port. We drank on till dusk while the 'muddied oafs' and 'flannelled fools' passed under the windows to and from the river, the track and the playing-fields. At one of them, being hard up, I auctioned all my books, many of them finely bound by Maltby and still to be paid for.

But on days when I had no engagement 'offal' continued until I went down.

It was Terence who introduced me to the Hypocrites' Club. This body – too short-lived to be described as an 'institution' – had rooms over a bicycle shop in St Aldate's. It has already been well described in the memoirs of my contemporaries. It was, when I arrived there, in a state of transition. Elmley, now Earl Beauchamp, whom I have mentioned above, a solid, tolerant, highly respectable man at Magdalen, was later secretary. He was at that time voluntarily rusticating with the yeomanry. The senior member – all clubs were required by the proctors to have a don responsible for them – was R. M. Dawkins, the much-loved professor of Modern Greek, who never, I think, set foot there. Most of the original members were heavy-drinking, rather sombre Rugbeians and Wykehamists with vaguely artistic and literary interests, but it was, at the time I joined, in process of invasion and occupation by a group of wanton Etonians who brought it to speedy dissolution. It then became notorious not only for drunkenness but for flamboyance of dress and manner which was in some cases patently homosexual. Elmley ordained that: 'Gentlemen may prance but not dance', but his rule was not observed after his sequestration.

All college deans reprobated the Hypocrites, especially 'Sligger' Urquhart of Balliol, who rightly regarded it as a rival attraction to, and source of corruption of, his own sober salon. Soon it was impossible to find a senior member and the proctors closed it. In its brief heyday it was the scene of uninhibited revelry. The difference between the two antagonistic parties may be expressed in parody by saying that the older members were disposed to an archaic turn of phrase, calling: 'Drawer, a stoop of ale, prithee', while the new members affected cockney, ordering: 'Just a nip of dry London, for me wind, dearie'. As I belonged to neither party, at the first, and only, general meeting which I attended, knowing scarcely anyone, I found myself, much to my surprise, proposed and elected secretary. The voters were all tipsy. I performed no secretarial duties. My appointment was a characteristic fantasy of the place, and after a time I had a tiff and either resigned or was deposed – I forget which. My predecessor in the office, Loveday, had left the university suddenly to study black magic. He died in mysterious circumstances at Cefalu in Alistair Crowley's community and his widow, calling herself 'Tiger Woman' figured for some time in the popular Press, where she made 'disclosures' of the goings-on at Cefalu.

The building which housed the Hypocrites was timbered and, I think, genuinely Tudor; it still stands at No. 31 and is preserved as an Historic Monument, not for its association with the club but for its antiquity. One ascended narrow stairs (rather as in London one descends to Pratt's) into a rich smell of onions and grilling meat. Usually the constable on the beat was standing in the kitchen, helmet in one hand, a mug of beer in the other. Above and beyond the kitchen were two large rooms. I saw the transition by which dart targets and shove-halfpenny

boards gave place to murals by Mr Oliver Messel (a frequent
visitor from London) and Robert Byron. There was a piano.
Folk music and glees gave place to jazz and, more in the fashion,
to Victorian drawing-room ballads.

The reader will remember the roll-call in the fourth chapter
of Scott Fitzgerald's *The Great Gatsby*. (A book incidentally,
which I never read until long after the author's death. In 1946
an American cinema agent said to me: 'You must have been
greatly influenced by Scott Fitzgerald.' In fact I had not then
read a word of his.) 'It is an old time-table now disintegrating
at its folds,' Fitzgerald wrote, 'and headed "This schedule in
effect July 5th 1922". But I can still read the grey names, and
they will give you a better impression than any generalities of
those who accepted Gatsby's hospitality.'

I could still present a catalogue of those who frequented the
Hypocrites in July 1923, their names are not grey to me but
few of them have become famous. I could make a necrology:

Peter Ruffer, the first of us to die, obese, musical, morose,
often contemplating suicide in his rooms in the Turl, killed in
the end by a quack doctor; Keith Douglas, also a musician,
narrow-faced, dressed for the Café Royal of 1890; David
Plunket Greene, enormously tall and gentle, always dressed far
beyond the height of fashion; Rudolph Messel, cadaverous,
wayward, generous; Richard Pares whom Sligger rescued from
bohemia and preserved for a life of scholarship prematurely
curtailed; Hugh Lygon, Elmley's younger brother, always
just missing the happiness he sought, without ambition, unhappy in love, a man of the greatest sweetness; and many
others . . . their names and the names of those still alive who
have drifted apart, might stir wistful memories in fifty or more
elderly men; no more.

The Hypocrites, like Gatsby's swimming-pool, saw the
passage, as members or guests, of the best and the worst of that
year. It was the stamping-ground of half my Oxford life and
the source of friendships still warm today.

I have mentioned above that I took early to the Union and to Oxford journalism. Later I combined these two interests by reporting the debates for the *Isis* and the *Cherwell* (they were then also fully reported in the *Morning Post*). My only scoop was on the occasion one Thursday evening when Mr John Sutro, then of Trinity, stood up to speak on the paper. It was evident that he had been drinking heavily and, as he spoke, the liquor worked strongly in him. After becoming increasingly incoherent, he received a note from the President: 'Had you not better sit down?' He did so and remained for a few minutes stupefied on the committee bench under the bust of Gladstone, until he caught a laudatory, if ironic, mention of himself. This he applauded loudly, then rose and with difficulty made his way out of the debating hall to collapse in the garden. I recorded this event, as the *Morning Post* did not. It transpired that his parents were regular readers of the *Cherwell*. A special copy had to be printed for them with the passage deleted.

I was no success as a speaker and never rose above the lowest rung in the ascent to office. 'An Oxford Union manner' is reprobated in the House of Commons as frivolous. It was far too grave for me to achieve. Also, I was too ignorant. I never heard any political talk at home nor did I ever read the political papers. I knew nothing of personalities, statistics or social questions (I once went canvassing for John Marriott and was ruthlessly exposed by a Liberal labourer whose vote I had impertinently solicited), and though the university was not fiercely divided, as it later became, on these matters, most debates were about public affairs. So little did I follow the news that at the beginning of one term I blithely greeted a man in Balliol with what seemed a pleasantry: 'I suppose all your sisters were raped during the vac', to which the sad and candid answer was simply: 'Yes'. For he came from Smyrna.

Nor had I any oratorical gifts. But most terms I put on my tail coat and spoke on the paper and quite often intervened spontaneously and ineffectually; I was not chagrined by lack of success and attended almost every debate as part of the multifarious life in which I was absorbed.

I proclaimed myself a Tory but could not have defined Tory policy on any current topic. There was already an active Labour party to which Richard Pares and many clever men belonged. Indeed, it comprised so many of the best brains that I advised a middle-brow socialist acquaintance before he came up that he would find the competition too hot and that he had better make his appearance as a Conservative. He took the advice and prospered.

The Conservatives had the Oxford Carlton Club with rooms at the corner of George Street. It was social rather than political and more than party loyalty was required for membership. It aimed, to large extent with success, at achieving in miniature the atmosphere of a London club. The Liberals, too, had a club called the New Reform at a corner of the Cornmarket, handsomely subsidised by Lloyd George and, as things turned out, wholly social. When the Hypocrites was shut, there was a mass migration there. I belonged at the New Reform and at the Carlton impartially; also to the Chatham, a small, ostensibly *élite* Tory discussion club without premises which met over mulled claret in various college rooms. (The Canning, with whom we shared our annual dinner, was an exactly similar body.) There was a quantity of silver – candle-sticks, snuff-box, cigar-box, loving-cup, etc. – which was delivered by a bank-messenger before meetings. I am told it disappeared during the second war. I also joined the White Rose, an occasional dining-club devoted to the Stuart cause. It had been under the Vice-Chancellor's ban since 1745, when two members were reputedly hanged on Magdalen bridge. We commemorated their anniversary, the Restoration, the birthday of the Bavarian pretender (to whom we addressed loyal greetings) and other events in Stuart history by dinners at the Golden Cross, which were regularly raided by the proctors. Those who could sing sang Royalist songs. I was as little concerned with the outcome of affairs of Westminster as with the Stuart restoration.

Most men vaguely professed some political sympathy. Terence had a tousled, corduroyed cousin in Jesus who combined communism with bibliography. Terence himself at that time held the revolutionary creed of a pre-Marxist Russian student. But few of us took any of this seriously; those few had ambitions of a career in public life and hoped to attract the notice of party managers in London. Most of us were very much more interested in the unseating for corruption of the city Member of Parliament than in the succession to the Primeministry.

Any male member of the university who cared to pay the small subscription could join the Union, and for this reason it was more cosmopolitan than other clubs and societies. There were very few, if any, Negro undergraduates, but Asiatics abounded, and these were usually referred to as 'black men' whether they were pale Egyptians or dusky Tamils. There was no rancour in the appellation; it was simply that these exotics seemed as absurd among the stones of Oxford as topeed tourists in the temples and mosques of the orient; there was no hint of deliberate personal contempt; still less of hostility. It struck us as whimsical to impute cannibalism to these earnest vegetarians. We may have caused offence. Certainly the only oriental whom I met, the Cingalese Bandaranaike, returned to Colombo fiercely anti-British. (This sentiment did not save him from assassination by his fellow countrymen when he lost the protection of the British Crown.) At the Union these emergent politicians made themselves at home and introduced a vehemence that was normally lacking in our debates.

I think the standard of debating was rather high and the divisions were more often a verdict on the merits of the leading speakers than an expression of preconceived opinion. Once, I remember, an eloquent American carried a motion in favour of Prohibition. The elections for office were not decided on the lines of political party. College loyalty, on the other hand, was powerful. In some colleges, and those the largest, relatively few men belonged to the Union. It was in my time rather easier for a candidate from St John's or Worcester to become President than for one from Magdalen.

The busts of illustrious former Presidents gave the impression that the chair was the first perch on the flight to eminence. I knew one man, a socialist, so obsessed with ambition that he stayed up an extra term, secretly employed (for he was poor) at New College Choir School. He never got elected nor has he since made a career in politics.

In fact, not many of the Presidents of my day have risen to great heights. My only contemporary to become Prime Minister (apart from the ill-fated Bandaranaike) was Sir Alec Home, then named Lord Dunglass. He never spoke at the Union nor did he, as I remember, take an active part in any of the political clubs. Of the Presidents of my time one committed suicide early, others became journalists or instructors at distant universities. I have vainly searched *Who's Who* for a record of their achievements. Four are widely known Jim (or Scrim) Wedderburn (now Earl of Dundee); Gerald Gardiner, Q.C.; Christopher Hollis and Douglas Woodruff.

Wedderburn combined gravity of manner with great lightness of heart. He was a protagonist in the admirable rag lecture on psychoanalysis by 'Dr Emil Busch' which has been described in detail by Christopher Hollis in his autobiography, *Along the Road to Frome*. A simpler but exhilarating joke of his was to substitute gin for water in the carafes which stood on the Union table, from which speakers often refreshed themselves to punctuate their *bon mots*.

Gerald Gardiner (Lord Gardiner) was one of the few members of the New Reform Club, of which he was President, who was a genuine partisan of Lloyd George. He was also editor of the *Isis* and President of the O.U.D.S. He was rather older than most of us. He had then the same elegance of appearance and cold precision of phrase and enunciation that have impressed themselves on so many juries. Like many outstanding men he was sent down by the proctors. His offence was to publish in the *Isis* an article by an undergraduette criticising the restrictions imposed in the women's colleges. He is, I believe, the only President of the Union to have been sent down during his term of office.

Christopher Hollis became, and has remained, one of my closest friends. I am here concerned with his performances at the Union. They were truly remarkable and, had we the American custom of electing an undergraduate as the 'most likely to succeed' of his year, my vote would have gone to him. But Christopher was never ambitious. Our confident expectations that he was destined for high office in public life have been disappointed. It was not that we overestimated his abilities but that we were ignorant of the qualities required for success.

He had a genuine interest in politics, which his long sessions in the House of Commons have somewhat staled, but was in other ways a sharp contrast to Gerald Gardiner; his appearance was unstudied, indeed unkempt, his tone of voice harsh; he was immensely genial and constantly funny; never a clown as were some Union speakers (not Gardiner). His jokes, like Chesterton's, were always designed to make a logical point. Much of his subsequent life has been spent in public speaking to a great diversity of audiences in all parts of the world. No orator can keep a consistent style in these conditions. At Oxford he had one particular audience and could address it in the confidence that every allusion and every turn of irony would be recognised. Ronald Knox alone of the Union speakers I have heard, excelled him.

Douglas Woodruff seemed an ancient. Gerald Gardiner was two or three years older than the rest of us and proportionately the more polished and confident; Douglas was ageless. I have often reflected that, by analogy to the legendary Wandering Jew, Douglas might be regarded as the Wandering Christian. I can conceive of him as equally at home in Ambrose's Milan, in the libraries of the mediaeval scholiasts, in the renaissance universities, in the courts of the Counter-reformation, in the coffee shops of Dryden, or in the Oriel common-room of the 1840s. With heavy head and hooded eyes, he drew in John-

sonian diction on a treasury of curious historical lore which
gave the impression of personal reminiscence rather than re-
search; I have since observed him abroad gazing at some famous
historical site, a space overbuilt, or a monument reconstructed
and totally unrecognisable to the modern eye, with a peculiar
air of familiarity as though he had known it well centuries before.

Douglas had a gift of speech which was witty and unemotional. If he had ambitions they were for influence not for
fame. He liked, in our small world, to be behind the scenes,
intriguing for others; a wholly benevolent grey eminence. In
his mature wisdom he was tolerant of the extravagances of
Christopher and myself but did not share them; a sober man
who found no one and nothing beneath his notice and very
little indeed to command his respect. In this phase of his long
and various life he belatedly supported Gladstonian Liberalism.
I came to know this sage well in after years, but at the university
I regarded him with remote awe. If Cruttwell had been cast in
his image I might have made a scholar.

The Union debates, in the early twenties, were still essentially an undergraduate activity. We went to dispute with one
another and demonstrate our own powers. Once a term, at the
presidential debate, a single elderly visitor from the larger
world was entertained and tolerantly heard. At the Eights Week
debate there were sometimes a pair of humorous senior members. (In what I have called the golden age of Ronald Knox
there were no outsiders at all.) But in the 30's the custom grew,
perhaps with the wireless, of providing more and more professional entertainers. At the time of writing, I am told, it is
common to have all four speakers on the paper drawn from
outside the university. The undergraduates merely sprawl back
and express their prejudices with jeers. We in my time were
much more interested in the performances of Christopher Hollis
and Douglas Woodruff than in those of Cabinet Ministers.

My first contributions to the *Isis* were light verses. It was
usual to adopt a *nom de guerre* and I chose 'Scaramel'. Under this
name I often wrote and drew. I stuck some cuttings in a scrap
book which has survived, and they do not seem to me much

better or much worse than most undergraduate journalism. I was engaged in one way or another with most of the magazines which appeared in Oxford.

The *Isis*, which in later years dropped the definite article and greatly changed in character, was then about thirty years old, firmly established with a number of advertisers, widely read and greatly looked down on by aesthetes and intellectuals. It was primarily a newspaper giving many pages to athletics. The first article was always 'Isis Idol'; what is now called 'a profile' of a prominent undergraduate – the captains of the various university teams, the Presidents of the Union and the O.U.D.S. and so on. This was followed by a leading article in which the editor was free to indulge his idiosyncrasies. Then came accounts of matches and meetings. The chief share-holder, who exercised some control over it, was an alcoholic figure called Gull who lived in St Aldate's. He had once been at St Edmund's Hall and was inordinately proud of having followed the Magdalen beagles when the Prince of Wales was out. The sole attraction, for me, of the *Isis* was that it paid its contributors.

In this desirable quality a rival appeared. The *Cherwell* had a history of many vicissitudes. It was intended to be a challenge to the *Isis*, performing the same function more brightly, and was issued irregularly whenever an undergraduate was well enough in funds to guarantee the printers' bill. Then at the end of my second year a barge drifted up the river bearing a strange figure. He tied up at Godstow; a middle-aged man, accompanied by a wife and unkempt family. He put it about that he was very rich and had taken to this manner of life for philosophical reasons. He claimed no connection with the university and he denied a normal education, or indeed any education at all, to his children, as a matter of conscience. His fortune was said to be derived from the manufacture of water-closets. John Sutro picked him up somewhere – he can no longer remember where or how – and was accorded the revelation that this visitant intended to take over the *Cherwell* and make it a prosperous concern. He called a meeting in his rooms in Trinity at which this man of mystery made the inflammatory statement: 'The first principle of the *Cherwell*, gentlemen, is that everyone who writes for it shall be paid, and paid very liberally.' He proceeded to propound the peculiar plan that it should start publication in July, in the middle of the long vacation. We did not wish to damp his enthusiasm, but pointed out that this was not the best season for an undergraduate magazine.

'I am aiming at a far larger public,' he replied.

So Christopher Hollis was installed as editor at Godstow and I, at home, posted off a weekly contribution (one of which was a quite funny short story in which an earnest student might find hints of my first novel) in the belief that we were earning £3 or £4 a week. Christopher on the spot drew some wages. I cannot remember whether I ever got anything. Certainly none of us got what had been promised and I do not think the printers were ever paid. Our proprietor walked the deserted streets of Oxford soliciting shop-keepers for advertisements for which he took advance payment in kind. Then with the autumn mists the 'closet-king' sailed away into whatever land of hallucination he naturally inhabited.

After that the *Cherwell* appeared intermittently, financed by John Sutro and edited by Robert Byron. Once it merged into the *Oxford Broom*, the creation of Mr Harold Acton, who has given a vivid account of it in his *Memoirs of an Aesthete*. The *Broom* published a short story of mine, which betrays the unmistakable influence of that preposterously spurious artefact, which quite captivated me at the age of nineteen, James Branch Cabell's *Jurgen*.

Many of my contemporaries were more accomplished writers than I. In one thing I was pre-eminent (for there were no competitors); this was in making decorative drawings. At Oxford I was much in demand to design head-pieces and covers for the magazines, book-plates, O.U.D.S. programmes and caricatures. My most ambitious work was a picture of the death of Mr Huskisson (run over by the first train) to celebrate the twenty-first birthday of John Sutro, the founder of the Railway Club. During one vacation I took lessons in wood engraving and was unduly elated when Jack Squire genially accepted some of my prints for the *London Mercury*. Others appeared in a handsome, short-lived publication entitled the *Golden Hind* which was edited and financed by a friend of my brother's, Clifford Bax.

During term I spent some time at the Ruskin School of Art, which had a somewhat tenuous connection with the university. Once a week we met to draw from the nude in a studio over a teashop in the Corn. The art master was supercilious; the models came up for the evening from London and were forbidden by the proctors to stay the night in the city for fear of their corrupting our morals – a superfluous scruple for they were remarkably unalluring young women. Peter Quennell was my companion in these studies.

Peter, who had decorated his first book of verse, drew worse than I and realised the sooner where his talent lay. It was many years before I despaired of myself as a draughtsman. My meagre gift had been overpraised at home, at school and at Oxford. I never imagined myself a Titian or a Velasquez. My ambition was to draw, decorate, design and illustrate. I worked with the brush and was entirely happy in my employment of it, as I was not when reading or writing. Later in this chronicle I shall note various attempts to escape from my literary destiny into pleasanter but less appropriate work with my hands.

4

> *For no one, in our long decline,*
> *So dusty, spiteful and divided,*
> *Had quite such pleasant friends as mine,*
> *Or loved them half as much as I did.*

Thus Belloc of his Oxford; so I of mine.

The record of my life there is essentially a catalogue of friendships.

'We kept a school and taught ourselves.'

The lessons were in no curriculum of scholarship or morals. Drinking had a large part in it. We preserved a sort of *mystique* derived largely from Belloc and Chesterton about the convivial swilling of beer and wine, quite unlike the contemporary transatlantic cult of whisky. Moreover there was at that time a real danger of Prohibition in England. It was said that a majority in the House of Commons had promised their constituents to support it, if it ever came to the vote and that it was only the astuteness of the minority which averted the disaster. There was thus an element of a Resistance Group about the drunkards of the period.

In a novel (*Brideshead Revisited*) which portrays some aspects of my Oxford life I gave a description of two undergraduates made free of a fine cellar and exulting in their acquaintance with wine. That was never my happy experience. I doubt whether, at the age of twenty, except by the label or the shape of the bottle, I could distinguish claret from burgundy. The passage quoted was written in 1943, at a time of acute scarcity, and in a mood of sentimental delusion. In fact we drank copiously but indiscriminately – and I use 'copiously' in relation to our age. We were very often very drunk but the actual quantities we consumed in our orgies were far less than I now regularly enjoy in complete sobriety. A few glasses of sherry, half a bottle of burgundy, claret or champagne, a few glasses of port, threw us into transports. A glass or two of brandy or whisky on top of them rendered us unconscious.

This was on rather frequent nights of celebration. The standard tipple, for all but the very rich, was beer. We enjoyed not only drink but drunkenness. And when I say 'we' I am speaking of a minority. There was a drinking set and I was of it. Most of my friendships were made in our cups. The first friend to whom I gave my full devotion did not enjoy drinking and as a result we drifted apart.

He was Richard Pares, a Balliol Wykehamist, with an appealing pale face and a mop of fair hair, blank blue eyes and the Lear-Carroll-like fantasies of many Balliol Wykehamists. I loved him dearly, but an excess of wine nauseated him and this made an insurmountable barrier between us. When I felt most intimate, he felt queasy. He withdrew, or was withdrawn, from our company and achieved many academic successes, university prizes, first-class Honours, an All Souls Fellowship, a professorship in the north; he would probably have been elected Master of Balliol had he not been tragically struck down by creeping paralysis. His subject was the West Indian sugar trade. Once, before his withdrawal, he had a dream in which one of us was convicted of the unknown vice of 'vanoxism'. It is John Sutro's recollection, but not mine, that it was connected with scourging raw beef with lilies. We founded a club named the Vanoxists who met for breakfast now and then at the Trout at Godstow, all of us united in nothing but affection for Richard.

His successor as the friend of my heart I will call Hamish Lennox, who was no scholar and soon went down to take a course in architecture in London; but he continued to haunt Oxford and for two or three years we were inseparable or, if separated, in almost daily communication, until like so many of my generation, he heard the call of the Levant and went to live abroad.

Hamish had no repugnance to the bottle and we drank deep together. At times he was as gay as any Hypocrite, but there were always hints of the spirit that in later years has made him a recluse. He eschewed London and London society and, without sporting or agricultural interests, loved the Scotch and English countryside as places of refuge.

Hamish's home was uncongenial to him. His father, the younger son of a Border family, was dead and his mother was high-tempered, possessive, jolly and erratic. (She later was the model for 'Lady Circumference' in my first novel.) Mrs Lennox had settled in Warwickshire for the hunting. She no longer kept horses, but she gardened with all the fury of the chase. 'I only keep this place going for Hamish,' she used to say, in flagrant self-deception, for he could rarely be persuaded to spend any time there and did not disguise his intention of getting rid of it as soon as it came into his hands. The spectacle of idleness in youth (and Hamish and I were very idle) threw her into frenzies of indignation. 'Why can't you boys get out of the house and *do* something? There's always something to be done about a place. When my husband went to stay anywhere, his first question was always what could he do to help. Why don't you cut wood? Why don't you clear the shrubberies? Why don't you take the roof off the potting-shed?'

To all these appeals we remained unresponsive.

She made friends with me as a link with her wayward son and constantly appealed to me to mediate between them; always without effect.

During Hamish's visits to Oxford we saw little of the university, spending our days driving in his motor round the surrounding villages and our evenings in the Oxford inns frequented by townees – the Turf, the Nag's Head, the Druid's Head, the Chequers and many others.

I could not have fallen under an influence better designed to encourage my natural frivolity, dilettantism and dissipation or to expose as vulgar and futile any promptings I may have felt to worldly ambition.

The candid autobiographer is in some difficulty in describing the friends of his youth; he must either present his readers with a long caste of characters whose names will be entirely unfamiliar to them or else give the impression that he consorted only with those who have since become notable. As I have said above, I was promiscuous in my choice of familiars. Many I have not seen or heard of for forty years and their names on the back of a menu stir no memory. They were an essential part of my adolescence. I can but serve the reader with a few samples who may suggest the character of my generation.

There was John Sutro mentioned above in an uncharacteristic lapse.

Like Woodruff, he has with age changed little in appearance, which was always singular and endearing, like a creation of

Waterton's; as though a whimsical taxidermist had secured some transitional anthropoid specimen, stripped it of its outer hide and replaced it with the skin of a rosy and robust baby, crowned the head with a soft brown wig and set it with large, innocent blue eyes, taken, one might think, from one of the Mitford sisters.

As I have indicated above, John was no ascetic. He was well-off and already a *bon vivant* though kept under stern parental discipline at home.

Some years later John joined a highly respectable London club of which one of his uncles was a member. In order to avoid recognition and a report to his home of his indulgences, he kept a false spade beard in the porter's lodge which he invariably donned before entry.

The Sutros inhabited a large mansion in St John's Wood, patrolled after dark by a night-watchman who sometimes embarrassed John in his late entries. Once John took into this house an Oxford friend, who lost the latch-key. Mrs Sutro would not go to bed until an emergency squad from Bramah had changed every lock in the house. None of his friends was ever invited to stay afterwards. Sometimes they turned up at North End Road in search of a bed, having been disappointed of accommodation at Hall Road. But we were entertained sumptuously at luncheon and dinner. It was there – not as described in *Brideshead Revisited* – that I first tasted plovers' eggs.

John is a lifelong friend, loyal, hospitable and above all humorous; a mimic of genius. In 1923 the telephone seemed an *outré* form of communication and it was John's custom to regale us with imaginary conversations on an imaginary instrument.

It can be said of John, as of no other man I know, that he has never wearied of a friend or quarrelled with one, but has continued year after year adding more and more to their company from both sexes and every nationality.

John is a Jew and it might have been supposed that he

would have indulged some resentment against Lady Mosley. In fact, after her release from prison, he was as ready to welcome her as were any of her friends.

He spoke in many voices. It was, indeed, rather rare for him to speak *in propria persona*. He is shortly to write his own book of reminiscences. I will not trespass on his territory except as far as it affects me, and that, I rejoice to say, is to a great extent.

The Oxford Railway Club, which he originated, has been rhapsodically described by Mr Harold Acton in his *Memoirs of an Aesthete*. As a sexagenarian I come late to autobiography. Many of my contemporaries have anticipated me. It would be otiose to recount in slightly different form anecdotes already so vividly told. But I still possess the menu of our first Railway Club dinner of November 28th, 1923. In later years, after we had gone down, our meetings became more elaborate and the membership wider so as to include friends of John's who had been at Cambridge or Sandhurst at the time of our formation. Chefs were then recruited from London restaurants and fine wines added to the fare. Silver cigarette-boxes were presented to astonished engine-drivers and reception committees met us at our destinations. But on that first evening we simply engaged a private dining-car on the Penzance-Aberdeen train, which passed through Oxford, stopped for half an hour at Leicester and took another private dining-car back to Oxford. We were content with the ordinary five shilling menu (seven courses in those days). On the return journey Harold's speech was the chief pleasure. Of the thirteen members who signed my menu (there must have been others, but neither John nor I can name them) I have seen only four in the last twenty-five years.

John was a genuine amateur of the railway system and knew his Bradshaw as my father and brother knew their Wisden, but for most of us it was merely an original way in which to spend a jovial evening. At that time Billy Clonmore (now the Earl of Wicklow) gave a supper party on the roof of the church of

St Peter's in the East. There was a club in Balliol named the *Hysteron-Proteron* whose members put themselves to great discomfort by living a day in reverse, getting up in evening dress, drinking whisky, smoking cigars and playing cards, then at ten o'clock dining backwards starting with savouries and ending with soup. A year or two later this craze – not that of the Hysteron-Proteron, but for finding bizarre venues for parties – came to London and was taken up by the newspapers who dubbed us 'the bright young people' and spoiled our fun. But in November 1923 it was all fresh and private. Nor were we all young. There was Dr Counsell with us, 'Doggins', who ran his own welfare service for undergraduates in the Broad, wore the tweed cloaks and rough silk shirts and ties of Hall Bros, and was permanent prompter at all O.U.D.S. performances; and the elderly and absurd lecturer in Tamil and Telegu, Sydney Roberts, who made himself much loved for no other reason than that after a life spent in conventional service in India he found enchantment in our extravagances.

The Railway Club was John's creation; it was also one of the many platforms on which Harold Acton, still in his first term, performed with inimitable zest.

He, too, has remained a lifelong friend. There are characters in my novels – 'Ambrose Silk', 'Anthony Blanch' – whom people to his annoyance and to mine, have attempted to identify with him. There are a few incidental similarities. The novelist does not come to his desk devoid of experience and memory. His raw material is compounded of all he has seen and done. But in neither of the characters mentioned did I attempt a portrait of Harold. Would I could do so now. His own *Memoirs* have performed that dangerous feat. He describes there how he descended on Oxford with a mission. He had already made a reputation at Eton and had a book of poems, *Aquarium*, accepted by a London publisher and in the press. He intended to stir us up and he succeeded abundantly.

Harold is as cosmopolitan in origin as Hubert Duggan, but he did not fret for female society. Slim and slightly oriental in appearance, talking with a lilt and resonance and in a peculiar vocabulary that derived equally from Naples, Chicago and Eton, he set out to demolish the traditional aesthetes who still survived here and there in the twilight of the 90's and also the simple-living, nature-loving, folk-singing, hiking, drab successors of the 'Georgian' poets. It is odd that he and I should have become friends, for my early tastes were somewhat of this kind. What, I think, we had in common was *gusto,* in the English use of the word; a zest for the variety and absurdity of the life opening to us; a veneration for (not the same) artists, a scorn for the bogus. He was always the leader; I, not always, the follower. His conspectus was enormously larger than mine. I was entirely insular. Indeed, at the age of nineteen I had never crossed the sea and I knew no modern language. Harold brought with him the air of the connoisseurs of Florence and the innovators of Paris, of Berenson and of Gertrude Stein, Magnasco and T. S. Eliot; above all of the three Sitwells who were the objects of his admiration and personal affection. While Mr Betjeman was still a schoolboy rubbing church brasses, Harold was collecting Victoriana. My preferences were then for Lovat Fraser (perhaps forgotten now; the illustrator and designer who carried on the manner of the 'Beggarstaff brothers') and for Eric Gill. Harold led me far away from Francis Crease to the baroque and the rococo and to the *Waste Land.* He was not then learned, as he has since become, but he was vividly alive to every literary and artistic fashion, exuberantly appreciative, punctilious, light and funny and energetic. He loved to shock and then to conciliate with exaggerated politeness. He was himself shocked and censorious at any breach of his elaborate and idosyncratic code of propriety. The one quality he despised, traditionally characteristic of aesthetic Oxford, was languor. He was a Catholic but no proselytizer; nor did he frequent the normal popish circles of the University, but it was, incongruously enough, at a meeting of the Newman Society, to which I had been taken by Esmé Howard (a New College friend, a cousin of my future wife's,

who died tragically young; a man who never set foot in the
Hypocrites) to hear Chesterton, that I first met him and, as
I have said, struck up, antithetical as we were in so many ways,
an immediate and lasting friendship. I was certainly a little
dazzled by his manifest superiorities of experience, but this
was never the source of condescension on his part or of envy
on mine. Among the 'offal' eaters at Hertford there was a
strikingly handsome 'hearty' for whom Harold conceived a
romantic attachment. It was the presence of this Adonis almost
daily in my rooms that drew him there, where neither the
company nor the fare was exactly to his taste. While we drank
beer he would sip water and gaze ardently at the inaccessible
young athlete.

Harold in return gave many luncheon parties in his rooms
in Meadow Building at which I quickly collected a new circle
of friends – many of them the Etonians whom I have mentioned
as driving mad and destroying the Hypocrites Club.

One of these was Robert Byron. He has been commemorated
by Professor David Talbot-Rice in the preface to the re-issue
of *The Road to Oxiana* and, more fully, by Mr Christopher Sykes
in *Four Studies in Loyalty*. The former treated him as a Byzan-
tinist; the latter attempted and achieved a full portrait. But
Christopher was more than two years his junior and did not
meet him before he had made himself known in the world. I
was his senior by more than a year. At the age of eighteen
Robert gave no discernible promise of the adventurous jour-
neys and the frantic craving for knowledge which obsessed his
later years. His name will recur in this narrative, for our paths
often crossed. Here I will attempt to display him as he was at
our first meeting. Then he was as insular as I – 'Down with
abroad', he used to shout when travel was mentioned – and
a good deal more ignorant. This ignorance was some advantage
to him because it gave him the constantly renewed enthusiasm
of discovery, even of quite well-known facts and spectacles.
I remember his baffled annoyance when he tried to introduce
to me as his own discovery one of my favourite books, E. M.

Forster's *Pharos and Pharillon*. 'But *how* do you know it? *Where* did you find it? *Who* told you about it?' He learned little at school or at the university and later was disposed to think that masters and dons had concealed from him for their own ends the information he subsequently acquired. Anything they had tried to teach him – the Classics and Shakespeare – he dismissed as an imposture. In later years he professed a respect for Fowler's *Modern English Usage*, but he never learned to write elegant or perfectly correct English. His talent was for narrative, the sharply observed scene, the pungent anecdote, the fugitive absurdity. Later his aspirations grew vastly wider, but at Oxford he was purely a clown and a very good one.

He was short, fleshy and ugly in a painfully ignominious way. His complexion was yellow. He had a marked resemblance, which he often exploited at fancy-dress parties, to Queen Victoria at the time of her jubilee. He dealt with his ill looks, as others have done, by making them grotesque. He affected loud tweeds, a deer-stalker hat, yellow gloves, horn-rimmed pince-nez, a cockney accent. He leered and scowled, screamed and snarled, fell into rages that were sometimes real and sometimes a charade – it was not easy to distinguish. Wherever he went he created a disturbance, falling down in the street in simulated epilepsy, yelling to passers-by from the back of a motor-car that he was being kidnapped. He contrasted in almost every way with the elegant and urbane Harold. Harold was rich and familiar with high international society; Robert was poor and determined not, Heaven knows, in any obsequious fashion, to force his way into the worlds of power and fashion; and he succeeded. Harold had spent all his life among works of art; they were quite strange to Robert and when he encountered them he was excited to irrational outbursts of adoration or reprobation; either: 'Why does no one know about this?' (when everyone who cared, did) or: 'Trash. Muck. Rubbish.' (of many established masterpieces). Harold sometimes became light-headed with wine. Robert in his cups was pugnacious, destructive and sottish, lapsing before the evening was out into an unlovely sleep. For all that he was much loved and, eventually, admired. I liked him and, until the fractious late 'thirties, when his violent opinions became, to me, intolerably repugnant, I greatly relished his company.

There was Billy Clonmore, a close friend of Robert's, whose extravagances were refined by a slightly antiquated habit of speech and infused with a Christian piety that was unique among us and lay hidden behind his stylish eccentricities. Billy was a reckless roof-climber and quick in a quarrel.

There was David Talbot-Rice who seemed to live a life of carefree pleasure but was secretly studious, so that he is now full of academic honours. He alone (with the exception of Edward Longford, who led a secluded life) courted an undergraduette, the clever Russian who became his wife.

Of those who have become writers the most illustrious is Mr Graham Greene. His life in Balliol was very private. I knew him very slightly in those years. I was never in his rooms or he in mine. In later years he has become my friend and Harold's and John Sutro's, but at Oxford he kept to his own, far from austere, set and held aloof from us.

Neither Graham nor I remember how we met. It was probably through my cousin, Claud Cockburn, who had been at school with him and came up, most inappropriately, to Keble in my second year. I had never seen him during the days I spent at Beechcroft with the Jacobses and I went dutifully to call with small expectation of finding anyone very agreeable, for I found most of my mother's family a dull lot. I met a tall, spectacled young man with the air of Buda-Pest rather than of Berkhamsted. His father had been there for the last two years on diplomatic business and Claud was already captivated by the absurdities of Central European affairs. He had not yet acceded to communism and seemed to have stepped from one of William Gerhardi's novels, to which in fact he introduced me. I introduced him to the Hypocrites, which he has described in his autobiography as a 'noisy, alcohol-soaked rat-warren by the river'. He was as noisy and alcohol-soaked as any of the rats and soon became a fast friend of Hamish, Christopher Hollis and all the 'offal'-eaters.

Mr Anthony Powell must be added to this list, not because of any intimacy I then enjoyed with him, but because of his later achievements. In reading his brilliant series of novels I have sometimes thought – and, indeed, have been so foolish as to state as much in a review – that the recurring seemingly haphazard conjunctions of human life, which comprise his theme, pass beyond plausibility. His hero's passage through youth and early manhood is continually recrossed in improbable circumstances by the same characters. After I had written the review expressing doubts of the authenticity of so many coincidences, I began to reflect on my own acquaintance with him and understood that his was genuine social realism. At Oxford we stood on friendly terms though barely in friendship. We have seldom met by arrangement and often there have been long periods when we never met at all. But this is a chart of our courses. Three years after going down, as I shall relate, I tried to learn cabinet-making at the L.C.C. school in Southampton Row. There in the same drawing-class I found Tony, who was studying typography. A little later, very hard up and seeking a commission to write a book, it was Tony who introduced me to my first publisher. When he married, it was to the sister of the girl with whom my first wife shared lodgings. During the latter part of the war he worked in the same department of the War Office as my brother-in-law and shared a house with him in Regent's Park. When he settled in the country he chose a house within a mile or two of Mells, with which I had formed close links. I suppose that in the looser society of the United States or in the tighter society of, say, France such fortuitous connections would be barely possible. It is one of Tony's achievements to record this interplay which, I think, is essentially English. I may add that I have been unable to identify as a portrait of any of our numerous common acquaintances a single character in Tony's opus. I remember Tony as a conventional, observant undergraduate, younger than his fellows, an amateur of genealogy and military uniforms.

I was not altogether surprised when Robert took to writing; Tony, Harold, Christopher Hollis, Peter Quennell and Douglas Woodruff were plainly headed in that direction. The dark horse of my generation was Mr Alfred Duggan. Little could have surprised me more forty, thirty or even twenty years ago than the revelation that Alfred was to become the industrious, prolific historical novelist who is honoured today. I have mentioned his younger brother, Hubert, who was a delicate dandy of the Regency. Alfred was a full-blooded rake of the Restoration. He was very rich then with the immediate disposal of a fortune greater than any of our contemporaries. He was, moreover, the stepson of the Chancellor of the University, Lord Curzon. This connection irked the authorities, who otherwise would have summarily sent him down. We were often drunk, Alfred almost always. He came up with a string of hunters; he kept an account at the Macpherson's garage for day- and night-chauffeurs. Whether in the saddle in the late mornings or at 'the 43' (Mrs Meyrick's night club in Gerrard Street) in the early mornings, Alfred was always tight; never violent, always carefully and correctly dressed, always polite, he lived in an alcoholic daze. The vultures of Balliol won what were for them great sums of money from him at cards. He paid punctiliously. When the card party broke up, Alfred would climb out of his window to his waiting car and be driven to London. In Gerrard Street he cheerfully signed whatever cheques were put before him and always honoured them.

He was, when I first met him, a professed communist. Brought up a Catholic he had at Eton made a formal recantation to the Archbishop of York who received him into the Church of England. Shortly afterwards he again recanted in favour of atheism. Lord Curzon discerned his quality. His memory was exceptionally retentive and in the shadowy years when he continued to drink very heavily and was seen sitting, apparently stupefied, turning the pages of an historical work in the library at Hackwood, his brain, like an electronic device, was in an inexplicable way storing up recondite information which became available when he heroically overcame this inherited disability.

He, too, will recur in this narrative. I write of him now as an undergraduate when at all his luncheon and dinner parties he had a ghostly place laid (often occupied) for anyone he might have invited when drunk and forgotten.

Cyril Connolly has not yet published an account of his university life. When he does so, I think he will express discontent. As he relates in *Enemies of Promise*, he had at school been an initiate of the esoteric culture of whose existence most Etonians are unaware. He had been much cosseted, as such initiates are, and this gave him a taste for the society of dons from whom he expected similar attentions. But dons look for accomplishment as well as for promise and Cyril never set seriously to work. He found gentle friendliness in Sligger Urquhart, but neither intellectual stimulus nor flattery. (Sir) Maurice Bowra, newly elected Fellow of Wadham, was his chief new acquisition. I knew Cyril then, but cannot claim him as a crony. He was, and is, temperate and, as I have mentioned, I then looked on hard drinking as the pledge of fellowship. Cyril was too fastidious for the rough company I kept.

He was suffering, I think he will tell us, from poverty. The differences of pocket money at school are negligible. At the university he found himself on an inequality of expenditure with his old friends from Pop. This never worried a man in precisely the same position, Christopher Hollis, but Cyril was haunted by an Anglo-Irish ghost of dandyism which he finally exorcised some years later by briefly identifying himself with Montparnasse and Barcelona. Balliol was ill-suited to his mood; it was not a luxurious college; next only to Keble it was the least luxurious. The architecture is dismal. Cyril would have been happy in Peckwater with an allowance of £750 a year. In Balliol, with modest means, he felt a stranger – or so

I believe. When he comes to give his own account, I may find myself quite at fault. As I have said, I did not then know him well. He and Maurice Bowra were both acquaintances who became friends after I attracted some attention as a novelist.

To give a picture of my generation I must name three whom I did not greatly like but whom, in my innocence, I was proud to know.

Basil Murray was a satanic young man, strange offspring of puritan parents, Gilbert Murray the Professor of Greek and Lady Mary Howard (of the Carlisle branch of the family). I use 'satanic' deliberately. There were times when he seemed possessed by a devil of mischief. There is a character derived from him in one of Nancy Mitford's early, out-of-print novels. He was highly intelligent. Too flashy and adventurous for the literary *élite* who formed a gentle, close set – Anthony Asquith, Eddy Sackville-West, Jack McDougall, Kenneth Clark, David Cecil – he was in revolt against their assumptions of superiority and founded, in imitation of Cambridge, a group of 'Apostles'; twelve men chosen by him for their brains not, as in their prototype, for moral earnestness. Christopher Hollis was a member; not I. None of them took the project seriously and it soon came to nothing.

Mr Peter Rodd had the sulky, arrogant looks of the young Rimbaud. As an ambassador's son he was highly cosmopolitan, but without any taste for conventional high society. Nor had he any artistic interests. He was a man of action with his thoughts on the high seas and the desert. Some readers have professed to recognize in the character 'Basil Seal' who appears in some of my novels a combination of Basil and Peter.

The third man was someone very different and it is true that the characters in my novels often wrongly identified with Harold Acton were to a great extent drawn from him. He was called Brian Howard, the patronymic being the capricious choice of his father, who was reputedly born Gassaway. I have no doubt that before we are all dead someone, not I, will write a memoir of Brian. He is a rich source of anecdote. All that has appeared so far is Cyril Connolly's *From Oscar to Stalin* (represented under the title *Where Engels fears to Tread*), a brilliant pasquinade of 1937 which, incidentally, provides a leper's squint into Cyril's own life as an undergraduate. Brian, when he came up, determined to eschew the arts and to pose as a sportsman. He never got into the Bullingdon, but he charged gallantly at the fences in the Grind. More than this, in the intensely snobbish era which immediately succeeded my own, he contrived to make himself more than the entertainer, the animator, almost the arbiter, of the easy-going aristocrats whom he set himself to reform in his romantic model, like the youthful D'Israeli inspiring 'Young England'. 'Put your trust in the Lords' was the motto on the banner in his rooms on his birthday and there are many placid peers today who may ascribe most of their youthful fun to Brian. Sometimes he embarrassed them, as when Trinity hearties broke up a party he was at and impelled the guests to the gate, he threatened: 'We shall tell our fathers to raise your rents and evict you.' At such moments I think he really believed that Gassaway was a Whig magnate. He was an incorrigible homosexual, subject to a succession of delusions, and died by suicide at the time when he at last became rich. He will reappear later in these pages. At the age of nineteen he had dash and insolence, a gift of invective and repartee far more brilliant than Robert's, a kind of ferocity of elegance that belonged to the romantic era of a century before our own. Mad, bad and dangerous to know.

The quality which these three had in common was insolence, a determination to treat with the world only on their own terms. In middle age their panache became draggled, but they never lost their self-confidence.

5

One day, a decade later, I was at Madresfield, a house which successive owners have liberally adorned with inscriptions. Maimie Lygon and I stood by a fountain in the garden on which is written: 'That day is wasted on which one has not laughed', and she remarked: 'Well, you and I have never wasted a day, have we?'

It would be false to represent my undergraduate life as one of uninterrupted mirth. There were quarrels and crapulosities and transient bouts of the despair of adolescence (in one of which, as I have recorded, I asked my father to remove me to an art school). There were also nagging debts.

The reader may well have wondered during the foregoing pages how I was able to afford to live the life I described. I could not afford it. My scholarship was worth a hundred pounds a year. My allowance from my father was nominally two hundred pounds augmented by a further fifty in birthday and Christmas presents and in response to urgent appeals. This was the average expenditure of undergraduates of my time, but I greatly exceeded it. My only economy was during the vacations. I never went abroad, but spent my time with Hamish at my home or at his. During term I spent lavishly and was always short of ready money. The Old Bank was not as accommodating to me as it has since become; an overdraft of a few pounds brought the sharp warning that no further cheques would be honoured. The Oxford tradesmen were more liberal. There was no need to pay on the nail for clothes, books, tobacco or wine. College battels – the terminal bills for rooms, coal, tuition, subscriptions and so forth, and for food and drink ordered in college – had to be paid promptly and usually engorged the greater part of my allowance. Even the shops showed restlessness after a year and had to be appeased in the traditional way by further orders. For pocket money, the need of which increased as I took to frequenting the George, a wretched restaurant which was the fashion, I made a modest income by contributing to the *Isis*, by designing book-wrappers for Chapman and Hall and book-plates for various acquaintances. My mother had a little money of her own. I drew on that. My brother was good for an occasional fiver. But I contracted larger loans. I did not go to my richer friends for these. Alfred Duggan would certainly have signed a cheque for almost any amount at any time, but delicacy forbade my soliciting him. I turned instead to my poorer cronies. When at the age of twenty-one Terence came into control of his patrimony I borrowed a hundred pounds. He gave it to me in a single note (the only one hundred pound note I have ever handled) and I carried it rejoicing down the High from his bank to mine. His communist cousin made an attempt to relieve me of half of it, but I evaded him. I paid Terence five pounds a year for several years until I was able to make good his capital investment. I made a similar arrangement with another Hertford man. But little of these (at the time and in the circumstances) large subventions went to settle my bills. I went down owing about two hundred pounds and during the next three years continued to run accounts in Oxford while starting others in London, and was not completely solvent and independent for four years. 'Embarrassment' would not be the right term for my financial position. I did not fret much or often about this condition, but found it an occasional source of gloom, annoyance and frustration.

The only serious regret of my Oxford life is the amount of time which I wasted on my books in my last term. Had I known I was to get a third, I would readily have settled for a fourth. As it was I entertained confident hopes of a second and spent many hours a day and some in the evening attempting to master the neglected texts. Christopher Hollis, a Brackenbury scholar, did the same with the same result. I think that in my time, and for some years after, the majority of Brackenbury scholars took thirds. The magic of F. E. Smith failed to work for us.

How much I could have enjoyed that last summer had it not been for the delusion of the Schools! As it was I looked forward to a ninth term, which, having come up in a by-term, I was obliged to keep in order to qualify for a degree, of pure pleasure. Hugh Lygon and I had engaged digs together in Merton Street next door to the tennis-court. One term's comparative seclusion, I thought, would be amply compensated. I was proved wrong.

I was uneasily aware as I left the Examination Schools that the questions had been rather inconvenient. I did not even then despair. Cruttwell and my other tutor gave a dinner party for the history candidates at which I arrived tipsy and further alienated their sympathies by attempting, later, to sing a Negro spiritual.

On my last night as an undergraduate I was at a large party in Balliol from which I was lowered on a rope by Patrick Balfour at 1 a.m. and climbed back into Hertford from the garden of All Souls.

My *viva* was in the last batch at the end of July. Hamish and I stayed at the Abingdon Arms at Beckley. I walked into Oxford in my subfusc suit and white tie, collected my gown in college and presented myself at the Schools. My questions were purely perfunctory. Next day the class-list was posted and Hamish and I set off for Ireland. Cruttwell's valedictory letter reached me at a house near Cappoquin in County Waterford.

I cannot say [he wrote] that your Third does you anything but discredit: especially as it was not even a good one; and it is always at least foolish to allow oneself to be given an inappropriate intellectual label. I hope that you will soon settle in some sphere where you will give your intellect a better chance than in the History School.

My father decided that a Third Class B.A. was not worth the time and expense of going up for a further term. The memory of his own failure in the Schools tempered his reproaches and he entered me at an art school for the coming autumn.

Chapter Nine

IN WHICH OUR HERO'S FORTUNES
FALL VERY LOW

ON THE DAY I went down from Oxford I resumed my diary
and kept it in a desultory way for the next two years. It reveals
a warmer and altogether more likeable character than its predecessor. The priggishness has disappeared and with it most
of the malice. Nevertheless it makes dismal reading, for, in
contrast to the tale of success at Lancing, it comprises a record
of continuous failure.

In the autumn and early winter of 1924 and again in the
same seasons of 1926 I spent longer at home than I had done
since 1917. During this period my father passed his sixtieth
birthday. The affairs of Chapman and Hall were going badly
and such meagre profits as were made came not from my
father's authors but from the scientific books in which he had
no interest. The intermittent but frequent presence of a dissi-
pated and not always respectful spendthrift disturbed the
tranquillity of the home to which he always looked for refuge.
My coming of age that first October was not celebrated.

That first autumn Terence produced a cinema film using our
garden for most of the scenes. The story was a fantasy of the
attempts of Sligger Urquhart to convert the king to Roman
Catholicism. Elmley, John Sutro and I were the leading actors.
The heroine was Elsa Lanchester (Mrs Charles Laughton), a
lithe, red-headed girl of precisely my own age, who was not
then a professional actress but managed with Harold Scott an
inexpensive and highly enterprising cabaret in Charlotte Street
called *The Cave of Harmony*. My father fully appreciated the

fun of our venture, so much like the private theatricals of his own youth; he delighted to find the cast at his table and when the film was shown him took particular satisfaction in recognising his own possessions. 'That's my chair' . . . 'Take care you don't break that decanter.' But as the leaves fell and the winter brought its attacks of asthma and bronchitis, gloom settled in the house. He had lately acquired a wireless set, and contrary to modern domestic conventions, it was he who always wished to hear it, I to turn it off.

The art school I had chosen was Heatherley's, then in Newman Street, which advertised itself as 'a Paris Studio in London'. It had a long history and an interesting list of former students, mostly literary men rather than painters. The Tate Gallery displays Samuel Butler's admirable picture of the original Mr Heatherley articulating a skeleton. The place was consciously picturesque, housing a variety of armour, historical costumes and lay figures which I never saw put to use. Its attraction for me was that students started at once in the life-school without the preliminary discipline of the 'antique' – plaster casts – which was still imposed in more professional institutions.

The great majority of the students were respectable girls who, like myself, were believed at home to be 'artistic'. The few men had ambitions of commercial draughtsmanship. No one seriously aspired to High Art. There was little of the comradeship and none of the high jinks I had expected. The tuition was negligible. The proprietor had a white beard, a very red nose and a hand which trembled so grievously that the charcoal was invariably shattered when he attempted a demonstration. The studio merely provided an opportunity for drawing. We sat on 'donkeys' ranged round the platform on which a model stood in the traditional attitudes. In the mornings the pose was constant for a week. In the afternoons there was a succession of ten-minute poses which we sketched in pencil. One afternoon a week was devoted to a 'composition class' when we were given a subject, usually some abstract idea such as 'conflict'. We then worked from the imagination and were criticised for 'rhythm', 'chiaroscuro' and so on. No formal perspective was taught.

For three or four weeks I worked conscientiously, setting out early in the morning for the Hampstead tube-station along the familiar path I had followed to Heath Mount and returning in the dusk. To give interest to my walk I took to placing pennies on walls and posts along the way and collecting those which remained (usually the total number) on my return. Tony Bushell was working near by at the Royal Academy of Dramatic Art and we lunched together, as we had done at Hertford, on cheese and beer in a public house in the Tottenham Court Road.

As a result of the exercises in the studio my eye grew sharpened and my hand more responsive until my drawings were by no means the worst in the class; but boredom soon overcame me. I enjoyed making an agreeable arrangement of line and shadow on the paper, but I was totally lacking in that obsession with solid form, the zeal for probing the structure of anatomy and for relating to one another the recessions of planes, which alone could make the long hours before the models exciting. In the first three mornings of every week I had completed my charcoal study and for the following two I merely fiddled, sketching in the margins various aspects of the hands and feet (sadly misshapen appendages which did not approach the classical perfection of Trilby's). The ascetic régime I had planned for myself became irksome.

Hamish had wandered off into Africa. I began to frequent the Café Royal in the evenings. My brother Alec introduced me to a bohemian world among whom I found cronies. My name was not on the lists of any of the conventional hostesses. No engraved cards summoned me to the thriving world of Pont Street. Most of the parties I attended were impromptu or assembled at very short notice by word of mouth. There was Mary Butts, a genial, voluptuous lady of the *avant-garde* who wrote short stories and at the time consorted with a man who had been in Alistair Crowley's black-magical circle at Cefalu. She had been married once in the inner circle of Montparnasse.

Now she had a large house in Belsize Park which served as lodging for a shifting community of mostly unmarried couples. Parties were frequent there. I have a memory of Tony Bushell sitting on the stairs eating her face-cream and of a garden full of interlocked couples.

There was also a Hindoo lady in Regent's Park, the daughter of a rajah, so emancipated as to be *déclassée* – but still preserving tenuous links with minor royalty. Women sometimes resorted to fisticuffs in her house.

There was also Gwen Otter in Tedworth Square, an inexhaustibly hospitable, unmarried woman of middle age and slightly reduced means, with the appearance of a Red Indian. Her drawing-room had black walls and a gold ceiling and piles of tasselled cushions in the style of the earlier Russian Ballet. She could not bear solitude and her house was always full, spongers mixing indifferently with well-known figures of the stage and the arts. She never sought celebrities. The best recommendation to her salon was not that everyone asked someone out but that few did.

Evenings spent in this company and in the nondescript assemblies that met most evenings at bottle-parties in various unfashionable quarters rendered me as unfit to work as my instructor was to teach, but I went to them and, short of money for a taxi, often slept on a sofa or walked home in the early morning from Chelsea or Kensington. But it was the lure of Oxford, still full of friends, which finally made me despair of myself at Heatherley's.

I can date my decline accurately. On 10th November I went for the week-end to Mrs Lennox in Warwickshire. On Sunday John Sutro came over from Oxford and invited me to lunch next day with him in his digs in Beaumont Street. That evening I recorded in my diary: 'I am more than half inclined to accept.' I did so.

Monday Nov 12th I went to Oxford and contrary to my intentions stayed the night. John's party consisted of Harold Acton, Mark Ogilvie-Grant, Hugh Lygon, Robert Byron, Arden Hilliard and Richard Pares. My arrival had been kept a close secret [and I was greeted with an enthusiasm that proved my undoing]. After luncheon which was hot lobster, partridges and plum pudding, sherry, mulled claret and a strange rum-like liqueur [something, I think, which John had discovered at Wembley Exhibition] I left Hugh and John drinking and went to a tea party at M.O-G's and then to the New Reform where I found Terence and Elmley drinking beer. I drank with them and went to dinner with Robert Byron in Merton Hall. I found Billy [Clonmore] and after dinner went to the rooms of a hunting man called Reynolds and drank beer. I then got a message from the O.U.D.S. from Hugh and John to come immediately to Banbury. I went to the station but could not persuade them to abandon the expedition and went to the Nag's Head where I had arranged to meet Elmley. Claud Cockburn turned up with mad Y-L and a beastly man with an eye glass all very drunk. When we were turned out we went to the old Hypocrites rooms for a drinking of whisky and a performance of Terence's film. After about this stage of the evening my recollections became blurred. I got a sword from somewhere and got into Balliol somehow and was let out of a window at sometime having mocked Tony Powell. When I got back to Beaumont Street I found that there had been a fire in John's rooms. Next morning I drank beer with Hugh and port with Preters and gin with Gyles Isham, lunched with Hugh and Desmond Harmsworth. Harold and Billy saw me off at the station feeling woefully tired.

It was nearly five months since I had seen any of these friends. They fêted me spontaneously in a way to rekindle all my love of Oxford. My later appearances were less of a novelty. Instead of being an unexpected and honoured guest I found myself assuming the common status of those who cannot at once sever the cord uniting them to the university and haunt it for years to come. I still dressed as an undergraduate. There was a new fashion that term – high-necked jumpers and broad trousers – and I adopted it. I returned every week-end that term and found a new friend who had just come up to Magdalen, a lean, dark, singular man named Henry Yorke who was later to dazzle us with his series of novels published under the name of Henry Green.

It was now my turn to give dinner parties and luncheons, to seek rather than to be sought, and these expeditions added to my debts. They also rendered me at the beginning of each week increasingly listless in the drudgery of the life-class. When we closed for the Christmas vacation I signed off at Heatherley's.

Hamish and I had often projected a private printing press on which we hoped to produce books which I should decorate and sometimes write. There were many such in the country then producing works which varied from the precise and beautiful to the slipshod and pretentious. Studying some samples at an exhibition I was struck by the small volumes of a one-man press in Sussex. This lonely artificer not only set type and decorated his pages with post-Pre Raphaelite designs in black and white but also reproduced script in delicate poly-chrome from plates on which the pale colours stood out in thick, opaque pigment more like paint than ink. The matter printed comprised unremarkable Georgian nature-poetry and little precious essays. I cannot now look at them without revulsion, but at that time, in the aftermath of debauchery, these innocent pages awoke tender memories of afternoons at Lychpole and recalled me to the precepts of Mr Crease which I supposed had been exorcized under the vigorous influence of Harold Acton. I wrote to this printer and proposed myself as an apprentice. He promptly accepted me unseen. My father, ever ready to forward any project which promised some settled interest, paid him £25. I went down on a preliminary visit and was not exhilarated by what I found. I had expected something like the austere and secluded St Dominic's Press at Ditchling, but the cottage which gave the press its romantic name was a modern villa very near Bognor. The younger son of the house, with whom I walked for a morning through damp lanes in search of lodgings, confided in me his ambition to become a fashion-designer. Worse than this the secret process used to reproduce the plates which had momentarily fascinated me proved to be entirely dependent on photography; the script

and the drawings were sent to a commercial firm who transferred them in intaglio to zinc sheets which were then inked
by hand and pulled in the press. It was not the dedicated world
of the handcraftsmen to which I aspired.

I returned to North End Road with the matter of my
apprenticeship unsettled and there was confronted by the
seasonal sheaf of bills and the knowledge that I had issued some
post-dated cheques which would fall due in the new year. In
this predicament I suggested a settlement to my father; he
should pay my debts, I would forgo my allowance and hence-
forth earn my own living.

There was only one profession open to a man of my qualifi-
cations. However incomplete one's education, however dissolute one's habits, however few the respectable guarantors
whom one could quote, the private schools lay open to anyone
who spoke without an accent and had been through the conventional routine of public school and university. I called at a
scholastic agency and received some twenty or thirty 'private
and confidential notices of vacancies': 'Reply promptly but
carefully, enclosing photograph, if considered desirable, and
copies of testimonials, mentioning that you have heard of the
vacancy through us.'

The idea of myself as a schoolmaster seemed wholly absurd,
but I recalled some of the curious figures who had passed
through Heath Mount and set to work composing applications.
I had no testimonials. I had forgotten most of my Greek; my
French and mathematics were negligible, I was unable to
present myself as a cricket-coach. English history was not a
subject of primary importance for public school common
entrance or scholarships. But, as the scholastic agent remarked,
few headmasters were able to find men with all the qualities
they demanded and with desperate levity I offered to teach
anything which anyone might require. After a week I was
summoned by telegram to an hotel in Marylebone to interview
Mr Vanhomrigh, the proprietor of a school very far away on
the coast of Flintshire. He was a tall, pleasant man of late

middle age. The only question he asked was whether I possessed a dinner-jacket. When the parents of Irish boys came to visit them, such a garment was required. Reassured on that point he engaged me at £50 a term. His school, he remarked, was so remote that there was no possibility of spending anything during term. Did I smoke? That was a pity, as tobacco was the only amenity not provided. It would eat into my savings which otherwise should be intact at Easter to supply me during my well-earned holiday. I wrote to tell the Sussex printer that I should not be coming to him. He insisted that my father must forfeit the sum that had been advanced, with the irrefutable argument that it was already spent.

I had no sooner accepted this post than Hamish turned up unannounced at my home. He had contracted malaria in East Africa, run short of money and returned third class, completing the journey across Europe without eating. He was unshaven, unwashed, without luggage, wearing a ready-made French overcoat over stained tropical ducks. We were of much the same build; he re-equipped himself from my wardrobe and for some days we went revelling in London together.

He still had the intention of setting up as a printer, accepted without reproach my temporary defection from the arts and proposed to live for a time at his home and to apprentice himself to Mr Newdigate at the neighbouring Shakespeare Head Press at Stratford-on-Avon. His return made my imminent departure for Flintshire seem a more bitter exile and there was another, stronger influence to make me regret it. In the course of the autumn I had fallen in love. I had in fact fallen in love with an entire family and, rather as Mr E. M. Forster describes in *Howard's End*, had focused the sentiment upon the only appropriate member, an eighteen-year-old daughter. I lacked both the experience and force of purpose to prosecute a real courtship. In less than a year our relationship became one of intimate friendship, doting but unaspiring on my part, astringent on hers.

Her name was Olivia Plunket Greene. Her younger brother,

David, had come up to Oxford in my last year, six foot seven inches tall, a languid dandy devoted to all that was fashionable. We had met from time to time, but lived in different sets. Her elder brother, Richard, had been at the Royal College of Music. I came to know him during my last term when he took over the lease of the old Hypocrites' rooms in St Aldate's. He was more piratical in appearance, sometimes wearing ear-rings, a good man with a boat, a heavy smoker of dark, strong tobacco, tinged, as were his siblings, with melancholy, but also infused with a succession of wild, obsessive enthusiasms. He brought to the purchase of a pipe or a necktie the concentration of a collector. During the next few years I saw him become a connoisseur of wine, a racing motorist, an exponent of the latest jazz, the author of a detective-novel. To each new hobby he brought the infectious absorption of an adolescent. He was never boring about his monomanias; instead he made them amusing for us all.

When I first met him he was in the dumps; unhappy in love, not in the inability to engage the affections of the clever and charming girl who eventually became his wife, but in his prospects of marriage, for he had no money and no job and her parents demurred at the engagement.

I find it very difficult to describe Olivia as I first knew her. Harold Acton in his *Memoirs of an Aesthete* mentions only 'minute pursed lips and great goo-goo eyes'; an inadequate version. She died unmarried in early middle age, having spent the last twenty years of her life in a remote cottage with her mother, seeing practically no one else. At the age of eighteen she combined the elegance of David with the concentration of Richard; her interests were narrower than his but more intense. A book, a play, a film, a ballet, a new, and usually deleterious friend, a public injustice, generally known and generally accepted, but suddenly discovered by Olivia, would totally engage her for a time; these crazes were mitigated by a peculiar fastidiousness, which did not prevent her from saying and doing outrageous things, but preserved her essential delicacy quite intact; also by shyness which made her unwilling to make any friends save those who were attracted by her and forced their way into her confidence. She nagged and bullied at times, she suffered from morbid self-consciousness, she was incapable of the ordinary arts and efforts of pleasing and was generally incapable of any kind of ostentation; a little crazy; truth-loving and in the end holy.

The parents of this family lived apart. I used sometimes to see the father at the Savile Club. He was a very handsome Irishman, a singer and professor of music and son of the Mrs Greene whose children's books, particularly *Cushions and Corners*, were a delight of my childhood. Their mother, Gwen, was in early middle age when I first met her, retaining without artifice the grace of youth. As the daughter of Sir Hubert Parry she had grown up among the 'Souls' in the heart of late Victorian musical and artistic society; until her marriage she had devoted herself to the violin. More important, she was the favourite and devoted niece (by his marriage to her aunt) of the theologian Baron von Hügel. She was not yet a Catholic and her uncle, who in youth had been in danger of condemnation as a Modernist, did not specifically urge her to become one. Instead he wrote her the spiritual letters which she edited for publication in 1928. The baron died at the time when I first became Gwen's friend. His name recurred often, but I did not then at all appreciate the greatness of her loss or the seed of mysticism he had cultivated in her. I merely knew in a vague way that she was 'religious'; a proclivity then shared by none of her family. What struck me most in her at that time was her humour and sympathy. Her children were devoted to her and she lived with them and their friends on terms of serene equality. There was no sense of the division of a generation such as I felt with my own parents and, *a fortiori*, with Hamish's or John Sutro's. I say 'serene', but in sharing their lives she suffered with them in all their intricate problems and misfortunes; suffered indeed more than they did. The serenity, I now recognise, came from her hidden life of prayer. I have met one or two others since with this rare quality. At the age of twenty-one I merely accepted her with the same incurious enjoyment as my contemporaries afforded.

Gwen's seemingly easy love of the young was something consciously sought and achieved. Some years after I first came to know her she wrote in her book about her father and uncle, *Two Witnesses*: 'We look at old people humbly wondering how we may escape where they so obviously fail . . . we long to avoid the judging mind. . . . Youth and age *are* separated, we cannot be as we once were; but we want to get closer to youth again, not to underline what separates . . . We have to make up, as older people, for the daring of youth's hope, for their radiant generosity, their trusting love. Once that same hope filled our every day. We want to live truly in a *young* world . . . let us reflect how terrible would be an old persons' world.'

I do not know that I ever offered her much daring hope or radiant generosity. Trusting love I certainly gave her.

The Plunket Greenes were not well off. Olivia had not been 'brought out' in the conventional way, but chose her own circle from among her relations and the friends of her brothers. It was a contradiction in the character of Gwen and Olivia that they were continually changing house – five times, I think, in the ten years during which I was practically a member of the family. When I first knew them they lived in Holland Park in a terrace now dissolute, then pleasantly secluded. From there they moved to a noisy flat in Mayfair, then to South Kensington, then to Battersea, then to St John's Wood. It was an expensive habit for people of slender means, even when the changes were prompted by the intention of economising.

Richard Plunket Greene was in much the same workless and penurious condition as I during that winter, aggravated in his case by the longing to marry. He, too, decided to put in time as a private schoolmaster. It was his example which fortified me to that desperate expedient. There was no question of Olivia marrying me, but my infatuation and her interest were at their height and I was just beginning to penetrate her reserve, when I set off disconsolately for Flintshire.

It would have suited my mood if the school to which I consigned myself had been one of those wholly disreputable institutions in which the country abounded. Instead I found it depressingly well conducted. There were, of course, eccentrics – monsters even – in the masters' common-room, but the boys were healthy, happy, well-fed and well enough taught to pass into the public schools of their choice. Half came from Ireland, half from the industrial north and they conformed precisely to traditional form. The Irish boys, children of the English and Scotch occupation, were volatile, good-looking, courageous, impudent; the Lancashire boys stodgy, plodding, cautious, mark-seeking; the Irish the more engaging, the English the more submissive. As the question of the dinner-jacket had suggested, the Irish were held in greater esteem by the head-master – or rather by his wife, who in these matters dictated the taste. To an uncertain young schoolmaster uncertain of his authority the progeny of the industrial north were preferable.

Not all the boys belonged to these categories. There was a carriageful at Euston, recognizable by their red caps, whom I was charged to take care of. At first they were subdued and ate large quantities of sweets. After an hour or two they cheered up while I became more despondent. Fellow passengers watched me with sympathy as I sat with them in the dining-car giving them ginger beer. I felt as convicts, if men of delicate sensibility, must feel when they are moved from one prison to another shackled to their escorts; a spectacle of warning. None of the little boys was sick. As they recovered from the pangs of leaving home, they began to question me about my proficiency at games. I had forgotten the example of Heath Mount that a schoolmaster can only commend himself by boasting. It was plain by the time we reached Chester that I had made a feeble impression. There we were joined by other boys, the Manchester contingent, who distracted their attention.

Eventually we reached our station on a lonely stretch of the coast between Rhyl and Colwyn Bay where the train stopped for our convenience. There was one very small taxi which I took. The boys had to walk. Each had a bag. 'Oh, sir, will you take my bag? Jolly decent of you, sir.' Some thirty pieces of various sizes were thrown in, at my feet and on my lap, piled up round me so high as to obscure the windows. Should I have refused to accept them? It seemed churlish to do so. It also seemed less than magisterial to arrive buried in hand-luggage. That is how I arrived. My doubt was resolved by the Headmaster's wife, who greeted me on her doorstep. 'The boys know they must carry their own bags. You should not have let them do that to you, Mr Waugh.' She regarded me with aversion and added: 'There is a telegram for you. I hope you can understand it. I certainly cannot.' She handed me the message she had taken down on the telephone. It was from Hugh Lygon and John Sutro and read: *'On, Evelyn, on.'*

I was destined never to earn the affection or esteem of this powerful lady. She it was who supervised the kitchen and the sick-room, nicely discriminated between the social status of the parents and, in fact, made the school the prosperous concern it was. The only department in which she was not dominant was the choice of assistant masters. Once her husband had found them, she took them in charge. He knew how hard they were to find; she knew how manifestly they lacked the requisite qualities. She was a woman entirely strange to my experience whose counterpart, when I took to travel, I was to meet in many imperial stations – the memsahib boss of distant communities of English exiles. The nearest I came to her favour was when, a month after my arrival, Mrs Lennox and Hamish drove to visit me. They came in a large new motor car and were markedly the social superiors of even the most respected Irish parent. I was in school when they rang her bell. Two minutes in her parlour convinced her of their high position. 'Some *very* nice friends have called for you, Mr Waugh,' she announced. 'I am sure Mr Vanhomrigh will excuse you from all duties while they are in the neighbourhood.'

But I was from the first an obvious dud. The Lennoxes, she assumed, were on an errand of mercy, as indeed they were. She had sources of information that confirmed her first, accurate estimate. I had never attempted to exercise authority. I had never written on a blackboard. I had never carved a joint – one of the most arduous duties. I used to stand at the head of my table desperately hacking while the plates for second helpings piled up before I had finished the first.

I do not know quite what Mrs Vanhomrigh hoped to get as her subalterns. In my way I was not, I think, much more or much less a dud than my colleagues; but she picked me out as one of her husband's least happy appointments and did not dissemble her antipathy any better than had Cruttwell.

But I anticipate. I have left myself, ignominiously emergent from a precipitation of bags, at the front door of the house where I was to spend two dismal terms.

When later I came to write a novel which introduced a private school in North Wales, I lavishly embellished the place with castellations. This was not the aspect of the buildings which awaited me on that dread afternoon. They were modern in structure, well kept but haphazard in plan. They lay at the summit of a steep road and themselves prolonged the ascent up the hillside so that, inside, one continually climbed staircases covered with highly polished linoleum, always to find oneself on a ground floor. Mrs Vanhomrigh (pronounced by those who sought her goodwill 'Vanummery') had, on one side of the hall, a little drawing-room, very well kept, clean as an operating theatre, as encumbered with ornaments as that of a matron of fifty years her seniority. There were few flowers at this season – in the summer the place was fragrant as an American 'funeral-parlour' – but much silver of the kind seen in the windows of Regent Street, designed for presentation; Mr Vanhomrigh's pledges of love, perhaps, or the gifts of parents whose doltish sons had got through Common Entrance. All shone bright as the linoleum. It was here she led me and with long, keen experience judged me and condemned me.

I suppose that, like all fallen humanity, she nurtured an unattainable ideal – a *prince lointain* – whom she would get for fifty or sixty pounds a term. She cannot have hoped for any-one very learned or very accomplished. To whom, I wonder, did she aspire? To someone twenty-five years old, in appear-ance a drawing by C. E. Brock in *Punch*, in character a hero from the novels of Ian Hay, who had only just failed for his blue at cricket and hockey; a bad second in Maths? A man, perhaps, dedicated to the Church – the son of a Rural Dean – who had decided on a more sporting life; a man with a pure, strong sympathy for little boys, who would one day marry a wife like herself and set up on his own, modelling his school on her precepts, taking the boys who were not quite up to her stan-dards? She may have hoped for this. She did not find him in me and her perennial disappointment was as bitter as when she first suffered it.

Except to her sharp eye and to the eyes of my fellow travel-lers from Euston, my inadequacy was not immediately apparent, for term began in a leisurely way. Mr Vanhomrigh had none of the vivacity of Mr Grenfell. He procrastinated and he improvised and it was several days before I found myself actually in charge of a form. During that happy period I sat in the common-room and engraved a book plate for Olivia. I also wrote some pages of a novel I had begun. I remember only that it was named *The Temple at Thatch* and concerned an under-graduate who inherited a property of which nothing was left except an eighteenth-century classical folly where he set up house and, I think, practised black magic.

Every night of his life, my father told me, he dreamed that he was back at Sherborne as a new boy. For some years I was haunted by the dream that I was back at Mr Vanhomrigh's. I had no strong, pure sympathy for little boys nor they for me. 'In charge of a form' is not an accurate expression. 'Con-fronted by' it or 'exposed to' it would be better. I was appointed to take the eldest in history, the younger in Latin and Greek. The latter I kept in subjugation, finding positive relish in making their lessons as tedious as the subject (very easily) allowed; the former were disorderly. I never fully succeeded in keeping them quiet. One of my major defeats was when I cried wrathfully to a moon-faced, vacuous creature: 'Are you deaf, boy?' to which all his fellows replied: 'Yes, sir, he is.' And he was.

The best way, I found, was to talk myself, without giving my pupils the opportunity to 'participate', as the liturgical jargon terms it. Memories of the History Sixth at Lancing and of the few lectures I had attended at Oxford, lent me words. One morning, early in my career, Mr Vanhomrigh paid a surprise visit to my form and sat at the back listening while I discoursed on the financial embarrassments of Charles I. I was quite eloquent about the principle that 'the king must live of his own', about the alienation of crown lands by Elizabeth and James, the feudal dues, the decline in the value of silver. In the presence of Mr Vanhomrigh the boys were unusually silent. Afterwards he called me to his study and said: 'I was deeply impressed by your lecture, *deeply*. But, you know, it was far over their heads. Also I noticed you constantly referred to "Stafford". I have always called him "Strafford".'

I no longer dream of those humiliations. Time has healed the scars even of one ghastly afternoon when one of my colleagues and I decided to take horse exercise. A groom brought out mounts from a neighbouring livery-stable. He asked me about my previous experience and, with disastrous candour, I admitted that I had not ridden anything since a child's pony at Midsomer Norton. Concern for the safety of his horse (not for mine) made him insist on attaching me to a leading-rein and it was in this contemptible situation that I was met by all the school returning from football.

I did not aspire to popularity. How far below it I stood, was evident on the afternoons when it was my duty to take those not otherwise employed for a walk. These excursions began in a crocodile. In the hills they broke up until reassembled, but, starting on the march, it was the custom to compete

for the privilege of walking with the master in charge. 'Can I
have a side, sir?' 'I asked first, sir.' 'He had a side last week.'

No one asked me for 'a side' and I strode lonely and silent
at the head of the odious little column.

On the other hand I was cheerfully accepted in the common-
room. We were a rum lot united like defeated soldiers in the
recognition of our common base fate. One, I remember, was
taking correspondence lessons in singing and made a frightful
row in chapel. The second master, a stern Scotchman, a new-
comer like myself but deeply experienced in the trade, disconcerted Mr Vanhomrigh by giving notice at half-term at the
same time elaborating a detailed exposition of the faults of the
school. 'I don't think our Welsh climate suited him,' said Mrs
Vanhomrigh.

But there was more jollity than bitterness in that common-
room. We greatly enjoyed the bust-up between the Scotchman
and the Headmaster. We were grossly ribald about Mrs
Vanhomrigh. We were not totally reverent of the Irish parents
for whom we donned our dinner-jackets. Some years later a
young friend of mine, Mr John Betjeman, served his turn as a
private schoolmaster. I visited him at his place of bondage and
said, not entirely facetiously: 'You will remember these schooldays as the happiest time of your life', but in my case there was
no happiness; merely hilarity.

I pined for Olivia, wrote to her often and was more than
once rebuked by Mr Vanhomrigh for searching the post for
her answers before it had been sorted. I was seldom rewarded.
It has been my fortune throughout life to love people who were
bad correspondents.

I have described her as 'astringent'. Hamish and I had fallen
into a mock-whimsical style of letter-writing which I can trace
in my diary, for I often used the same phrases there. I recorded,
for example in mid-March: 'The fields are full of preposterous
white things on legs which the farmers call "lambs" and keep
to amuse their sheep.' I wrote the same words to Olivia, who
snapped like a lizard on any affectation. 'I have rather a

thing against lambs,' she wrote. 'I think they are common.'

Once my colleagues and I went to dinner at the big hotel in Llandudno to celebrate the departure of the Scotchman. The wine we chose was one which I had last drunk with Olivia at the Café Royal and I fell into a melancholy at the sight of the label – Clos Vougeot 1911 – seeing myself as 'Comus Bassington' in Africa with his 'much crumpled programme of a first-night performance at the Straw Exchange Theatre'.

Thus the weeks passed in deep self-pity.

At length with a little money I took the long train journey to Euston, abandoning, without detriment to them, the little boys left in my charge, travelling alone and blissfully in another carriage.

That Easter holidays I spent mostly with the Plunket Greenes in London and on Lundy Island, where they rented a disused lighthouse, and with Hamish in Warwickshire. Olivia scolded me for wasting my time as a schoolmaster instead of becoming an artist, but it was clear in our walks across the windy island and in our long sessions in the lamp-lit parlour – conversations which often lasted literally until dawn – that my infatuation had become a matter of only mild interest to her.

In London, my brother, Alec, told me that Charles Scott Moncrieff, the translator, needed a secretary. He was then living at Pisa. I do not know what secretarial duties I could have performed, ignorant as I was of the languages from which Scott Moncrieff worked, and incapable of using a typewriter, but I urged Alec to press my claims. My mother thought I should find myself in an undesirable set of expatriates, but all my hopes became concentrated on this project.

My wages were soon spent and I found myself, contrary to my resolutions and promises, again falling into debt. I used to telegraph for cases of drink to my Oxford wine-merchant, which we drank at small parties in London studios.

In Warwickshire Hamish and I had his house to ourselves, as his mother was taking a cure at Harrogate. He went daily to his printing and we spent long, happy evenings carousing.

Returning to Mr Vanhomrigh's was as bitter as my second term at Lancing. There seemed no prospect of surprise. In this foreboding I was wrong. A very surprising man, about ten years my senior, had come to take the place of the disgruntled Scotchman as second-master; a dapper man of sunny disposition who spoke in the idiom of the army. He later provided certain features for the character, 'Captain Grimes', in my first novel.

Grimes, as I may now call him, was conscientious in school; at dinner he treated Mrs Vanhomrigh with a benign condescension which left her dismayed but disarmed; after dinner he came with me to the village pub and drank copiously. The other habitués of the house spoke Welsh. Grimes and I spent many evenings together. At first he was something of a mystery to me. Not only was he paid more than the rest of us; he seemed to enjoy some private means and I was puzzled why he should choose to exile himself among us. But he was a man without deceit. His weakness (or strength) was soon revealed. After a week or two a whole holiday was ordained in honour of Mr Vanhomrigh's birthday. It was no holiday for the assistant masters. The whole school was packed into charabancs in the early morning and driven to the slopes of Snowdon, where games were played and a picnic luncheon devoured and scrupulously cleared up. Great licence was allowed; boys and masters chased one another and scuffled on the turf. At length at nightfall we returned wearily singing. When it was all over and the boys in bed we sat in the common-room deploring the miseries of the day. Grimes alone sat with the complacent smile of an Etruscan funerary effigy.

'I confess *I* enjoyed myself greatly,' he said as we groused.

We regarded him incredulously. '*Enjoyed* yourself, Grimes? What did you find to enjoy.'

'Knox minor,' he said with radiant simplicity. 'I felt the games a little too boisterous, so I took Knox minor away behind some rocks. I removed his boot and stocking, opened my trousers, put his dear little foot there and experienced a most satisfying emission.'

A memorable confession which, meeting him in after life, I found he had entirely forgotten. Such episodes were not rare in his chosen career.

Soon after the school-treat I had a letter from Alec confirming my appointment in Pisa. I gave my notice to Mr Vanhomrigh who accepted it without any expression of regret.

'I never give notice,' said Grimes. 'It's always the other way about with me. In fact, old boy' (using a lapidary phrase which I later transplanted), 'this looks like being the first end of term I've seen for three schools.'

June was hot. The mists which the term before had hidden the hills lifted and revealed a countryside of great beauty. We had a deserted beach where we had to conduct the boys for morning bathes, but from which we could swim alone at night. For a few long, brilliant summer days my life seemed full of hope. Then came two sharp blows.

I had sent the first chapters of my novel *The Temple at Thatch* to Harold Acton, asking him for criticism and hoping for praise. His reply was courteous but chilling. 'Too English for my exotic taste,' he wrote. 'Too much nid-nodding over port. It should be printed', he recommended, 'in a few elegant copies for the friends who love you such as myself and . . .' Here followed a list of the least elegant of my friends, the set who had assembled in Hertford for bread and cheese, whom Harold had always delicately deprecated.

I did not then, nor do I now, dispute his judgement. I took the exercise book in which the chapters were written and consigned it to the furnace of the school boiler.

Hard on this came a letter from Alec saying that he had misunderstood Scott Moncrieff, who did not need and could not afford a secretary of any kind, least of all one with my deficiencies. 'It is the end of the tether,' I wrote in my diary.

Not rancorously but very sadly I contrasted my lot with that of my friends. Christopher Hollis was travelling round the world as a member of a university debating team. Tony Bushell was playing juvenile lead opposite Gladys Cooper in a successful London drama. Richard Plunket Greene had at last won consent to his marriage on the condition of his leaving the precarious private school where he was, and taking a post as music-master at Lancing. Opposition, once overcome, turned to benefaction. Aunt after aunt among his fiancée's family stumped up for a marriage settlement. Robert Byron was making plans for an adventurous motor tour across Europe with two rich friends, Alfred Duggan and Gavin Henderson (Lord Faringdon); the tour which was to set light to the great bonfire of his later enthusiasm for the Byzantine world and to provide the material for his first travel-book. Harold Acton was in the full glow of Oxford popularity and esteem. I alone, it seemed, was rejected, at the end of my short tether.

Grimes sought to enliven me with stories of his own ups and downs; experiences that might have been taken for hallucinations save for his shining candour. Every disgrace had fallen on this irrepressible man; at school, at the university, in the army, and later in his dedicated task as schoolmaster; disgraces such as, one was told, make a man change his name and fly the kingdom; scandals so dark that they remained secrets at the scenes of his crimes. Headmasters were loath to admit that they had ever harboured such a villain and passed him on silently and swiftly. Grimes always emerged serenely triumphant. The catalogue was diverting rather than consoling. I envied him his unclouded happiness but not his exploits.

One night, soon after I got the news from Pisa, I went down alone to the beach with my thoughts full of death. I took off my clothes and began swimming out to sea. Did I really intend to drown myself? That certainly was in my mind and I left a note with my clothes, the quotation from Euripides about the sea which washes away all human ills. I went to the trouble of verifying it, accents and all, from the school text:

Θάλασσα κλύζει πάντα Τ'ανθρώπων κακά

At my present age I cannot tell how much real despair and act of will, how much play-acting, prompted the excursion.

It was a beautiful night of a gibbous moon. I swam slowly out but, long before I reached the point of no return, the Shropshire Lad was disturbed by a smart on the shoulder I had run into a jelly-fish. A few more strokes, a second more painful sting. The placid waters were full of the creatures.

An omen? A sharp recall to good sense such as Olivia would have administered?

I turned about, swam back through the track of the moon to the sands which that morning had swarmed under Grimes's discerning eye with naked urchins. As earnest of my intent I had brought no towel. With some difficulty I dressed and tore into small pieces my pretentious classical tag, leaving them to the sea, moved on that bleak shore by tides stronger than any known to Euripides, to perform its lustral office. Then I climbed the sharp hill that led to all the years ahead.

INDEX

Faringdon, Lord, 229
Fawr, Cadwgan, 9
Fitzgerald, Scott, 181
Flecker, J. E., 112, 167
Forster, E. M., 37, 198–9
Fraser, Lovat, 197
Fremlin, Rupert, 126, 165
Fulford, Roger, 102, 106–7, 113, 126, 128, 131

Gardiner, Lord, 185
Gertler, Mark, 122
Gibbens, Dr, 168–9
Gibson, Wilfred, 76–77
Gielgud, Sir John, 71
Gill, Eric, 122, 145–6, 197
Gosse, Anne, 14
Gosse, Edmund, 13, 65–66, 73
Gosse, Hannah, 13
Gosse, Philip Henry, 13
Gosse, Thomas, 12–13
Greene, Graham, 119–20, 200
Greenidge, Terence, 176–9, 183–4, 207, 208, 213
Grenfell, Granville, 81–82, 87
'Grimes, Captain', 227–8, 229
Gull, Mr, 188

Harmsworth, Lord, Desmond, 213
Harris, Dick, 100–1, 106, 112, 114, 124, 125, 128
Hilliard, Arden, 212–13
Hoare, Miss, 37–38, 49, 54–55
Hodgson, Ralph, 112
Hollis, Christopher, 185, 186, 189, 202, 203, 207, 228–9
Home, Sir Alec Douglas, 185
Howard, Brian, 204–5
Howard, Esmé, 197
Howard, Lady Mary, 204
Howitt, Rev. W., 114, 117

Hügel, Baron von, 218
Hunt, Holman, 7

Isham, Sir Gyles, 213

Jacobs, Barbara, 116–23
Jacobs, W. W., 75, 118–19
Jacobs, Mrs W. W., 118–19
Johnston, Edward, 146

Knox, Mgr Ronald, 45, 69, 93, 129, 143, 186

Lanchester, Elsa, 209
Lauder, Sir Harry, 99
Lawrence, D. H., 77
Leibnitz, 143
'Lennox, Hamish', 192, 216, 225
'Lennox', Mrs, 212
Lloyd George, David, 67, 183
Longford, Earl of, 200
Lowell, Amy, 77
Lucas, E. V., 75, 79
Lunn, Sir Arnold, 143
Lygon, the Hon. Hugh, 167, 181, 207, 212–13, 221
Lygon, Lady Mary, 205–6

MacCarthy, Sir Desmond, 66
MacGregor, Mary, 68
McDougall, Jack, 204
Machin, P. F., 165, 178
Mahon, Denis, 3
Mahon, Theodosia, 3–4
Mallowan, Max, 165
Marriott, Sir John, 182
Marsh, Sir Edward, 76, 112
Melville, Lord, 11
Messel, Oliver, 180
Messel, Rudolph, 181
Mestrovic, 121
Meyrick, Mrs, 202

INDEX